sahela re

Celebrating
30 Years of Publishing
in India

Praise for *Sahela Re*

'A tale finely told, where writing and music form body and soul. With a rare combination of poetic imagination, sociological insight and historical understanding, *Sahela Re* is a nostalgic but unsentimental evocation of the vanished golden age of Hindustani music and a lament for its present predicament. With truly creative unconcern for political correctness, it shows that, ironically, the golden age was in a colonized feudal society and its withering has come about in democratic India. It brings to life women artistes who pursued their beloved art uncompromisingly, following their emotions and dreams at a heavy personal cost. A tale that will haunt you long after you've read it.'

– GEETANJALI SHREE

'Mrinal Pande, well-regarded Hindi writer and mediaperson, is also a trained Hindustani classical singer. Drawing from her knowledge of the art form and its history, she explores the world of Hindustani music with deep understanding and empathy. Her narrative mixes the tragic and the comic, and reveals the grace and grandeur, the sufferings and ironies, the darings and failures of lives involved in music. *Sahela Re* is a human document. A rare fictional account of a lesser-known ethos, the novel is a triumph of creative imagination.'

– ASHOK VAJPEYI

'Like a lyrical detective, the writer takes us on a journey into a forgotten and forsaken world of music. As the book unspools, the hidden notes turn out to be as beautiful as the ones heard.'

– NAMITA DEVIDAYAL

sahela re

A NOVEL

mrinal pande

translated by

PRIYANKA SARKAR

HARPERPERENNIAL

An Imprint of HarperCollins *Publishers*

First published in English in India by Harper Perennial 2023
An imprint of HarperCollins *Publishers*
4th Floor, Tower A, Building No. 10, DLF Cyber City,
DLF Phase II, Gurugram, Haryana – 122002
www.harpercollins.co.in

2 4 6 8 10 9 7 5 3 1

Originally published in Hindi as *Sahela Re* in 2017
by Radhakrishna Prakashan Pvt. Ltd.

P-ISBN: 978-93-5629-632-9
E-ISBN: 978-93-5629-633-6

Typeset in 11.5/15.7 Adobe Caslon Pro at
Manipal Technologies Limited, Manipal

Printed and bound at
Replika Press Pvt. Ltd.

MIX
Paper from responsible sources
FSC® C016779

This book is produced from independently certified FSC® paper to ensure responsible forest management.

To my three wonderful gurus,
Dipali Nag, Ramdas Mungre and Pandit Vasant Vamanrao Thakar.

FAMILY TREE 1

(Benares-Kolkata waali)

- Nathua Baadi
- Gulab
- (children:)
  - Motiya (aka Martin)
  - Hira Bai (aka Victoria Hewitt)
    - Anjali Bai
      - Shakir/Kanja (Anjali Bai's unacknowledged son, fathered by Tajuddin)

FAMILY TREE 2

(Sherkothi waali)

- Husna Bai (Ammajani)
  - Allarakkhi
    - Haidari Begum
      - Amaal Jaan

FAMILY TREE 4

Rai Bahadur Kunwar Shardul Vikram Singh (aka Bade Sarkar)

- Anantvijay Singh
  - Radhaprasad
  - Madhobilata (Putul)
- Manjhle Chacha
- Nanhe Chacha (Pramod Bihari Singh)
- Shammo I[...] the elde[...]

FAMILY TREE 3

Kalisadhan Banerjee
(aka Kali babu)

Sukumar Banerjee — Lotika Banerjee (Wife)

Shantul
(Prosenjit)

Bantul
(Indrajit)

FAMILY TREE 5

Pandit Ambadutt Tripathi

Gauri Tripathi — Paritosh Sukul (Husband)

Sanjeev

Vidya

nmo Bibi

Dammo,
the youngest

Sahela re, aa mili gaayein,
Sapt Suran ke bhed sunaayein,
janam janam ka sang na bhoolein,
abki milein toh bichhdi na jaayein.
Sahela re…

(Bandish Raga Bhoop)

O Friend, come let us sing together,
let us uncover the secrets of the Seven Surs,
let us not forget the bond that has survived many births,
may we never part when we meet again.
O Friend…

New Delhi

Dear Radha Dada,

How are you? I hope you remember your old friends, Vidya and Sanjeev, even after becoming a star publisher.

If you are wondering why someone would get in touch to remind you of the past, you have a point. Remembrance happens when it happens. Period. I asked you once if one remembers differently in English and Hindi – how Sanjeev and you had laughed at me!

You'll probably tease me for being sentimental. Truth is, I have remembered you often, and for many reasons. Sometimes while reading a good book you have published, or while listening to music, especially while lazing in the winter sun.

Take for instance late last night, when I chanced upon Husnara Begum's Shuddh Kalyan, '*Mandar baajo, baajo re…*', being broadcast on the radio from an unknown station in some corner of the world. A whole sea of memories gushed in, and as I drowned in the music, I so missed Bhaiya and you.

Communications disappear fast in the digital world, and with them, memories. It has kicked out the art of writing letters by hand and replaced it with the email. And now one no longer knows what would happen if a system marked shared memories as spam and swept them off into some vast trash bin in cyberspace.

So, before you begin to inch towards the delete button, let me quickly spell out the second reason for getting in touch so shamelessly.

You may be aware that I have been researching the history of musical theatre for a while now. I have been trying to connect the threads related to the events leading up to its formative years, and changes over time that may have muffled the past. The problem is that our Education Department will reject a proposal such as this saying the subject does not conform to the parameters of the fellowships on offer currently.

I am left with only one option to finish my research on time: ask a publisher for advance royalties and add my own savings to fund my research. I don't know about the state of the printing market. All I have heard is that digitally produced books from the West have started eating into even our meagre incomes. Even so, Dada, would you be willing to publish my work when completed and, in the meanwhile, also help me with an advance?

Please do not hesitate to say no. I realize I am pushing boundaries by writing to you suddenly after such a long silence and making demands. But I realize it is impossible for me at my age to see such an ambitious project through all on my own. And yes, as you might have guessed, I don't wish to write to Bhaiya for help.

That was all I had to say. I'll understand even if you choose not to reply.

With love,
Vidya

Lucknow

Dear Vidya Rani,

Your mail hit my inbox like a comet. I was surprised and, of course, quite delighted all at once. I remember your mother calling you Dhumketu, a comet. It was such an apt name coming from one who understood you the best.

And now, it is my turn to air grievances. I have been noticing that you have chosen to write most of your acclaimed academic tomes in English. So far, you have not published any of your well researched work in an Indian language. All that notwithstanding, I want you to know that whatever be your proposal, any publisher would be glad to receive it. That you thought me worthy of this honour, believe me, I am really grateful for that.

However, first things first. May I ask why you are still annoyed with your brother and my friend, Sanjeev? Honestly speaking, who are you actually angry with? Is it your Gandhian father, whose deep, unspoken dislike for mehfils, that to him reeked of a feudal hedonism, dragged your mother away from the two things which had been a big part of her upbringing: good music and musical baithaks?

Or are you angry at your mother, who meekly chose to curtail her singing after marrying your father, and took care to sing only behind closed doors, even singing under the shower whenever he was home. Remember, she was also the one who escorted Sanjeev and you to the Akashvani Sangeet Sammelans when he would be away?

Or is this humble descendant of your grandfather's friend the real reason behind your anger? I, who'd enter your home through the back door like some contagious mosquito, bringing you all news about who sang what and all the gossip from those banned mehfils? One who so respected generational ties with your mother's family that he saw to it that, despite your father's hostility to it, you both got addicted to music?

Maybe you'll put on your calm Buddhist nun-face and say that you don't hold grudges against anyone.

But Munni, if you are not angry with any of us, then why have you avoided your poor brother for so long? Is it because Sanjeev was as gifted as his mother, but unlike her, would not let his talent succumb to a slow death under the burden of family expectations which he had been struggling to shrug off since his early years?

Why was it surprising that when the Stanford scholarship offer promised to open up so many horizons for him, he accepted it without even checking with your mother and you?

Are you disappointed with him because he decided to leave?

If fulfilling a deep desire by honest means is a crime, then aren't you and I guilty of it as well?

True, Sanjeev left without providing much support for your widowed mother, leaving you, the remaining sibling, with several responsibilities. Also true that both mother and daughter may have had to suffer nasty asides about the irresponsible behaviour of a son with such promise. But don't you see that, just like you, when Sanjeev saw an opportunity to fulfil his dreams, he could not afford to stay put any longer?

Or maybe somewhere in your mind you already understand this? And wait! Before your fingers start inching towards the delete button in irritation, hear me out.

My advice as well as precondition to advance royalties is that you rebuild your relationship with Sanjeev, just as you have done with me. You might be surprised to know this, but Sanjeev and I keep bumping into each other in different parts of the world. Let me tell you, I can sense he has been waiting long for the ice to thaw. I feel crushed each time I face his sad eyes with many unasked questions about you.

Anyway, think it over. You must know that I am not doing any favours by agreeing to publish your work on music. I am always happy when a good manuscript falls into my lap. And yes, I free you of all financial worries. Just send me your bank details.

Once again, please let go of your anger.

Radhaprasad

~

Delhi

Radha Dada,

Thank you for replying to my rather rambling mail. Well, if the sister of your best friend – a friend who is in a land far, far away – writes to you out of the blue, that's reason enough to be surprised.

You are right. Sanjeev was the reason why I kept my distance. I guessed that the two of you must have been meeting every now and then, and I was a little scared that whatever he may have said to you about my silences could have bred misgivings in your mind. I was almost sure you might divert my mail to the spam box without even looking at it. Your reply reassured me.

To be honest, I no longer know why I have been cross with Bhaiya for such a long time. Could it be that, entangled in the web of familial memories sitting in a house that is slowly turning into a spinster's unkempt abode, all cobwebs and dusty drapes, I simply forgot to let in fresh air or sunshine?

Once upon a time, our shared love for music used to be sunshine and fresh air in this house. Amma taught us to gulp in music like an elixir whenever we could despite Babu-ji's well-recorded dislike for frivolity of any sort. Even after his death, when we fell on hard times, the legacy of music from Amma's ancestors remained like a silken strand that drew the three of us and you close together.

Believe me, Amma's reason for not going to live with Sanjeev was not because of a deeper attachment to me or a displeasure towards her son. It was just that she did not want to leave her own world of classical music and her traditions for an alien land. She had seen many of her friends who chose to live out their twilight years abroad turn into lost souls, hovering between two worlds. All of them told her they felt alone and humiliated when they were trotted out by their children among their friends or colleagues as specimens of a certain lost cultural tradition. To Amma, the very thought of becoming oriental exotica of some sort became more and more revolting as she aged.

I know that in her younger days, Amma with her father were as much a part of the musical events at your dear Dada-ji's house as his own sons and daughters and their grandchildren. Amma talked often to Bhaiya and me about the mehfils she had watched from behind the bamboo blinds in the women's quarters: the gharana ustads and divas like Roshan Ara Begum, Alladiya Sahib and Bhaskar Bua performing to a rapt audience. Most of those talented maestros are gone. It would be awful to see Amma's eyes grow misty in her later years at the sight of the frail and listless ustads and pandits getting felicitated in wheelchairs in front of TV cameras. 'Too late,' she'd whisper, 'too late!'

As you know so well, so long as Babu-ji was alive, there was an unannounced but absolute curfew on what he referred to as the kind of 'mehfilbaazi' in Amma's natal home. But once, after Babu-ji's death, when Amma got to know that Roshan Ara

Begum had come down from Pakistan, she swallowed her pride and shyly let on how eager she was to see and hear the grand old lady of the Kirana gharana perform. 'One can never know when we'll get to hear such musicians next,' she muttered as she was wont to do, always leaving her thoughts half unsaid. Ultimately, Sanjeev Bhaiya and I somehow managed to get three passes. It didn't take much persuasion to get her to leave the house to hear the great Roshan Ara Begum sing at the Talkatora Stadium in Delhi.

It was then that we saw a glimpse of an entirely different bygone era of music, and the deep ties between the musicians and their ardent admirers from Amma's generation.

When Roshan Ara Begum began and her voice struck pancham, the pristine fifth note, it pierced our insides like a koel's sharp coo that leaves you breathless! The entire hall reverberated with the divine sound of her pancham for a while, and even the hardcore critics, ustads and pandits we'd seen quibbling over every little note, always eager to trash Pakistani singers, sat stunned and mesmerized by the magic of that one note. Each note in Roshan Ara's seemingly simple alap that followed was like a robust blossom slowly unfurling its petals. And as we relished the fragrance of the composition, the silky voice leapt up into the higher octaves, and then suddenly, slyly, before we could recover our wits, it once again slid back to the lower and then the lowest scales. And all this, while her face remained joyful and serene, as if she were playfully tossing flowers in the air, even as she was savouring the juices of her favoured zarda within her scarlet mouth.

The drummer became possessed too. His beats came fast and thick, powerfully underscoring the completion of each cycle like bolts of lightning! Together, the singer and the percussionist swayed like a cobra and a snake charmer oblivious of the audience, totally conjoined in their own world of togetherness.

Roshan Ara was squat and dark of complexion, and her rather puffy-looking face was not really one from which one expected such rich music to emanate. But as she sang, her face had the soft sheen of a freshly plucked aubergine bathed in morning dew.

Oh, she loved glitter! Her ample body was sheathed in an outfit shimmering with gold. Her arms were laden with it; her neck and ears too. With the mildly flirtatious air of the beautiful woman passing gently by while strewing subtle inviting gestures for her paramours in Ghalib's '*Yaar ko chhed chali jaaye, Asad*', she began to sing for her long-lost followers. Her face wore an inscrutable smile as she broke into the lilting thumri, '*Paani bhare ri kauno albele ki naar?*' (Who is the dandy whose beloved is drawing water from the well?).

After every shower of 'Wah! Wah!', she'd bend her neck ever so slightly and do a shy salaam.

After a while, she paused and said, 'All my singing is just good fortune, bestowed upon me by Him. I am no expert as such. I had a father for an ustad who could melt your heart with his songs. Singers like Dhela Bai, Kesar, Gangu and Moghu Bai from Goa trained with me at my father's feet. All of us received the same talim, and music flowed in our baithaks, day and night.

'I do not know how it is here today, but khayal and tappa are not that popular in Pakistan any more. Among fauji marshals and brigadiers, it is usually some naat, or Bulle Shah's '*Heer*'. That is what I am requested to sing mostly. This is like old times. Ya Khuda, what days those were!'

A few years after that, Bhaiya went away and settled abroad, and some years later, Amma died. But even today, I lose sleep each time I catch the sur of a long-forgotten bai, ustad or begum sahiba on the radio. As their pukar, their glorious call, falls on my ears, the faces and scenes from old baithaks begin to unfurl like a film in the mind.

Surrounded by fickle neo-converts to Indian music, you can imagine how my soul longs to delve into those age-old ragas and musicians' lives fast evaporating in a grey mist and record their stories.

And that dirty mist is swirling all around us.

An aged dancer in Delhi, adept at networking, once talked me into attending a music fest sponsored by the Ministry of Foreign Affairs where she was the presenter. The performances were to be followed by drinks, which they've renamed as 'Ras Ranjan' to ward off the evil eye of the media teetotalers. Today, this ministry is considered to be the gateway to glamorous foreign tours at the government's expense. In turn, bureaucrats in the ministry expect artistes to dance to their tunes because they are paying. When the name of a yesteryear singer came up, my friend the dancer casually said, 'After Partition, that daughter of Chand Bai moved to Pakistan and settled in the red-light area of Moti Gate.' I could see other ageing dancers and singers, who cavorted around famous patrons, nod in agreement.

Later, as the heavy drinking began and guests began chatting each other up, one heard a bureaucrat's wife tell the presenter, 'You were so right there. The aged ustads in gaudy kurtas or singers with heavy make-up and jewellery appear so uncouth, uncivilized and embarrassing when they perform abroad. This department should also teach these musicians proper English and better stage manners before sending them on foreign tours, or they are only good enough to sing at neighbourhood weddings.'

These words were greeted with laughter.

Then the seminar began. The topic was, 'The Syncretic Ganga-Jamuni Tehzeeb in Hindustani Music and the Role of Women'. The daughter of an important politician was the main speaker. Organizing seminars around themes where music, media and women are tossed together is supposed to help strengthen the national profile through 'soft diplomacy'. So, of late, I have noticed an effort to confer a peculiar aura upon our traditional courtesans, not as women who sang their way to reach the top in our performing arts, but as India's earliest financially self-supporting feminists.

However, as soon as a female speaker comes on stage, several acidic gutters open up. Particularly if the talk moves on to the personal lives and mehfils of professional deredar tawaifs.

Once at such a talk show, a minister's daughter, a poor singer burdened by many airs and wiles, and known for shamelessly copying Begum Akhtar's naturally sonorous voice, began by talking about the contributions of the male ustads from the big gharanas (even theatrically touching her earlobes while uttering their names) and then spoke of professional female singers. She spoke not about their individuality but rather leeringly about their messy personal lives. And once she had set the ball rolling, other speakers delved lower. Talking about one Zohra Begum, one critic with a red caste-mark on his forehead said, 'And why refer to her as "begum"? She should be called a "bai". Her mother was actually the precocious daughter of a rich man who eloped with her Muslim ustad. Zohra Begum was born just six months later. When her father died, the greed to sing on the radio made her turn into Zohra Begum.'

As though on cue, a salivated titter went around among the young male audience in the hall.

You tell me, Radha Dada, how can these people crazed with sex and samosas even dare to take the names of Khan Sahib and Shyama Tai who embodied melody? As for Shyama Tai's elopement, you and I both know that it was her father's alcoholism and abuse after her mother's death that led her to run off to a faraway village with her master.

Singers like Khan Sahib and Shyama Tai are not Hindus or Muslims. They didn't just sing in courts or dargahs but also in the temples of the Dattatreya.

The last speaker thanked the one before him, and while masticating a paan, his mouth full of its juices, said that the authentic core of Indian music emanates from the sacred religious culture of our rishis and munis. Whatever knowledge of sur that the infidel Khan sahibs had acquired was from the company of pandit Hindu families like Shyama Tai's. 'Do you know,' he added viciously, 'when Khan Sahib's car met with an accident and his blood-soaked body was laid on the ground, he was found to be in the pose of reading the namaz?' The audience tittered again, just as the speaker had hoped.

What remains to be heard after this? What forgiveness?

You may argue that that is how it has always been. But Radha Dada, at least earlier, music lovers had a deep-seated reverence for the art and the artistes. These days, the VIP seats at music concerts in capital cities seem to be filled with people who arrive late, and during the performances, are often coughing, talking to each other, or stroking their expensive jewellery and checking their mobiles.

After considerable thought, I decided that the research conducted under the government fellowship could go to hell. This organization might not be willing to fund my research on this topic. But before I begin, I need to get the picture right. So, could you please do me one last favour? I enclose a list of names. These are some knowledgeable veterans in the field. I will need to write to them, and if they allow me, meet them for more information. Could you add any other name you can remember to this list? And yes, where can I find the address of the agent who worked for your grandfather Kunwar Sahib's sugar mill – the man your mother helped get a job in a packaging warehouse after his acting company had failed?

In an online interview on music, Kolkata's Sukumar Banerjee mentioned that, according to him, the cupboard of an aged songstress contained a treasure trove of critical information on the tawaifs of her times. As far as I remember, he said she now lives somewhere near Rampur and had enjoyed a considerable fan following in her heyday. I must get in touch with her as well, if I can.

From now on, I will keep apprising both Sanjeev and you about my work regularly, to thaw the ice of our long-drawn cold war. It doesn't matter if the correspondence is one-sided or even if the two of you delete the emails without reading them.

Vidya

~

California

Dear Vidya,

I received a mail from Radha after a long time. Attached were the casual updates on your well-being. No, it doesn't matter that it took so long to reconnect.

Why don't you consider tying together the history of music from the bygone era into a narrative of an art form and the age that created it? This must not have been an easy decision, but I know that you will not let anything deter you once you have decided to quit academia and move on. Just begin your work and leave all worry about travel and other expenses to me. I shall be happy to see you reap the results of your labour.

Before you kick up a fuss, as you always do, about not taking favours, though, let me tell you that Radha has sent me a scanned copy of your first letter and proposal, probably without your permission. He is right. I have waited a long time for the ice to thaw. I will consider this letter that you sent Radha as proof of the end of a long, silent fast.

I was especially happy to know that you thought of my old, talkative friend Radha as a potential source. During our college days, nobody could challenge him when it came to trivia about the world of singers and courtesans, and anecdotes around their various performances. My friend might have settled in Lucknow, but he has travelled the world. He has made several unexpected appearances in America and rekindled my memories of all the master musicians and their songs.

You mentioned watching a YouTube interview of Sukumar Banerjee, the reclusive authority on old musicians. One could say that Sukumar is way ahead of Radha when it comes to telling stories on music and musicians. In my opinion, while gathering information about music and its practitioners, Sukumar and Radha are as vital as the Bard and Homer. You will find every possible information that's vital in their commentaries. What they don't know, you can be sure, is not worth knowing.

Please do not stop this chain of communication, Vidya. Time is passing and we are all greying. Let us talk and share our thoughts on music and much more before the end.

I am amazed at myself for having written such a long letter.

Affectionately,
Sanjeev

PS: Radha asked Sukumar for the address of the old courtesan with the largest repertoire of the old world of classical music. It is attached to the mail. Please also heed this (unasked for) advice: Write to her first and ensure she has not passed on. And ask her with due humility when you could meet her. According to Radha, she must be close to ninety. So, if it turns out she is still there, it would be prudent to meet her as soon as you can. Most of the people from that generation have one foot in the grave. And if someone like you does not record the history of that generation of greats, we will have to contend with whatever the likes of the people you mentioned hand us.

Good to know that we will be talking about such interesting things in your book. I know you well, so won't ask you to let bygones be bygones. All I ask is that you keep writing to me.

Sanjeev

~

Delhi

Dear both,

Thanks! I am hoping that the advance I have received will cover the expenses. Besides, I have some savings too, so you need not send money from overseas. Thank you for asking, though.

The addresses were useful. I have written to all of them. Sending you a scanned copy of the first reply.

Vidya

~

Lucknow

Dear Vidya,

When the ice is finally melting, let me tell you that I didn't advocate the case for my friend and your brother for no reason.

It is difficult to understand introverts like Sanjeev. I also know that a deep friendship between people with different temperaments is marked by frequent bouts of quarrels and healing. You might not know this, but when your brother and I were very young, one of my eccentric uncles, Nanhe Chacha, had started a bookstore in our town. It was a part of a franchise that ultimately and predictably failed. It had to. Like any self-absorbed son from a rich family, Chacha was usually absent from his own shop. However, bookworms kept discovering new and rare books in his shop and, of course, we became regular visitors there. Turning a deaf ear to the accountant's insults, we would drink copious amounts of tea or coffee with friends there while aggressively discussing politics and music. We laughed loudly enough to startle the serious browsers around us. We ignored their polite glares because, like Scheherazade's, our stories were unstoppable once they started pouring out. We usually ended up missing our buses or trains, our important lectures.

Your brother was the uncrowned genius of the group. In the initial days, he was so solemn and sincere that the store's accountant, Shyamal Babu, advised us to be like him.

But that was not to be. Sanjeev ended up becoming like us. Meaning that he too was seen laughing loudly, cracking jokes, and offending and turning away many buyers. From our initial interactions with him, we had sensed that behind his intense and fakir-like airs (that women find so compelling) lay an exceptionally funny, witty man, and maybe the DNA from your mother's ancestry was responsible for this. Your father was known as a serious though courteous man, so his sense of humour Sanjeev certainly inherited from his mother's family. I still remember several of her incisive, mostly one-sided quips about men and matters.

And then you, Vidya, landed in our lives like a comet, always a fighter. You fought not just with Sanjeev but even me like it was your birthright.

I have learned from a shloka from the Shiva Mahimna Stotra that we recited, that the heart is an unseen yaksha within us. And the yaksha is exceedingly difficult to control. May it be guided by noble influences. My yaksha, it seems, had gone to sleep. Unhampered by it, I plunged into a world of profit-and-loss sheets. Then your mail shot into my inbox and the inert yaksha inside me began to stir and heave once again. The Teen-Taal composition in Raga Chandrakauns that Nanhe Chacha had created for you at our request came to mind: '*Kaahe karti ho jhagda ri chhokariya?*' (Why do you fight so, girl?). Do you remember it? The composition worked as a mantra to bring out the giggles in you which tamed that uncontrollable temper of yours. Each time you got down to fighting with me with your claws out, if he was around, your brother and I would make Nanhe Chacha sing this accompanied by an organ:

Singh raashi ki param katkhanni, karey naag ki asvari,
daant nikaare ghar se nikasin kaam jagat ki patkhwari.

The one with Leo at the centre of her horoscope is able to ride a snake,
her fangs bared, she comes out of her den only to make her enemies quake!

According to Nanhe Chacha, it was all in the stars really. Our family priest had warned your nana-ji that you were born with a temperament more suited to a male. You will be stubborn, he had predicted, and fearless, and a solitary worshipper of knowledge your entire life.

Legend has it that, upon hearing this slightly alarming prediction, your nani was livid. But so what? After all, even the great bard confirms, it's all in our stars.

So both of us poor men have long known that you would never ask anyone for favours or money or assistance in any of your many ventures. Rest assured, I will extract every penny's worth of the advance I have given you from the book once it is published.

All of us, and in this I include Amma, Babu-ji and my Baba's souls as well, will experience an immense peace when they see your labours bear fruit and you calm down, all passion spent, as some poet said. Let that calming be our shared bonus. Now, just get started.

Affectionately,
Radha Dada

Boston

Dear Vidya,

I truly am gobsmacked! I cannot believe that the chronically lazy Radhaprasad would reply so promptly. If an extremely miserly publisher like him has so hurriedly approved your book proposal, then I imagine he expects good results.

Love,
Sanjeev

Delhi

Dear both,

I just returned from the pilgrimage of Tapish Miyan's The New Czecho Musicals Factory in Rampur. I'd like to immediately share with the two of you what turned out to be an astonishing and rare experience. This will, of course, also help me sort my own thoughts. So just listen in, even if I occasionally seem to ramble a bit.

My train reached the station five hours late, and before I could even think of hiring a rickshaw or a horse cart, a bearded young man leapt in front of me. He had the sing-song accent of the Indian-English most small-town Indian youth seem to affect. 'Miss Vidya, I presume?' he asked.

When I nodded, he told me that he was Nawaz, grandson of Tapish Sahib of The New Czecho Musicals Factory and cast a surprised glance at the size of my tiny strolley.

'Is that all?' he asked. 'The car is parked outside. There were strict instructions from Bi Sahiba and Baba that you are not to carry your own bags or take a rickshaw or some other transport. I came early so you do not need to do any of that. Come.'

And that is how the trip began.

While driving his car, in his rambling English, Nawaz introduced me to his family history. The sum of it was that his great-grandfather, Tareek Uddin Khan Sahib, was a maker of violins. He used to travel often to Germany and Czechoslovakia to train with masters and learn more about the art of making violins; also about how to procure the necessary supplies, like strings and bows. During his time, the names of these two countries were synonymous with music in his household. In 1993, ten years after the death of his great-grandfather, when Czechoslovakia split up and Germany united, Dada Huzoor, Nawaz's grandfather, changed the name of his factory from The Tareek Musical Hall to The New Czecho Musicals Factory. They make fewer quality violins now; mostly guitars and furniture.

'We get demands for violins from Goa and Kerala mostly. They are old customers, so we have to oblige them. But now they have started going in for cheaper Chinese violins. If we charge two thousand, the Chinese charge two hundred. There's that much of a difference. So Abba and Chacha now work on furniture mostly. But Dada Jaan insists that we continue making quality musical instruments until the time we can. So we've all been apprenticed at the shop. Every child in our family can make some kind of an instrument.'

Then his mobile rang, and Nawaz Miyan's attention was diverted.

'Look, bro,' he said to his friend, 'the kind of music our family has grown up around is now only heard by a few Southies whose hands still keep the beat in concerts. The general public here prefers the "*Huzoor tera suroor*" type songs it can dance to at family weddings. So we have decided that, like you, we will enter popular contests like *India's Got Talent* for promoting our band. Something different, yo. I am just waiting for the oldies in my family to stop breathing down my neck. What?'

Once their intricate issues were sorted, Nawaz brought his attention back to me. The little I could glean from his conversation was that he spent most of his time listening to Punjabi pop on his earbuds and watching reality shows on TV. He didn't relate much to the old Urdu-speaking world of his Abba or Allarakkhi Bi. In fact, he was surprised that an English-speaking person like me would come running all the way from Delhi to meet the oldies.

'Like, yo man, I really dig Kalpana Rao and Honey Singh! I listen to Kalpana's "*Raat jaane na do*" on loop every day. Man, she is cool!' Nawaz Miyan told me that he had started a funk rock band along with four other friends. They are popular DJs in the city and much in demand at local weddings. He dreams of going to Mumbai to meet the composer Vishal Dadlani.

'He is the guru of cool, man! Can you help?' he asked.

He was dismayed to hear that his idol was a stranger to me. He dropped me home and disappeared inside the house.

The house where Tapish Sahib lives with Allarakkhi Bi, who is living out her last days, is almost thirty miles from the city. The ancestral kothi is made from old lakhori bricks and has a distinctive smell – a combination of mould and fragrant tobacco from the hookah. The garden outside looks derelict, but the kothi is huge with beautiful carvings. I was told that the lady of the house was mostly confined to her bed. She was surviving on the help provided by a few old employees who had been with her in her earlier home, Sherkothi.

Allarakkhi Bi looked like a wrinkled prune plonked on a pillow drenched in oil. The ruins of her once-famous good looks still retained the magnificence of the fortress. She met me with a lot of affection – kissing my forehead, blessing me. Finally, exhausted, she fell back on the pillow. When her old caregiver Ramdei appeared, Bi told her to show me to my room so that I could freshen up, and then she collapsed out of fatigue. She also asked that I be given some hot tea.

The sum of what Ramdei told me in her thin voice on our way to the room was that it was after a long time that she was seeing Khan Sahib and Bi Sahiba talk to anyone from outside. Otherwise, by morning, after suffering from arthritic pain all night, Bi Sahiba would be reduced to a fly without wings. Khan Sahib has also gotten old, and his limbs have given up on him. What was there to say? Everyone had gotten old. But how could she stay on in Sherkothi without doing anything, when her mistress was lying here in this condition?

'Bi Sahiba has a daughter. She studied in English in Bambai. When Badi Malkin, the grandmother, died, Bibi Allarakkhi Jaan stayed with her daughter in Bambai city for a long time. But Bibi didn't like it there, and so she returned to her roots. She finally sold the kothi to a distant relative of Khan Sahib, and he brought her here and has been looking after her with a lot of love and respect. So what if it is not her house? At least she is safe here, and it is all because of Khan Sahib's kindness. He is an old-world man, which is why he is so faithful. Not like the men today.'

When I came out of my room after freshening up, I heard Bi Sahiba call for Ramdei repeatedly.

'Ramdei! Have you gone completely deaf?'

The old caretaker yelled back, 'Coming.' Supporting her knees as she stood up grimacing with pain, she whispered, 'To be honest, there isn't much life left in Bi Sahiba's body, but she seems to be losing her mind too. Otherwise, one never heard her raise her voice even once. Her regal manners were unmatched in the old days. She is going downhill each day. I have sent a postcard to her daughter informing her about her mother's condition. Forget all past resentments and come along with your daughter to visit your mother one last time, I said to her. You might have fought with her earlier, but how can you forget a mother? Now I hear that the young one is taking leave from work for a few days, and they are both coming here. How can her child who was raised across the seven seas know of the glories this haveli has seen? Don't know if Bi Sahiba will live to see another summer.'

The tea arrived. We sipped it in silence. Then, Allarakkhi Bi stirred and began reminiscing about the old days, almost as if she were trying to snatch her memories from the air.

'I left Benares so long ago, yet Benares refuses to leave me. We come from a family of deredar tawaifs. My mother was the famous tawaif Husna Bai; we called her Ammajani.

'Before we moved to Benares, we lived in a village. We continued visiting the place even after our move. But how can any place compare to Benares?'

Taalillah Benares chashm-e-baddoor,
bahisht-e-khurram-o-firdaus-e-mamoor

May God keep Benares from the evil eye,
it is heavenly bliss, paradise embellished.

'Ghalib Sahib expresses it so well,' said Tapish Sahib.

Bi continued: 'Hira Bai, mother to the famous singer Anjali Bai, was a close friend of my mother's in Benares. I heard they live somewhere here, close to the mountains in the north. Such a beauty, and a most virtuous lady. Whichever poet's words she sang became popular among her numerous listeners. The mehfils where the two friends, Husna and Hira, performed seemed to glow with the light of a hundred lamps.

'I must have been seven or eight when a rich zamindar here fell for my Ammajani. When he could no longer contain his love, he claimed her as his and brought her here. My mother and I came here, leaving behind dear Hira Bai and her daughter, my friend, Anjali Bai. The bond that broke then could never be repaired fully. Life!

'The village you saw on your way here from the city did not always look this forsaken. There was a time when it was beautiful. There were fewer people, and the air was clean. At night, if you slept on the terrace after it was sprinkled over with fresh water, the open sky above gleamed like a plate of pearls. Those travelling in cars could barely see our kothi. Only if they tried hard could they do so, from behind a thick canopy of trees.

'Our Sherkothi was constructed after clearing a number of farms on the outskirts of the city. Two gates were erected on either end. One was called the Sherwala Gate, the other was called the Ghanti Gate. The Ghanti Gate was called thus because a big brass bell hung from it; it isn't there now. It was sounded every time the Maharaj came visiting, so as to inform those at home. The Sherwala Gate was called so because carved lions sat on either side of it. Because of this gate, the kothi got to be known in the area as Sherkothi, "the kothi with the lions".

'Kalika Prasad Singh Ju was the full name of Maharaj Ju whose mistress my Ammajani was. He was the fifth son of the king of the famous clan from Champanagar in Pancha. His mother was from Bihar.

'His wife, the Maharani, never approved of Maharaj Ju's relationship with Ammajani. Maharaj Ju, too, tried his best to keep Ammajani away from Maharani Ju and her followers. This is why he had this kothi built for her. But destiny played a game of its own design. One day, Maharaj Ju went out for a drive without telling anyone. And then came the news of his death. A lion of sixty isn't so old that his heart would burst from his car bumping into a tree.

'Later, when songs started being recorded for the gramophone, back in Benares, Hira's daughter – my friend Anjali – made quite a name for herself. She was invited to many mehfils across Bombay, Calcutta and Madras. I heard that later, annoyed by some household dispute, she finally moved to the Deccan and settled there, and passed away quietly. May Allah give her peace!

> *Hawas-e-ser-o-tamasha woh kam hai humko,*
> *liye jaati hai kahin ik tawakko ai Ghalib.*

> I do not have a lust for travel and spectacle,
> what sweeps me away is desire, O Ghalib.

'Maharaj Ju had been so smitten with my mother's voice that he had built the Sherkothi exclusively for her and installed her here with a lot of loving care as his woman. Ammajani stopped singing at mehfils in her grief at the passing of her mentor Maharaj Ju, but she started taking me to mehfils to sing for the sake of livelihood. We could not earn the kind of reputation that Hira Bai and Anjali Bai had earned since we were not in Benares.

'Ammajani had the heart of a fakir, much removed from worldliness. Having sensed that, Maharaj Ju had made Ammajani the legal owner of the kothi. He made sure that all the paperwork was complete and in order. Had he not done that, his wife the Maharani would have lost no time in banishing us to some faraway forest, tasked with warding off crows!

'Maharaj Ju called Ammajani Husna Bai. He had faith in her and gave his mistress the freedom to invite music teachers to polish her music and learn new compositions. So she invited many well-known ustads, masters of the Benares style of singing, to Sherkothi. Later, I also trained with them.

'My childhood passed well under Ammajani's care. I didn't want for anything. My training started at the tender age of nine. I was briefly sent to Bombay for further training, but after that I was back in Benares, and a year later, followed my mother to Sherkothi. All through, I received the best training in khayal, thumri, dadra, tarana, kol and tappa from the finest masters. I learned all the finer points of intricate lesser-known taals like Pancham Sawari that has fifteen beats to a cycle, and Ashtamangal that had eleven. Such rare creations were taught by major ustads only to courtesans from certain gharanas. And these were treated as our most coveted possessions.

'Arre ... bring the cup to my lips a bit slowly, Ramdei, otherwise the tea will spill on the sheets. I can't even lift a glass of water any more. Ammajani used to say whoever lands on this earth will eventually be devoured by the earth. Are you listening, Ramdei? Don't laugh. I, too, laughed at Ammajani when she said this.'

Ramdei wiped her eyes and then wiped the tea which had spilled. 'The old woman is beginning to lose it. The daughter should come to visit her now. She could die any day.'

Bi continued: 'Maharaj Ju had two great passions in his life – music and hunting. One time, he had hunted some fifty lions. Carvers from Mirzapur had come around then, and very carefully carved from heavy stone the two lions and placed them on the pillars flanking the Sherwala Gate of the kothi. Fond of hunting and travelling in the jungles of the Terai, Maharaj Ju was, by temperament, a loner. He despised visiting people, or creating any kind of spectacle like others did during festivals at the kothi. If our massage-women, usually wives to the village barber, sang some lewd and raucous songs on Holi or some special occasion, only that much was tolerated. In the end, after his death, Ammajani said goodbye to her ustads, old servants and Maharaj Ju's people, and moved here permanently with me.'

For a long time, Bi lay on the pillow with her eyes closed, as if she were asleep.

Outside, somebody, maybe Nawaz Miyan, switched on the FM radio. Some girl was singing a peppy item number on the show, *India's Got Talent*, and perhaps swaying to it.

Now, it is Makhdoom Alam Khan 'Tapish' Miyan's turn.

'What should I tell you about myself? My father was well known locally and was loyal to Maharaj Ju. After Maharaj Ju, he continued as a part of Badi Bi Sahiba's, as in Husna Bai's, inner circle, where she personally supervised her daughter's performance in mehfils. He was a retainer with impeccable manners, and handled all the affairs of the mother and daughter, including those who were admirers of their art. He also arranged for regular supplies from the city. Organizing Bi Sahiba's mehfils has been the job of our family for generations, actually. I am just continuing the good work in an age when one's own progeny abandon their parents.

'If I wanted, I could have moved to Bareilly where my other son lived. But the generous soul she was, Badi Bi Sahiba bought him a factory of motor parts there. By Allah's grace, it is doing well. But since our family has sworn loyalty to this family, I continue here. How can I leave Bi Sahiba alone in her last days?'

Then came many anecdotes from the time of the British. The old will open up their hearts to strangers as one would in front of Allah.

'I have heard that, earlier, master composers received invitations from abroad to make instruments for the army bands of the British in Muradabad. Bagpipes that we called mashakbeens, different kinds of organs, drums, etc. When the British heard that the families of sword- and armour-makers of the Mughals lived here, they showed them the designs for the instruments. The artisans laughed and said that even their apprentices could make those. That is how musical instruments started being made here, and even the British had to accept the genius of Indian craftsmanship.

'Ammajani had spoken with some British resident we called Razdan Sahib – his name sounded somewhat like McLaughlin or something like that. She was keen on setting up a factory for making violins for my grandfather. She argued, "Can't the hands that handle an instrument like the sarangi make violins? After all, both are string instruments."

'In South India, violins are used a lot in Carnatic music. The British laughed when they saw Carnatic musicians with holy ashes smeared on their foreheads sitting on the floor and playing. They supported the violin with their big toe instead of playing it standing, with the instrument wedged between the chest and chin as the sahibs did. But they were great players, and soon, even the British had to admit their mastery over the instrument.'

I am back, and I have brought with me the world spread between Benares and Sherkothi. After spending four days with them, I have started to feel as though the threads between a number of anecdotes, such as the ones above, are beginning to come together. But there's still much left – new addresses to locate and many new and old musicians to write to.

Any reactions?

Vidya

Lucknow

Dear Sanjeev, Vidya Rani,

You have dug up the memories of beauties and relics and are making my old heart sing, '*Julam kar dala ri mori guiyaan...*' (Ah! You subject me to such luscious cruelties, my love...)

To tell you the truth, I have been in awe of you – the hot-tempered Vidya Rani of our shared childhood. I remember how when she received seven gold medals at her convocation, all other scholars present in the hall stood up to clap for her for ten minutes; the world of academia was shaken, as was I all over again. Surpassing all male intellectuals and getting a full professorship at such a young age was no mean feat back then. Your colourful account of the meeting with the senior Allarakkhi Bi is masterly. It also brought to mind so many old incidents from musical mehfils I attended back then.

The first trio of impassioned music lovers that comes to mind is that of our Nanhe Cha, our friends Shantul-Bantul's father Sukumar Chacha, and my father. The template of their rocking musical gatherings had come straight out of their fathers' baithaks. Before Sukumar Chacha and Baba, their fathers – meaning Mr Kalisadhan Banerjee, aka Kali Babu, and my grandfather Kunwar Shardul Vikram Singh, aka Bade Sarkar – had been close friends. Your nana was conferred an honorary membership, something like a position of a permanent special invitee, of these baithaks. And he was authorized to attend them whenever he wanted to.

There is no renowned artiste of those generations these bosom pals had not invited to perform at these mehfils in their homes. And there is no gharana these friends had not had intense debates over while picking apart the various singing styles. They often walked out in a huff and stopped talking for a few days, but then came back and resumed the bickering.

Look at the irony: your father never attended these sittings, nor did he allow his music-loving but extremely obedient wife – your mother – to attend these mehfils. The women of our house, meaning my buas and mother, and Shantul-Bantul's mother, our Lotika Chachi, on the other hand, had issues with the men holding or attending these adda sessions in each other's homes, but could never muster the courage to put a leash on their men. Those days, musical mehfils were considered an essential part of the old nobility with a refined taste cultivated over generations. And women married into these families were expected to accept that as a given. But both the men and their wives continued their friendships for generations, sharing their homes, food, and anecdotes about the baithaks and those who attended or performed there. Truth be told, in that era, it wasn't just the cars or furniture that were passed down from one generation to another, but even friendships and enmities.

I was around eight when Dada-ji, that is Bade Sarkar, passed away. But I still remember that these two unmatched connoisseurs of the arts and close friends, Bade Sarkar and Kali Babu, would come to the baithaks at our house and talk about the singers, critics, old statues and buildings for hours. In the excavation at the university site in the city, which was being supervised by Kali Babu, many rare artefacts were being dug out. Both friends were very attached to these old artefacts. While Kali Babu's interest was professional, Dada-ji was simply interested in anything to do with the arts.

Bade Sarkar was an old patron of ancient sculptures and paintings, and it was no secret for Kali Babu that many rare sculptures of gods and demons, among others, had been sold to form part of his private collection at prices that were almost state secrets. Every time his secret came out, Dada-ji would argue, 'Bhai Kali, I am just a lover and patron. Why would I want to know the source of the sculpture? It is unwise to ask about the lineage of the server after having drunk the water.'

My sister Putul would also have a few pleasant memories of this twosome. You should tape them sometime. Our fathers and Sukumar Chacha's generation inherited this mad passion for the arts and music, and there was a certain level of snobbery common among their women. When the singers and bai-jis entered the house, humming and dancing, along with their musicians and students, even our old governess and help would avert their faces and laugh, and Dadi's eyebrows would come together in a frown immediately. The women of the house called Sukumar Chacha 'Mir Bigadu', the one who leads friends astray.

On most days, as dusk descended, thalis would get sent out for the two of them. Their wives and daughters-in-law who had been raised in this tradition of friendship knew well the art of knowing and respecting the tastes and preferences of guests. Which is why they knew how to get fish and meat cooked and served in bowls for Sukumar Chacha the way they had done for Kali Babu earlier. Dadi would sigh too, like her mother-in-law used to, and say, 'All this is bound to happen in the company of Mir Bigadu!' and at the same time, direct the servants to look after him well.

Going against his pandit father's desires and family tradition, Sukumar Chacha had decided to take up a job at a tea estate instead of at the university. This was because this less demanding but better paying job was best suited for fulfilling his questionable love for music and alcohol. Until the end, Dadi always had this one grudge (among many others) against Mir Bigadu's mother – Mrs Kalisadhan Banerjee – that despite being born into a family of great intellectuals, her son took to chasing singing women like his maternal uncles. Yes, he did make a lot of money, but he did not produce even a single book like his ancestors to propitiate their souls.

Anyway, that era and those folks are long gone.

After his retirement from the job at the tea estate, Sukumar Chacha has settled down in his ancestral house in Calcutta. The elder son Prosenjit (Shantul) lives in New York and visits rarely. The younger son Indrajit (Bantul), who had turned into a bead-wearing hippy with a flowing mane ages ago and left home, is now running some sort of food shack in Goa with an Israeli woman, I am told. He also organizes pop shows at the beach for his perpetually bored comrades and earns fairly well from it. He hasn't met or spoken with his father in years. Lotika Chachi, who was forever fighting with her husband and kept pampering him, is not alive. Only her emotional blackmail could have summoned the wayward boy home.

So now Sukumar Chacha lives alone in the Kolkata house, cared for by a few old retainers trained by Chachi. Of late, his body has started to fail him. But when I voice my worries, he says, 'So what? Just like an old car needs constant maintenance and repairs, this body does too.'

Putul is still in Kolkata. But the light in her seems to have gone out after the death of her husband. Her arthritic knees have also turned her into a more or less immobile recluse. Whenever I go to Kolkata for a special function or the book fair, I stay with her. I also try to meet Chacha. Even when I can't, Putul keeps enquiring about his well-being over the phone.

When I went to Kolkata a few years ago, Chacha told me that Shantul had paid him a visit with his third wife Savitri (aka Sheeba) the year before. Half French, half Bengali – her father was French and mother a Bengali – Savitri is a professor at a well-known Ivy League university. She wears a Himachali topi over her buzz-cut hair, Chacha told me, and ties her sari so it stays five fingers high above the floor. 'It is good that your chachi did not live to see her newly minted daughter-in-law's American Marines' crewcut hair above a cigarette-smoking face,' Chacha said.

I hear that this beloved of Shantul's is also an accomplished, well-published feminist scholar, and was a student of Jacques Derrida. She speaks half a dozen European languages (but not Bengali). Chacha said she deconstructed him, the entire household and, in fact, all of Bengali literature – from Saratchandra to Mahashweta Devi – in just one week. Finally, with great difficulty, folded hands and a prayer on his lips, he bid her farewell after Durga Puja. I know that her keen eyes are trained on Chacha's treasure trove of scholarship on music, which she will rob as soon as he dies. As God wills!

After Chachi's death, our fun-loving Sukumar Chacha now spends most of his days in bed, listening to music alone in his room on the first floor.

While earlier, you couldn't shut him up, now he rarely speaks. That house is a testament to how a home turns into a ruin without a woman's presence. When Chachi was alive, the house would get mopped twice during the day with the Bengal Chemicals' phenyl, and in the evenings, it would be redolent with the smoke of camphor. Now, the house is probably not even swept every day. It has turned into a kingdom of dirt and mess. Once when I was visiting him, Chacha had to ring the bell thrice before Bhritya showed up with his pot-like face. Then, almost half an hour later, Chacha's favourite Makaibari tea was presented to me in a china set. The condition of the tea and saucer indicated that, after Chachi's death, the dishes in the house were not getting washed. The spoon was so dirty that I had to excuse myself from dipping it into my cold tea by saying that I didn't take sugar.

But Chacha is one of a kind, a rare being. He continues to be interested in his hobbies despite his physical and familial despair and loneliness. And what a memory! The pictures of all the singers still hang from the cobwebbed walls of his house. He has kept music CDs of new artistes in shelves on either side of his huge double bed, along with a music system with Bose speakers that Bantul got him. He told me that he preferred the intimacy of the voices of the ustads and bais of yore over that of these pretentious and idiotic musicians. His only regret is that he has not been able to write about that era of music experienced by many generations of our families.

A college-going boy comes over every day. Daily, he reads out the newspapers, writes letters and emails. But his pronunciation has put the fear into Chacha that the person who, while transliterating from Hindi or Urdu to English changes Mashkoor Ali to Majboor Ali, and turns Badi Moti Bai – with a dental T – meaning a pearl, into Moti Bai – with a palatal T – meaning a fat woman, can only prove to be a disaster while taking dictation!

I tried telling him that even if he wrote however he wanted to in English, then I or someone else could go through and turn it into a proper manuscript. Later, it could be edited and could even be translated into other languages. Please, at least start writing.

Chacha's reply was: 'Why should I write? For whom? iPods and YouTube have birthed self-proclaimed Tansens and Kansens in every house, who churn out blog after blog on the Hindustani music tradition in English. I don't find any curiosity in them about identifying shrutis or knowing more about the professional musicians who ruined their lives for their music. Even if some stupid publisher publishes it, the book will need to be publicized at a graveyard, exclusively for ghosts.'

I would suggest that Vidya get in touch with Chacha immediately over email to start the process of discussing the book. It is probably the promise of her pen that has been keeping him from knocking on death's door. I will let you know if his stance softens later. Then, you can even meet him when you think the time is right. You'll have to arrange to live in a hotel, though, because his house is now ruled only by the servants.

Who knows how many scholars like Chacha, who have stood at the cusps of eras, might be alive in other faraway cities? We can only hope that the shade these figures provide can bring some peace to wayward minds. Instead, like Shantul, we can go on Facebook and pick demonesses from distant lands as our companions for life who then sit and deconstruct our ancestors with their Derridean weapons. What else can one do after that other than taking medicines like Shantul Moshai to control blood pressure? After such knowledge, what forgiveness? Even Chacha Eliot had said that.

You remember that time when Sukumar Chacha and Nanhe Chacha had joined hands to create a score based on Raga Adana,

'Jack and Jill'? What a unique composition. They sang it on Shantul's birthday, and then stretched the notes on 'And Jill came tumbling after' into an elaborate overture or alap followed by fast-paced taans!

'*Tehi nau divasah gatah!*' Those were the days, my friend.

And then, today's supreme scholar, Vidya Bai, in her crushed frock and wild hair, screaming 'Radha Dada!' would come and hug me so warmly.

How can I forget those little arms?

I'll wait for your letters.

Radhaprasad

~

Delhi

Dear brothers,

Thanks-thanks-thanks!

This is what they mean when they say, 'When it rains, it pours!' Amma would have said you probably did not deserve it but for the grace of an elevated Jupiter in your horoscope! While you seek it, all the knowledge is being lined up for you by your gurus.

It looks like this book might just write itself. Radha Dada's letter can itself be considered a scholarly article.

And another great surprise. Around the same time, I get another letter from Sukumar Babu that I am attaching here. It is a gem in itself!

Love to all,
Vidya

Kolkata

My dear Vidya, my blessings to you.

May you always be happy! When I got a letter from Radhaprasad from Lucknow after many years, I felt pleasantly surprised. I hear the renowned professor and scholar, Vidya (don't be shocked, thanks to the internet even this old man can manage to keep abreast of ratings and happenings in the academic world), is planning a book on Hindustani music and old singers. I felt even happier when soon this was followed by your letter. As your beloved brother and his Sancho Panza, my darling Radhaprasad, might have told you, this old lion, who used to prance through the mehfils of Lucknow and Kolkata, has now lost some of his old vigour. And his knee pain and breathlessness keep haranguing him. Death like an old landlord is forever shouting for more and more, so finally the tenant may leave and be done with it!

Frankly, I myself have lost the desire to write a memoir. But I still like listening to old musicians on TV and seeking out publications to remind me of the bygone era. I had once even thought of chronicling the thousands of anecdotes about musicians and mehfils passed down over the generations and the rare experiences I had with the artistes in my own time. You have woken me up at the right time.

Recently, my eldest son's third wife, Savitri, gave me some good advice. 'Baba, if you can't write in Hindi or Bangla on the computer, then write in English. Finding a translator will not be difficult.'

It is not that she has some great admiration for my command over English. Rather, her husband had told her that one of my many youthful vices was regularly writing critical essays on Indian classical music for many English newspapers in Lucknow and Kolkata, and that these essays had birthed bitter debates both within the family and the academic world. Her materialistic mind calculated that it was immaterial whether the book was good or bad; if it guaranteed creating a debate or a controversy, publishers would queue up for it and a fat advance against royalties was certain.

'Nowadays, even parents are encouraging children to write in English instead of in Hindi or Bangla' – is what she said to me.

I told her, 'Bouma, royalties be damned. At this age, neither the dollar nor the rupee can help me sleep. But the problem is that presenting that era to readers in English will be tricky. Our Hindustani is a colourful, vibrant costume. Forcing on it an Englishman's tie, coat and hat would be like turning it into a clown.'

How do you translate spontaneous outbursts of mehfil attendees such as: '*Aaye haaye! Yeh toh Huddu Khan Sahib ki gamaktaan hai!*'; '*Arre vaari jaaun, is adayegi mein toh ayn-mayn Patiale ke Faiz Mohammad ki chhab hai*'; '*Wah! Kya rangeeli firat hai, jiyo raajjja!*'? Does saying, '*Aaye haaye*! This echoes Huddu Khan Sahib's voice' or 'My my, his style seems to have the influence of Patiala's Faiz Mohammad', or 'Wah! How colourful! Live on my king!' – capture the beauty of these gems? No! At least, not for me.

By the way, talking nonsense, even without an audience, is also an old man's favourite occupation. Nonsense is important. Our Rajab Ali Khan Sahib, the great been player, used to tell us back then that, no matter how out of breath they may seem, new musicians should always listen to old Brahmins and old musicians. Who knows when you might find a pearl amid those ramblings!

It won't just be politically incorrect but also dangerous to offer that advice in this age that is somewhat hostile to Brahmins. But the latter, that is listening to old singers, continues to be good advice. I had also picked up much from the different kinds of roars I'd heard from the old lions of my generation. How to win over your learned audience by subtly inserting a forbidden pancham while rendering Raga Bageshri, how to string the note gandhar in Raga Maru Bihag in a way that it wrings tears out of your listeners, and so on.

If your enthusiasm has not turned cold even after this long and rambling letter, then let me present to you this bandish written by one of my ustad sahibs from Agra, sung by not just performing musicians but also scores of moody beggars, mirasis, even pir-fakirs and paramhans yogis:

> *Gunan ki ladai ladiye, sab guni maaro taan,*
> *baat karat kachhu howat naahin, yahi go yahi maidan.*

> Wrestle not with words, but robust full-throated notes,
> this is the only arena there is – here no match can be won with mere words.

There is but one stage and it is this. May God give you a long life and the patience to write about it. But my time is nearly over.

Let me give you some homework. You can also consider it an admission test of sorts. Sending you to meet Bi Allarakkhi was one of my initial clever moves. I have always wanted to know about the mysterious life-story of Hira Bai. She was a close friend of Bi's late mother, Husna Bai, and being the other famous courtesan of Benares at the time, her true adversary. I have also been curious about Hira Bai's daughter Anjali Bai. I have heard fragmented stories about them and some, mostly uninformed, gossip. The mother-daughter duo of Hira Bai and Anjali Bai was not just one of the best known in those days, they were also shrewd performers who turned themselves into self-made crorepatis. What today's generation would call 'not just great singers but also very market-savvy performers'.

From the snippets of gossip from the rumour mills, I have gleaned that Hira Bai came from a family of mirasis somewhere in the Himalayan regions, and her talented daughter, Anjali Bai was born to her out of her union with a British forest official posted there. One doesn't know where Anjali Bai may have been born, but it is said that she had been baptized at a church in Allahabad and given a Christian name.

And since in those days the church did not baptize illegitimate children (I hear now, though, that they even get same-sex couples married), she must have been a legitimate child. Later, after her father suddenly committed suicide by jumping into a hill river, she and her mother – who like many native mistresses of British officers was referred to as a Bibi, a socially unrecognized wife – may then have found themselves destitute and arrived, as did many others in the same situation, at the well-known Dalmandi locality of Benares. The rest is history.

I have plenty of evidence to prove how Hira Bai managed to get the blessings of the many ustads who were deeply impressed with her style and fluent English diction, how under their tutelage, her naturally melodious voice was honed further, and how Hira Bai managed to handle the sharp tongues of other female singers and shrug off the rivalries and jealousy. After this, began her good period, when she started getting invited to sing at various major mehfils. Soon, Hira was the toast of the town.

But her early days have always been shrouded in mystery, and I need to know more about her.

There is no doubt about the fact that Hira and Anjali were not just extremely sophisticated tawaifs but also intellectuals. Hira Bai was an erudite and talented shaiyara, and some of her compositions are sung to this day. At a time when the biggest custodians of music and art were kings, emperors and zamindars, it was only at Hira Bai's mehfils that writers competed to present their poetry and ustads to sing their then-latest musical compositions.

Who was this genius? How did she manage to conquer the male bastion of Hindustani classical music at a time before feminism, when good women were expected to be docile homemakers and not-so-good ones to become objects of male desire? Where did Hira's intellectual sophistication stem from?

Vidya, you have to solve this mystery for me.

The rest that follows is about the rise and decline of the fortunes of Hira, her daughter Anjali, and the other singers of their time that coincided with the growth and decline in raga-based music.

But that part I will share with you, along with evidence, only when you find and share Hira Bai's secrets with me.

I would advise that you make Hira and Husna Bai the core of your project. Writing about their lives and work will give you an entry point into the world of Hindustani music of an entire lost era.

I think it was Nietzsche who said that all art aspires to the state of music! Even before him, our own Vyas Baba, the writer of the epic Mahabharata, had said of his work that no other work of art has what his epic has, and what it does not have, will be found nowhere. His epic, it's true, reads like a musical score.

So, if you can, please try and find out about Hira Bai's early years. Did you know that Radhaprasad's Nanhe Chacha was also my father's closest friend? They had a friend, one fabled man known only as Bachchu Babu. He had crafted an exhaustive list of the best bais in Kashi in forty rhyming couplets. He had, it is said, achieved this feat after conferring with many other experts (including Kunwar Sahib and your nana), and Hira Bai's name features in that list.

But let's stop the jokes, and to come back to my request – don't laugh it off. There is a method in my madness. I believe my elders who said that, among the fabled sixty-four lakh birth cycles each human must go through, every one is allotted a special life. That of a Vaishakhnandan or a donkey, a beast capable of trudging a long path without stopping, even as it carries the heaviest burdens.

You could think of the burden of this commissioned research as you living out that donkey-life.

Radhaprasad's old man and his friends were big fans of Hira's daughter, Anjali Bai. For the men of our generation, this woman, with a cold, calculating heart, and with an equally moving beauty, remained as much of a mystery as Monaco's queen, Grace Kelly.

When you start unearthing the stories of that time and the sacrifices all of them made for their music, you will start getting a clear picture about our classical music of that era for your readers.

Only then can we get into a deeper discussion on music. You are lucky that the pastor of the church in Allahabad, Father Michael Gomez, is the son of a former colleague and a music lover at the tea plantation. He was a close friend of my younger son Bantul in school. The two had started a pop group called Hellraisers – a name most fitting. Later, the kind-hearted Michael followed the path of the Lord, but I have heard that Bantul continues to raise hell from his ancestral home in Mapusa in Goa.

Instead of my own son (or maybe at his behest), Michael calls me up every now and then to check in. I am forwarding you his address. His help might smoothen the process.

Since the time I received the letters from both Radhaprasad and you, I have been wondering whether it is also the will of God that I hand over the bundle of all my information to Vidya Mai before I climb on to my pyre.

Please convey my fond blessings to your brother, sister-in-law, and their children.

Lots of love,
Sukumar Banerjee

Delhi

Dear brothers,

After I received Sukumar Chacha's letter, I called up Allahabad's Father Michael Gomez.

The pastor was quiet for a long time. I kept thinking while holding the phone that any minute now he would rudely say that all this was not his work, or something like that. And he did have every right to say that.

Instead, he suddenly said, 'I can hear you. Do you have any information about the year or time when this Hira Bai's daughter Anjali Bai was baptized in our church?'

I told him that, as far as I had been able to find out, Anjali Bai's parents got married soon after the Mutiny of 1857 at a church in the Kumaon region. It is possible that their child was born within five years of that, say between 1860 and 1865. And her baptism must have been held sometime around those years at Allahabad's Methodist Episcopal Church. There might still be some old records in the church that could give me the names of the parents and some information about their marriage.

This was followed by another long silence. I thought that the call had disconnected when, again, all of a sudden, he said, 'I'll have to see. Would you please call me after two days?'

Did I have a choice?

When I called two days later, Father Gomez's mobile was switched off. One of his attendants answered the landline, and after swirling a ball of tobacco around in his mouth and spitting out some of it, he informed me that 'Maankil Sir' had gone out for some urgent work. He had been told that when the call from Delhi comes, he should say that the papers related to the baptism had been found. 'He will call you back when he returns. Sahib doesn't keep his phone on roaming.'

I remained hopeful. Father Gomez might call any day. Why should a pastor lie?

He did return my call two days later. He told me that I could go over and take a look at the register any time the following week. If I couldn't make it next week, I'd have to wait for a month as Father Gomez had to leave town on work for three to four weeks.

Was I mad? I told him that I was going to meet him next week somehow.

After a moment of silence, he said, 'All right.'

'But I am not very familiar with the city,' I said immediately. 'I'll need help with finding a place to stay.'

The same cool tone advised that I take a rickshaw to the church from the railway station. Any rickshaw puller would be able to get me to the Episcopal Church. He stayed in a cottage on the church's grounds. I could first freshen up there, then go through the register in his office, and then take a train back to Delhi the same evening.

I realized that, despite his courteous behaviour, he was trying to tell me to do my job and then leave. It suited me. I could leave by evening. Not like I wanted to camp there! So, I am off to the station to book a ticket.

How can I miss a long-sought entry from the gatekeeper to a magical world Sukumar Chacha's letter had hinted at? But I will not stay overnight. Even if I have to travel both ways without reservations all through a winter night. I do have my self-respect.

I'll send you both my report once I return. Let's see what I can get my hands on, whether I manage to even find something, whether I manage to return with all my limbs intact from that soporific land of tobacco chewers.

Much love,
Vidya

~

Lucknow

Vidya Rani,

May you have a long life. This is the correct approach to work. Being proactive is the way to get the job done, and we can smell a great book emerging from this upcoming mysterious adventure of yours.

Can't help but add (heh heh) – don't stick your head out of the train window and don't eat anything offered by a stranger.

Happy journey!

Much love,
Radha

~

Boston

Dear Vidya,

Good work. Keep us both informed. We'll wait to hear from you.

Dada.

~

Delhi

Dear brothers,

I returned this morning. I will not bore you both with the hair-raising story of a ticketless journey from Delhi to Allahabad in a Kolkata-bound train with compartments packed like sardines. And truth be told, my arrival there was not exactly going to be a joyous occasion for my host.

I took a rickety rickshaw from the railway station, which, for various reasons (including the mud in the middle of the road formed by an unseen pipe that had burst, and a spectacular bull fight watched by the entire mohalla), kept stopping and took an hour to drop me off at Father Gomez's Episcopal Church.

Father Gomez surprised me by turning out to be a polite, soft-spoken, generous host, and like his friends, Bantul and Shantul, and their father, Sukumar Chacha, an expert on Western music. I got hot water to bathe, clean towels, a good breakfast, and a photocopy of the baptism register. By the time I sat down in the compartment for my return journey the same evening, Father Gomez's wordless support had melted even my heart hardened by my jousts with the bureaucracy.

After a refreshing bath at the church, I ran straight to the church's library. I found the place to be cleaner and better ventilated than expected. I then hoped that the old records had been just as well preserved. And within two and a half hours, I did manage to find that old register from the mid-nineteenth century, carefully preserved at the Allahabad Methodist Episcopal Church.

On 3 February 1860, the official chaplain of the church, Henry J. Stephens, had recorded the baptism of Baby Camellia Angelina, daughter of Edward K. Hewitt (forest officer to the Imperial Forest Department, Kumaon and Terai areas, to Her Majesty's government) and his wife, Bibi Victoria Masih, aka Hira Bai.

It amazes me how the material for this book seems to be overcoming various hurdles and coming to light almost on its own. I have never felt this close to any of the sources or characters of any of my works. I am also somewhat scared of how a dry academic like me will be able to shape all this into a readable book.

I am always jittery before setting out to write something new. But this once, I am beginning to feel strangely close to all the characters who keep beckoning me, as it were, to record their story even when I sleep. When I begin writing, it feels almost as if they are dictating the story to me.

Father Gomez told me that, before what the British described as the Sepoy Mutiny of 1857, many pastors of the London Missionary Society had taken up the work of proselytization and building churches in the faraway Kumaon region, which was fast becoming a vacationing spot in the hills for British families tired of the heat and dust of the northern plains. Thirty years ago, when the Asiatic Society handed over their work to the Methodist Episcopal Church, it became the Indian Methodist Church, of which Father Gomez is a representative. This gave him direct access to the pastor in Ranikhet.

But I remained apprehensive. Despite this connection, it might be difficult to find old paperwork in a church located a long distance away in a place like Ranikhet. The only consolation was being told that the Methodist Church is still known for its orderliness. So there's hope that I might find the paperwork related to the marriage of Anjali's parents in Ranikhet after all.

I have also taken care to note the address and phone number of the current pastor of the Ranikhet church, one Roger Masih, from Father Gomez. It was clear from our conversation that they were not just colleagues but close friends as well. Father Gomez has promised me that he will request Brother Roger to help me collect information from the church register and the locals about Camellia Angelina, daughter of Edward K. Hewitt, and the child's mother, Hira Bai.

In return, I have promised to send Father Gomez an autographed copy of the book as soon as it is published. That his affection for both Sukumar Chacha and his good-for-nothing son, Bantul, remains deep and constant was evident from the way he spoke of them. He said that the book will be precious for him.

After all this, the return journey was smooth. My mind remained focused on Hira Bai.

Next stop, Ranikhet!

You must not complain any more that I do not keep you in the loop.

Love,
Vidya

(*On my way from Delhi to Ranikhet*)

Dear brothers and Chacha,

'Kindly wait, you are in queue…'

'The Vodafone number you are calling is busy…'

'All lines in this route are busy…'

It was nothing short of a miracle that, after listening to these recorded voices almost half a dozen times, I finally managed to get through to Brother Roger Masih of Ranikhet's Methodist Episcopal Church.

And he, like Father Gomez, asked me to visit either next week or three months later, during the summer vacations, because he was going to be away at a conference in a fortnight's time.

Who wants to lose time and risk losing a precious source? I booked a ticket online immediately. It will be cold there, but the chances of getting a seat on the train running from Delhi to the foothills at Kathgodam are better during winters. Besides, I don't want to put this work on hold until summer. Who knows, by the time Brother Roger returns in the summer, he might get transferred out of Ranikhet.

I have been told to take a Gosain-ji taxi (that seems to be the brand name) from Kathgodam to Ranikhet. (At the taxi stand, I will find someone known to Brother Roger.) I have also been told to give Brother Roger a missed call after crossing the Khairna bridge. My destination would be an hour's drive from there. Either he'll pick me up from the bus stop or one of his men will escort me to the church in the taxi. The church is just five minutes away from the bus stop.

The rest, after I return…

Love,

Vidya

~

Kolkata

Dear Vidya,

Well done, and I hope that you will carry enough winter wear to keep yourself warm. Don't fall sick after returning. Ranikhet is so picturesque! I wish I could go with you.

Take care.

Sukumar

~

Lucknow

Dear Vidya,

You are turning into Alice in wonderland. Waiting to hear about your adventures.

Radha Dada

~

Delhi

Dear brothers and Chacha,

As I write this email to you from Bhagwan Singh Karki's diner and Internet Café, 'Corky's', I am indeed reminded of the Alice in wonderland forever turning into a dwarf or a giant.

You are right. This city is so green even in winters, and so picturesque that it absolutely resembles a wonderland, all covered in mist and the evergreen deodars. The history of this area may begin with a few cold, hard facts in Tourism Department handbooks, but could suddenly turn into a fable when you arrive and talk to the people who live here. And one can never quite tell which is which.

Until now, the stories I have heard locally of Victoria Masih, née Hira Bai, mother of Baby Camellia Angelina, are about some sudden meeting between the white hunter-forester and the local beauty, followed by love and then marriage. From the stories I have heard, Hewitt emerges as a rich hunter-playboy, and the tales either shock or inspire laughter, depending on where you stand.

The local sources are exactly like the moody ponds here. Calm on the surface, but when you step into them, you seem to get sucked into an unseen whirlpool.

My conversations started with the taxi driver. For him, I was a profitable city-dwelling tourist. I had to turn down his offer to take me to the best places with correct rates for local shawls and tweeds, or honey and fruit juice from the Chaubatia orchard. I then presented my real motive for visiting Ranikhet. At that, the driver's gaze seemed to register disapproval and suspicion.

'Fine then, madam.' He drew in a long breath and started looking at me in the rear-view mirror like he could look into my very soul.

I don't know how my credentials became bearable to him by the time we turned a corner, but suddenly, he offered me tea at a wayside kiosk, over which we got chatting. It is thanks to this rather long tea break that I can send you this mail from his favourite Internet café. I'll send you more updates from Ranikhet. Here, as the driver says, the connectivity is 'a little so-so'.

From Ranikhet

By the time my super-milky ginger tea arrived, all the sunbathing locals in the vicinity had congregated. As soon as I uttered Hira Bai's name, it was as though a thousand streams had burst forth. This is what I have gleaned from that impromptu conference.

Until the time the first English officer sent by the Governor General around 1850 reached Kumaon, this land was an uncharted and unknown territory even for other Indians like me. The British officers looking for a hill station to cool off in during Indian summers heaved a sigh of relief upon discovering this bit of Scotland in India. Their leader was adamant about appropriating this land overnight and settling new colonies here. These smart sahibs had even brought their own boats and fishing lines.

Until then, this place was visited by people from a few nearby villages only as a site of pilgrimage, to pray to the local gods, not for staying. It was forbidden to swim or fish in the sacred ponds situated next to the temples. But the Englishman paid no heed to that. He sweet-talked the simple village head into his boat and rowed it to the middle of the big lake near the temple of Goddess Naina. There he hung the village head over the water, holding him by a leg, and got him to agree to sell the village at a very low price. He even got him to sign the sale documents on the spot.

After that, this area became the English sahibs' holiday home and hunting grounds.

Aha, when the outsiders landed here and began to build houses, many beautiful and young local girls and boys started to disappear, leaving behind wild speculations. The locals were fearful of the ways of the white men and stayed away.

By this time, I had transformed into a 'didi' from 'madam'.

'Call me Bhula, madam. Bhula means younger brother,' said the driver, as the taxi started climbing uphill.

After crossing an ancient steel bridge, Bhula and I started gathering information from various village markets along our way. We had chai; we also ate pakodas and roasted corn on the cob. I am deeply grateful to the proprietors and customers of Amitabha Hair Cutting Saloon, Bisht Gift House, Latwal Chowmein, Pande Mishthan Bhandar, including the drivers of Gosain Taxis, who shared precious bits of information about the land's history with me.

Throughout our journey from Kathgodam to Ranikhet, Bhula kept assuring me that the pastor was a very sharp and well-organized man and would have surely sent someone to pick me up if he had said so.

And as promised, as soon as we turned the next corner, a short man with a tilak on his forehead, a colourful woollen cap on his head, and a muffler around his neck, was there at the bus stop to 'reeseebh' us. And as soon as Bhula saw him, he shouted, 'Hallo, Dajyu ho!' and stopped the car right next to him. Just then, a gigantic bus went past the car at an alarming speed, almost touching it. I got so petrified by this bus full of yawning old men, college kids doing the lal salaam, the newly wedded young brides and screaming children, that I could not even greet 'Dajyu' properly. By the time I came to my senses, my flamboyant escort, after having offered a shy greeting to me, was seated next to Bhula and tugging on his arm like it was a pump.

'You have made it in good time, dear! It took Hiralal Shah-ji almost four hours to reach here from Kathgodam. He was telling me that there was a traffic jam near Ratighat again. The hills there had been crumbling for a while ... Heard that a bus had fallen into a ditch there. Almost forty or so...' he said, and made the sign of death with his hand. Bhula made the appropriate sounds and started the car after shaking his head, while saying something along the lines of, 'Such is a driver's life…'

Our taxi took off after a hair-raising jerk. The escort got busy in updating Bhula about the latest gossip. Both of them were familiar with the route, so there was no bickering over that.

The taxi had now started climbing upwards towards the neat and clean cantonment, leaving behind the crowded bus stop, and the row of taxis and trucks, all of which had ear-splitting horns that the busy marketplace reverberated with. After half an hour, with another jerk, we stopped near a small bungalow-style house close to an extremely beautiful church.

By the time the escort and the driver started saying their affectionate goodbyes, a man in a habit arrived. Both of them folded their hands respectfully and said, 'Namaskar, Roger Sir!'

Aha! So this is Brother Roger Masih.

'I hope you didn't face any troubles on the way,' he asked softly. I thanked him for recommending such a good guide and taxi service. He smiled at my fellow travellers and said, 'They are all our people.'

'Achcha, Didi, see you later. Have to go and get another tourist "paalty",' my newly minted brother Bhula said, and my other brother Dajyu gave me one last affectionate look and took off to get the other 'paalty'.

In addition to being Brother Roger's house, one of its wings, where he directed my luggage be kept, also serves as the church's guest house. While walking towards the guest house, I learned that the English had built the churches in Almora and Ranikhet almost at the same time. The founding pastor Bishop Buddon's unmarried sister Missy Buddon also lived with him.

Missy Buddon was highly educated, and she started a Montessori school for local children in two of the chapel's rooms.

After the revolt, since Ranikhet had already become a major cantonment for the British army, many new churches were built for them. Most of the local children go to these missionary schools to this day. And though the locals might turn their noses up at their focus on English, now even the Sant Kabir Academy, the Koormanchal Academy and several other new schools have started announcing that they will be teaching in the English medium. Many local politicians have their eyes on the foreign donations that missionary schools receive. Anyway, the number of churchgoers has dwindled, and a number of old churches have now been converted to shawl- or tweed-making factories, or army warehouses. Many buildings that were English theatres or dance halls built in the last century have fallen. For a few years, they were used as cinema halls, but with the advent of TV and video, the movie theatres closed down. This church still held regular prayer meetings.

The only difference is that earlier, prayers in Hindustani were held every morning for the natives and in English in the afternoon for the British, and now the prayers happen only on Sunday mornings.

This church in the cantonment area, surrounded by lush greenery and broken, somewhat rundown houses, still stands out like a jewel on a crown. There is a beautiful marble statue of Mary with a rosary in hand, surrounded by blue hydrangea bushes. The brass plaque on the side informs you that the statue was built by Commander William Norton in 1885 with the help of English soldiers who had embellished the grotto with stones picked out from the Gagas river.

This land – of dappled sunlight, of hill bulbuls tweeting now and then or mynahs singing *churr-churr*, and the verdant firs playing their own orchestra – has made me forget all my fatigue.

I freshened up, had breakfast, and then went off to speak with the reticent father, who was surrounded by piles of registers in the spick and span library of the church. Our conversation revealed that Brother Roger knew the church and the area like the back of his hand. He has been reading the old books and gazettes of the church at the local club's library. He came from a family based in the Hira Dungri colony built to house local converts. I decided that, if I have the time, I'll pay the colony a visit and research it. You would say I had come aiming for the stars and settled for much less. But what can I say if this disappointing lesser being is so colourful?

That's all.

Love to everyone,

Vidya

Ranikhet

Dear brothers,

I am on my way back, but I can't resist telling you about a magical meeting I had with a local Tagore, Kabir and Wajid Ali Shah.

It was Brother Roger who took me to meet the old and knowledgeable trio at the local library. They have been gathering all kinds of information from various sources about the area for years. They had, in the course of their search, been involved in several memorable public debates. Brother Roger had warned me that the three were slightly eccentric old men, but if I could keep my calm and give them proof of my total commitment to and seriousness about the project, they might relent and send me some useful information about Hira Bai and her family.

Everyone in the town seemed to know that, every evening, from four to five o'clock, this group first sat and read various newspapers available at the library, and then from five to six they could be found drinking tea at the local Krishna Sweet shop. Meeting this group proved to be a sort of eureka moment for me.

The members of this venerable group are Pitambar Dutt, retired headmaster, Himmat Singh 'Nirbhay', a former correspondent of the Hindi daily *Jan Jagran*, and Lala Paramlal Shah, owner of many shops and houses in the area and the head of the local grapevine.

Pitambar Dutt is tall and thin, rather dark of complexion, sports a sharp, vulture-like hooked nose, on either side of which are shining eyes set amid dark circles. He has sunken cheeks and a quivering but authoritative voice with which he must have chiselled and polished many impressionable minds. His catchphrase is 'I mean'.

It has been almost ten years since Pitambar Dutt's retirement, but he continues to go for his daily walk at exactly seven thirty in the morning, for 'health reasons'. I found him, attired in pants, a coat and a slightly tilted French cap on his head, to be the group's most vocal critic of the current education system.

'See, it is mainly primary education, I mean, school education, that, as the sociologists of this backward area say, "adds bhyalue and orientation to life", you understand?'

He is very cross with the proliferation of expensive coaching institutes. Why should a student, if classes are held regularly and he attends them well, need further honing? When he was the principal, he had even banned those obnoxious students' guidebooks from entering the school premises.

Himmat Singh, the journalist, who is younger, and has been a hockey forward and football goalkeeper for years, agrees with him. He is of medium build, walks fast, and speaks slowly. He was a part-time correspondent for a popular Hindi newspaper in the plains, is a lover of paan, ideologically left-leaning, and has a sharp tongue. He was relieved from work last year for levelling accusations at the owner of the newspaper about certain unacceptable policies which asked correspondents like him to collect news and advertisements from those who wished to be quoted in his stories. These days, he is planning to write a literary history of the Koormanchal region. His friends have some doubts about whether he will be able to finish it. Even so, they are all impressed with his fearless reporting and the straightforward, hockey-stick-like, hard-hitting language he plays with in the stories he files.

Unlike these two, the third friend, Lala Paramlal Shah is a laid-back, uncomplicated, fun person. He has a perennially happy, round and fair, somewhat effeminate face, with rosy cheeks. He could be perfect for playing Sita in the local Ramlila. As a young man, he probably had played the part. He is of medium height, pot-bellied, and always has a rolled paan leaf in his mouth.

When he laughs, which is frequent, his merry twinkling eyes narrow down to slits and his pot belly behind his expensive pashmina kurta jiggles, while specks of aromatic red paan-spittle come flying out of his mouth. He sports a large emerald ring on the little finger of his small, plump right hand, and I see an old, yellow sapphire ring on the index finger of his left hand. He is obviously a well-read, well-informed man with great taste. He also has a good knowledge of mammals and horses, and is known to be an expert on music and local cuisines, and a connoisseur of musk.

'I have but two interests, Vidya-ji,' he said masticating his paan, 'good food and good music!' To which his friend Himmat Singh said something along the lines of it being unsurprising that a well-heeled man with a vast ancestral legacy enough to feed seven generations should have 'burjuaa' interests like music and food.

Paramlal burst out laughing at his friend's comment. 'These red flag-wallahs live a life bereft of music and the fine arts. No wonder our friend has turned hostile to anything that makes a man happy. Which is why, dear,' he said to Himmat Singh, 'your party is losing not just in God's own country, but also in India's culture capital, Bengal.'

The reprimanded Himmat Singh 'Nirbhay' kept staring at the ceiling for a long time, as though to check if, as he appeared to suspect, there were hidden cameras there. Finally, he shook his head to say that it will be difficult for a man steeped in capitalism to understand Marx's long-term vision. For a rich man, navigating *Das Kapital* would be like Kalidasa trying to cross the vast sea of history in a tiny boat.

Having graduated from Lucknow University, Paramlal-ji is considered the local expert on Indian classical music. He seems to be on first-name basis with the foremost classical singers in Benares and Patna. Turns out, he had been friends with Sukumar Chacha in his university days.

'I have always been a chatterbox. Sukumar Da's father was a renowned English professor at the university. He was also steeped in music. His son has inherited this. I, a junior student come down straight from the hills, was an absolute rustic. I was greatly in awe of a sophisticated senior like Sukumar Da. He came from old money, and was an eccentric; one never knew when he'd summon you and ask you to touch the floor in a Lucknowi farshi salaam! All I know about classical music is largely thanks to Sukumar Da, as his disciple. I still have this treasure trove of rare old records—'

'—which our dajyu Paramlal only lets others touch during Holi or other special occasions after many requests,' Comrade Himmat Singh added, squaring off some old score.

By then, all three had convinced me that they were experts in their own fields. I happily promised to meet them the next day.

The interview I had to face the next day was almost on par with the interviews I had given for major university jobs. We talked for over two hours, and during that time, it became clear that the three had a comprehensive knowledge of my familial and educational background, the work I had done. And sitting in this remote town, the obvious effort they had made to know me better totally won my heart.

The three friends bid me farewell with a lot of enthusiasm and handed me their addresses and mobile numbers, and after taking my contact details, promised that they would divide the work among themselves and send me all the local anthropological information relevant to my search at the earliest.

I am now leaving for Delhi.

With love,

Vidya

~

Delhi

Dear brothers,

I had been waiting with bated breath for letters from the experts in Ranikhet. And today, within just a month, I have received letters from the three with all their carefully collected findings.

I can probably dare to enter Sukumar Chacha's court with the fairly comprehensive information I have gathered from them.

Attaching copies of all three letters.

What do you think?

Love,
Vidya

Ranikhet

To the most respected Vidya Didi, at whose feet I, Thakur Himmat Singh, prostrate myself and say namaskar.

It isn't just my hope but my firm belief that my letter will reach you before those of my other friends. The reason is that, though we started working on this project at the same time, as is his habit, our honourable headmaster began double-checking and evaluating every bit of information that he received from his sources. And I know for sure he must have started writing to you only after having worried about a correct format. By this time, he may have, as usual, found his favourite pen that some chief minister had gifted him – the one he calls 'Nirjhar Jharini', the forever-flowing spring – only for it to be taken away either by his grandson or some other relative. At this point, as has happened many times earlier, his blood pressure would have risen, and any work to be accomplished that day would have had to be shelved. And everyone here knows that this could mean a postponement running into weeks.

But once he picks up the pen, every sentence written by our 'Padda' does full justice to his subject. Which is why a few locals jokingly call him Padda the Pope. They say that it does not matter what your accounts or books say, what Padda the Pope says is the ultimate truth.

My other friend, Comrade Lala Paramlal, is a different type. He is indifferent to money or good things, but interested in them in a deeper way, if you know what I mean. To tell you the truth, he is like one of whom it is said, '*Nari mui dhan sampati naasi, mund-mundaaye bhaye sanyasi*', i.e., his woman died and his property vanished, so he tonsured his head and became a wandering sadhu. There is a saying here: You can keep trimming a forest, but it will still grow –thus also man's mind. This saying fits Lala Paramlal like a glove. Even at his age, should the desire to listen to a particular type of folk music begin to stir his heart, he will pick up his backpack and his iPhone and take off. He will not tell anyone when he'll come back from these trips. He even told me when I asked him later about his trip to a certain village of traditional Baadi singers. Till the time his wife was alive, she kept getting irritated by all his eccentricities. She had no patience for music of this type. She once told my wife, 'My Munni's father does not come out of the room once he takes to his harmonium and starts singing aa aa aa. The food goes cold, but who is to tell him that? It is as though he is just not there.'

I have heard that once, during the spring month of Chait, when a Baadi girl, what they call folk singers these days, was going around singing the usual springtime Rituraina songs, my friend got so enamoured of her voice that he followed her to her house with a tape recorder and returned only after several weeks.

It is for these very reasons that the locals here say that estimating the amount our mercurial Paramlal-ji will dole out for Holi or for borrowing his harmonium or durries for Holi baithaks is as difficult to imagine as someone killing a tiger and immediately making a seat out of its skin!

It was my duty to warn you, but as professional human beings, both these friends are twenty-four-carat diamonds. You have my word that whatever information these two send you finally will be a hundred per cent correct.

Now let me come to the matter at hand.

Our local poet Gummani had written about the ancient town of Almora that it was the English who changed its map from this to that.

This is also true for this entire mid-Himalayan region after the 1857 Mutiny. And it was around this time, after the Angrez had got full control over our forests, our land and water sources, that the unique love story of an English forest officer called Edward Hewitt and two local Baadi women singers, Gulab and Hira, began.

It is true that during the Mutiny, the hills did not see the kind of violence the plains did. A major reason for peace in this area was the commissioner of the time, Ramsay Sahib, called 'Ramjay Sahib' by the locals. What I have gleaned from official records and after talking to the old people in the family is that it is important to mention an incident to explain what the times were like. During that troubled period, a rich, far-sighted merchant, also a relative living in Nainital, became the informal treasurer for the English. He provided boarding and lodging to the badly battered British families and also loaned them cash. Ramjay Sahib got him the title of 'Raisahib' with all the benefits from the English once the hullabaloo died down in the hills. And we and his successors lived in great style thereafter.

A study in contrast to our ancestor was the town postmaster, Amin Khan, beloved of all. He was an extremely honest man. And despite daily treks through jungles, where tigers and bears roamed freely, despite bad roads, no letter ever got lost, no money order was not delivered on time. Ramjay Sahib had been angry with the Muslims from Ruhelkhand since the Mutiny, so suddenly he accused postmaster Amin Khan of giving the Terai rebels shelter and providing them with local newspapers. Amin Khan was fired without any evidence. Our Padda had heard from his aunt that, to save postmaster Amin Khan's job, a few locals went as far as Calcutta and returned with a recommendation letter from the postmaster general asking that his suspension be revoked. But Ramjay Sahib rejected the letter on the grounds that Amin Khan's community had proven to be enemies of the British during the Mutiny and, if reinstated, a popular postmaster might get the locals to regroup and rebel.

At that time, the English commissioner had the last word. Even the officials in Calcutta could not oppose him. On top of that, Ramjay Sahib came from old money and was the son-in-law of a commissioner called Henry Lexington. He was called the King of Kumaon, and his word was the law. It is said that the Mutiny enraged him so much that he snatched and tore the papers from the hands of a lawyer trying to defend Muslim rebels in his court. He said that there the law was what he said, not what was written in some books. So, our Amin Khan was removed from his post despite the people's requests and sent home to Najibabad. Nobody knows what happened to him.

But the Sahib then offered posts in the police to the dangerous criminals who had helped the police in catching the runaway rebels after the Mutiny. This was their reward.

There was no jail sentence for them thereafter, no hearing.

A few from my father's generation used to say with great pride that English rule was better than free India's. To which one of my comrades, who is also Padda's cousin, Hira Ballabh, had said, 'You ate their shit, and now you're acting proud about it?'

There was a furore outside. But within our homes, the women said that the way he said it may have been harsh, but what he said was correct. They were shit-eaters indeed!

He was a ferocious officer, Ramjay Sahib. He declared martial law in the area as soon as he heard of the rebellion of the Awadh army and subjects and of Awadh's Begum conspiring with Delhi's Badshah. Because of his reputation and the fear of the gun-bearing soldiers, the rebels could not carry out any violence here. The locals who made even the slightest noise were immediately hanged from trees without a hearing. There still exists near Nainital a spot we call Phansi Gadhera, the rivulet for hanging.

Next door, Garhwal's blood was hotter. A few rebels there were even executed. There were shoot-at-sight orders for the rebels. Nobody knows the number of Pahadis killed at this time.

There were no newspapers available that could report incidents as they happened. What is certain is that, instead of in the hills, it was in the foothills in the Terai region that many of the rebels who had escaped were killed.

Then, Ramjay Sahib drew up a well-thought-out war plan. He spread the news of rebels being hanged from trees, as also many princes and their generals. At this, most of the people who had risen against them quietened down. He also declared that he would be rewarding the most ardent supporters of the English. The result was as he had expected.

It was the sixteenth year of his rule, and by then, he knew each and every person and every part of the area well. When he freed the murder convicts languishing in the area's jails to fight the rebels advancing from Kaladhungi, he assured them that, if they helped the police catch the rebels, they would get police jobs. It was these convicts dressed as policemen who brought shame to the police force for looting. It spread a fair deal of discontent too. But that is a story for another time.

Among the local kings, the Nawab of Rampur (unlike Delhi's Badshah Zafar and Lucknow's Begum Hazrat Mahal) proved loyal to the English. However, the rebellion of the landlords they had considered loyal in Delhi and Lucknow had shaken the faith of the English in Muslims. The moles among them told Ramjay Sahib that a few rebels had marshalled two tanks under the guidance of two local Muslim leaders, Kale Khan and Fazal Haque, and were on their way here through the forests. When he received this secret message, he advised many of the English officers in Terai, Meerut, Bareilly, Muradabad and Rampur to come here to the hills with their families.

The elders say that, after this, there was such an influx of the English in Nainital that there was no place to house them. Not even hotels. They ran out of electricity and water. The state and the number of English families who had been forced to run away from their homes overnight was pitiable indeed. But Ramjay Sahib was dedicated to the cause of protecting his own people. To save them, he could go to any lengths, even bend the rules.

With the removal of the East India Company and the establishment of the British Crown, administrative work started anew. But the English had been both the Company's officials as well as the Queen's officers. The Queen pardoned most of the rebels and declared that the British now ruled Indian waterbodies, forests and agricultural land. They ruled us as they were united, but we kept fighting like cats and dogs among ourselves.

It is said that when Lord Mayo came to this area for an inspection, he was so happy with the administration that he gave Ramjay Sahib a promotion, and he ruled the area like a king until 1884. Our headmaster will write to you in detail about his forest administration and about Hira's lover Hewitt Sahib's many jungle adventures.

It was the Terai, where the forests that had until then been considered God's property, which was now under British rule. The first character in the drama of this new administration was Hira Bai's first husband and our hero, Edward K. Hewitt, forest officer to the Imperial Forest Department, Kumaon and Terai areas, to Her Majesty's government. He met our heroine, the Baadi Bibi Victoria Masih, née Hira Bai, on a forest inspection tour. This visit could not have been understood without this historical context, a vivid though complicated history of the region that I have provided.

Do let me know if you need any additional information related to my findings. Strike while the iron is still hot, or as they say here: '*Bagh ki khai bakri ka rakt abhi hai hi, do aankhar chahe toh bol de bakhat hai hi*.' The blood of the goat eaten by the tiger is still here. Add your two words if you wish – the time is still here.

Warm wishes,
Himmat Singh 'Nirbhay'

Ranikhet

Greetings to the most honourable Vidya Devi.

Hope you are well. Himmat Singh told me that he has sent you his information. That is what we knew would happen. The reason is that, being a seasoned journalist, it is second nature for him to collect information and turn it into a story and send it to its destination a lot more quickly than us lesser mortals. It is my personal opinion that journalists these days, in their haste to publish their stories, don't do justice to them, and all that their readers get to scratch is the surface. Even then, I would say that Himmat Bhai is as fearless, honest and hard-working a journalist as his name suggests. Hence Paramlal and I had asked him to send you the history of the 1857 Mutiny in Kumaon.

We hope, actually are confident, that by the time we have collated and written down the interesting story of Hira Bai, aka Victoria Masih, and her husband Edward Hewitt, Himmat Singh's letter would have apprised you of the history of the Mutiny years in the region.

So, now I present to you the story of our main characters, and also record the administrative changes made here after the Mutiny, which shaped the destinies of Victoria, née Hira, Edward K. Hewitt, and their daughter, Baby Camellia Angelina, née Anjali Bai.

A connoisseur of forests, hunting and women, and known to his friends as 'Eddie', our Hewitt Sahib was the spoilt third son of a respected English lord. As you know, according to the law of primogeniture, at that time, it was only the eldest son who inherited all the property in England. So many of the younger sons often took up jobs in colonies. Since Hewitt was the black sheep of his family, facing charges of the rape and murder of one of his maids, his family decided to pack off this troublesome son to the East India Company's army stationed in India. The family name was saved, and the worrisome Eddie landed in India as Hewitt Sahib. Not unlike spoilt sons these days who get plum jobs abroad through family connections instead of jail time, he soon got the opportunity to lead an army battalion in Afghanistan expecting it to be a cakewalk.

But the Afghans turned out to be tough fighters who posed stiff opposition to these outsiders. Eventually, the British army faced a massive defeat at the hands of Dost Mohammad's son, Amir Ali. Most of Hewitt's soldiers were sold off as slaves in the bazaars of Kabul and Kandahar. Bearing the burden of this shame, he made his way back to India. He now found that he could no longer cope with the discipline in the army. Invoking the name of his family yet again, he sent a letter to the Viceroy in Calcutta asking for voluntary retirement from the army and expressed the desire to take up a civilian job. He was lucky that the rulers were looking to expand Queen Victoria's reign to Burma and Sri Lanka and wanted to post more Englishmen not just in the army but also in the government. They also wanted to acquire the rich forests in the Himalayan region. The chances of finding minerals in the hills were slim, but the forests promised high-value wood, and rare birds and animals to chase and hunt.

The Company bosses decided that a few English loyalists would be posted to the Forest Departments being instituted in the region, so that timber for rail lines in the new colonies and musk, lion skin and herbs for British nobles could be procured easily by the government. So, soon after his resignation from the army, Hewitt managed to get a senior position in the Forest Department in Kumaon.

This posting felt far better than his expectations. Clean air, simple people, beautiful women, and lush verdant forests that offered a lot of game. This hunter loved the region so much, that he stayed here for many years like Ramjay, and he, too, lived like a king.

It is important to clarify here that, before coming under the dominion of Queen Victoria, these forests and lands were under the rule of the local king. But only in name. Neither the king nor his subjects disturbed the land because they considered it sacred. They only picked up things they needed, that too, after asking the gods for permission. The job of tax collection was carried out here by two officials who also paid their share of the taxes out of their salaries.

All this changed after the Mutiny. Under Hewitt Sahib, all these lands, rivers and forests were declared the sole properties of the Crown. The public could now actually draw up papers to buy or sell ancestral land and springs. Government officials told the people that this was a new system. The local representative of the Queen, responsible for sending reports to his superiors in Calcutta, was called the 'bandobasti' or a fixer-upper. The first thing he did after joining office was make sure that the Public Works Department stopped functioning. Bandobasti was now the de facto landlord. He was the man who pushed the files to the English officer concerned only after getting a certain commission. Even after he got the relevant approvals, he would start working only after receiving a bribe. People were told that no work could get done for free. If they didn't have money, they could make offerings of forest honey, fruits, borax or walnuts to get their work done.

Before the British arrived, stepwells, wells, ponds and temples were also considered sacred public property. But the Queen's rule turned all forests and lands, from Madras to the Himalayas, into the domain of the Crown, and the public became outsiders and potential enemies. The bandobasti secured the safety of other forests by giving outsiders who were willing to pay bribes the permission to extract wood, bamboo and kattha from these forests. In forests elsewhere, even plucking a leaf without official permission was forbidden. He delegated the job of catching and fining trespassing villagers to patrols. They were also like their masters. They beat up many. Many went to jail, but there were no hearings. The contractors and forest rangers filled their coffers.

The three main officers of the time – Kumaon's Hewitt Sahib, Garhwal's John Campbell Sahib and Terai-Bhabar's Peter Clutterbuck Sahib (Clutterbuckganj was named after him) – were all expert hunters.

After Hewitt's posting, his friends and he would set about in their sun hats and boots to hunt and pick up women on the pretext of inspection whenever desired.

The locals who had seen the mutineers' executions were afraid of these red-faced, tall and broad, gun-slinging Englishmen. The government was earning more than expected from the taxes collected by these officers from cattle grazing. Which is why even when these officers started interfering in the lives of the locals and started grabbing their women, the government looked the other way.

Hewitt Sahib would sometimes give a few people the right to gather pine cones, wood and grass. But there was a condition attached to it. The permission was only given to those who had a woman or a young boy in their family the Sahib fancied. Those whose girls had suddenly disappeared were even allowed to graze their cattle. In those times, these farmers and forest-gatherers used to hold their animals dearer than their women. So they would bear with all of this with a heavy heart. They could get themselves another wife from the money they saved after selling the goods gathered with the Sahib's permission. They had to run their households, didn't they? And who could they complain to anyway?

I have heard that Hewitt used to say that these forests were not built by the gods but by the English, and nobody else had the right to take anything from them. Such an absurd notion. You can call this a comrade's viewpoint. I have only stated everything I heard.

The lives of the people of the region underwent a change. The panchayats held to address mishaps stopped. Where can a woman tied to her husband and children go? The moment they would see a white officer galloping in on his horse, all the women in the fields and all the singers and dancers in the marketplaces would run for cover. If someone caught his fancy, the Sahib did not care if she was someone's daughter or wife, a courtesan, an upper-caste or a low-caste. There were those who entered temples, and even homes and kitchens, with their boots on, to pick up the women.

The Sahib also proved to be an expert in squeezing the rich forests and making money. He introduced the locals to the saw. It began to be used to fell tall, ancient deodar trees. 'Why do you fear divine reprisal?' the Sahib sneered. 'Look, I am paying you such hefty salaries.' The deodar and oak wood made into planks for the railway tracks in Burma and Lanka started getting shipped at a steady pace. If you did as they commanded, the English not only paid the wages but also distributed generous amounts of alcohol and meat.

The Pahadis had never seen so much hard cash before. And the English did not just pay money but also gave them brass tokens with holes called hundis to make trade easier. The locals made a song in the Nanda Devi mela: '*Aag lago sarkara double mein pado tot*' (Fie upon this government that has made a hole even in coin).

I have also seen a string made out of these hundis in my dadi's wooden trunk.

My dadi told me that when, after Hewitt Sahib's death, these hundis were demonetized, her mother-in-law sold off a bucketful of them to the kabadiwallah as brass junk. In a temple in Ranikhet, a brass bell that Hewitt Sahib had presented to the local deity, in lieu of saving his life from a man-eating lion, can still be heard. I'll show you the temple on your next visit.

The rest of the information is immaterial. Hope your family and you are healthy and happy. Paramlal-ji will soon send you his findings, with which most of your questions will get answered. Even so, if there's anything else you'd like to ask, please let me know. All three of us are very happy to be of help.

With best wishes,
Pitambar Dutt Pant
(Former headmaster)

Ranikhet

Dear Sister Vidya-ji,

Affectionate greetings. Hope all's well.

It was such a pleasure meeting you, and your simplicity, courteousness and love for music made me very happy. In my opinion, the current practice of endless distribution of music through technology and social media without much research is only hurting music, not helping it. Some self-appointed culture vultures think they can make our music international with just the click of a mouse. But classical music, Vidya-ji, is sacred. To this day, the path to its heart is long and difficult. Modern music that's learned without sweating over each note, each microtone, without a guru, is available at every nook and cranny like paan masala. But classical art forms will not reveal their innermost secrets to amateur hobbyists and lovers. The notes of music are like gods. They will only reveal themselves to devotees who have been praying to them for years.

Now, to the matter at hand.

The closest friend of my long-lost youth, Sukumar Chatterjee Babu had once said that converting a love story into a factual narrative is as difficult as it is for a cow to catch a lion. This old man can see the truth in it as he writes about the century-and-a-half-or-so-old love story of the English forest officer, Eddie Hewitt Sahib and the two Baadi singers, Gulab and Hira.

I grew up hearing my mother say that nothing truly dies in a land where men and women die every year by suicide, disease or in accidents. Their romantic tales, however, live on. All you have to do is invoke their names and all their stories will tumble out like a cascading waterfall. I find this connection a little odd. But I now find that this was no exaggeration. Not just Hewitt and Hiruli (an affectionate version of Hira in the local dialect) but many lovers have come into this world and gone. It is the stories of their love sung while sowing and harvesting crops that have made them immortal.

It would have been better had you been able to listen to the songs written by these Baadis from their own mouths. But times are such that it is I who will have to present the love story of Eddie Sahib, Gulab and Hiruli to you in my prosaic text. Please forgive me for my mistakes.

I had first heard the love story of Eddie Sahib and Hiruli many years ago at Vasant Panchami from a Bharti Singh who sang about it while going from house to house, collecting grains and money. This strange, mysterious tale drew me in so deep that I later followed another Baadi singer, Partima Devi, to her house to record it on a tape recorder.

The Baadis are an old clan of local musicians with immense contribution to the area's folk music. They claim to be descendants of the gandharvas who had started music in this world on the command of Lord Shiva. They claim that, while establishing their ancestors in this land, the lord of their clan, Shiva, ordered them to become musicians instead of taking up farming. Also, that they would go around with their families, and through their music, draw out all the bad omens from the land to make it more fertile.

Since then, the Baadis have been living like wandering Shaivite sadhus. The men wear circular discs called mundras in their ears and keep dreadlocks, and their women wear ghungroos and dance while singing old ballads to collect money, salt, grains and clothes from the homes of farmers. They marry among themselves. The men and women interact freely and drink a lot. Which is why householders steer clear of them.

Soon, in this era of high tech, this tribe is going to become extinct. That I can see. In Uttarakhand, many of their songs continue to live on in the hearts of its people, and elderly Baadi singers are accorded respect if they are present at a puja or on any auspicious occasion. But that is all.

When I heard one Partima Devi from this tribe, she was singing a song in which a singer-dancer named Gulab was complaining to the supreme god, Shiva. Dancing to the beats of her dholki, she pleaded to Shiva like a daughter would to her maiden home, 'May the curse of us Baadis be on you, Oh Shiva! Why did you not give us a part of this land? It is on your orders that our backs, which are like the treacherous mountains, are open to wounds of all kinds.'

I just stopped. This brave landless singer was cursing the Supreme God in such a strong voice about her hard life. I asked her to stop and ran home to get the tape recorder. When I requested her to sing the entire song, Partima Devi looked at me and said, 'I have so many long stories about Gulab and Hiruli, Babu-ji. But we are nomads. We wander about for survival. Where will we find the time to sit and talk like you babus? If you want to listen to the full song, please offer something. Come with me to our camp and buy us all mutton and alcohol. Then you can fill your boxes with songs about Gulab, Hiruli, Hewitt Sahib – anyone.'

And that's what I did.

I was so attracted to this singer who had the gumption to even reprimand the god of gods, Shiva, that I lost no time in fulfilling all of Partima's demands and lived with her family and brethren in Dang Chaura village for a full two weeks. I returned to the buzzing grapevine in the city. Some said that I had decided to marry a Baadi woman, others that, after spending a few days with her, I may have been thrown into some abyss. Or maybe I had murdered her to be rid of her!

Anyway! People ignored me for a few days wondering what I had been up to. Even my wife gave me the cold shoulder for two months. Then, things slowly came back to normal. Had to. And I was not ashamed of what I had done then or even now. Had I not gone off, how could I have narrated that eternal love ballad, which had been waiting for the right listener all these years?

This is how the song, 'The Ballad of Hira', opens:

> There were two young women in Dharali Village, their names were Gulab and Hira – they were aunt and niece. Beautiful, doe-eyed, they had grown up drinking the water from the Sirkanth river. And then, many young men started to drink in their beauty. The women got tired of hiding behind the boulders around the river. The stones near the waterfall were worn smooth by the young men clambering over them to take a peep. One day, the aunt was married off to a Kumaoni in Naikyana village. Poor Gulab missed her niece Hira; she wilted as she remembered the waters of the Sirkanth river and the taste of ragi bread.

Then, the song goes into great detail about how, in the Naikyana village, Gulab, tired of her mother-in-law's beatings and husband's disinterest, returns to her maiden home in Garhwal accompanied by her brother Nathua Baadi and other family members. On the way, they bump into Hewitt Sahib who is out on a forest inspection on his horse.

> Gulab put a hand around her niece's neck and joked, 'Oh Sahib, don't ogle at us girls; first take off your yellow-and-black-striped trousers, or our lambs grazing in the forests might mistake you for a tiger, take fright, and go jump off the rocks. And the young shepherds who are our brothers-in-law, who still get their hair combed by their mothers, will get beaten black and blue at home for no fault of theirs.'
>
> Entranced by the charming girl's laughter, the Sahib first laughed, and then actually took off his pants and threw them away. Then he winked at the girls and rode away. The young girls just laughed all the way home, joking with the young shepherds.
>
> Four days later, the Sahib arrived at Gulab's older brother Nathua Baadi's house in Bhagirathi valley on horseback.

> He entered his cave-like house without even taking off his boots and said, 'I am Hewitt Sahib, master of the jungles. I am enamoured of your beautiful sister, Gulab. I have come here to make her my wife and take her to my bungalow with apple orchards that never fails to impress onlookers. Now, name your price!'

I must clarify here that, in those days, it wasn't considered improper among tribes to buy or sell a girl with her consent if she had left her first marital home or had been abandoned by her husband. So, the story the song tells from here, to which I have added some information collected from local sources, is this: After debating with the greedy Nathua Baadi, the Sahib's raazinama was prepared and Nathua Baadi's sister Gulab went to Hewitt Sahib's home. There weren't too many happy days in Gulab's destiny. She died within a year from complications in pregnancy and left behind a brown-skinned emaciated infant. People began to wonder if the child was Hewitt's or the outcome of her liaison with one of her Baadi lovers. But by then, the Sahib's eyes had landed on Gulab's young and beautiful niece, Hira. He went to convince Nathua again for his marriage with Hira. People say that, the first time, Nathua had managed to extract five hundred rupees from the lovelorn Sahib, and the amount had been so big for the nomadic shepherd that he had been ecstatic. But now that he had seen the luxuries in the Sahib's house, he gauged the right price for this union.

Then there was also the question of Gulab's child.

Everyone knew that Hewitt Sahib was a creature of pleasures. If he did not like the bargaining and brought some other woman home, what would happen to the child? The pragmatic Nathua thought of all this and finally said that the Sahib can offer whatever he thinks is right, but there is one condition. Kumaon had not suited his Gulab. The niece Hira was also scared of the place. He would be grateful if the Sahib could get a transfer to Garhwal so that his young Hira could live close to her natal family. And if he agrees, the Sahib should get a pukka home made for the Baadi's family so that nobody raises any fingers at the maiden home of such a powerful officer's wife.

After some consideration, the Sahib agreed to this condition. But he was no fool. There was a reason behind his consent. He had been hearing that there had been several complaints made to the headquarters in Calcutta about his indiscretions, and Ramjay Sahib, too, had secretly warned him through a few letters to be a little more circumspect.

The people of Garhwal at that time were simpler and more trusting than the people of Kumaon. There were numerous forests and forest resources, but the natives there had no business sense. They did not realize how much money could be made from their sacred groves. So Hewitt agreed to move to Garhwal and sent a request for a transfer to the highest officer in Calcutta.

This is how Hewitt, after terrorizing Kumaon, came to Garhwal.

But Hewitt was also well aware of the social disapproval for native wives. So before shifting to Garhwal, he got Hiruli converted at a big church in Ranikhet. And after the priest baptized Hiruli as Victoria Masih, he married her there so as to redeem himself somewhat in Ramjay Sahib's eyes. After becoming Victoria Masih, Hiruli Baadi entered the Sahib's grand house in Mussoorie with his son from his first marriage to Gulab. The boy was christened Nathaniel (the Baadis called him Nathu Sahib).

After arriving in Mussoorie with Victoria and Nathaniel, Hewitt Sahib not only found a nice place near a slope for Hira's Baadi relatives but also had Hira's younger brother Motiya converted to Christianity, had him baptized as Martin, and got him admitted to a new convent school where he learned English. Even though he was born to a family of uneducated and backward folk, Motiya was a good-looking boy and blessed with a sharp brain. In a matter of a few years, he was proficient in various languages and learned new manners that pleased Hewitt Sahib. Nathu, Hira's stepson, followed him everywhere, and the wily Martin took advantage of this. In the village, he became famous as Martin Master and soon rose to be Hewitt's most trusted secretary. Meanwhile, Nathua Baadi was happy to have a good life in his new home and let Martin call the shots.

Now, it was Hewitt Sahib's turn to make a lady out of Hira. It is said that he disliked the English women born out of wedlock who came to India only to marry a rich English officer, and their fake airs, and the prejudice the English had against the natives. He married Hira instead of keeping her as a concubine just to spite them. Then he sent her brother to a missionary school to teach him English the way the English spoke and took his newborn daughter to Allahabad for her baptism. He kept a Muslim tutor, Mahmood Baksh Tankha, to teach Hira English and manners and Urdu like the begums of the nawabs of Terai. He played a big role in taking Hira outside Garhwal.

I don't know whether Mahmood was a good tutor or whether Hira was as studious as her brother Motiya, but I have heard that, within just a year, she started speaking in English fluently. As a reward, Hewitt Sahib doubled Mahmood's fees. I have heard that the Sahib also threw a big party at the Mussoorie Club after his daughter's baptism, which was attended not just by the native nawabs who were in the hills to spend the summers but even the district's highest English officers who had come after getting over their rancour because, by now, whether because of Hiruli's luck or her daughter Camellia Angelina's, Hewitt Sahib's trade in timber, musk and lion skin had become a massive success.

The Sahib adored his lucky daughter. It is said that the pale-skinned Angelina of the green-blue eyes used to resemble Hewitt's English mother. He bought for her expensive clothes from Calcutta and new books for his son Nathu. But the angry Nathu threw those books away because he wanted silks like his sister. Gulab's son hated his stepmother Hira and her light-skinned daughter vehemently.

Once, when he said something to his father about pampering the Muslim teacher too much, Eddie, even more short-tempered than him, beat Nathu up with a stick. Since then, a strain began to develop in the relationship between father and son. Nathu started to act up and throw new tantrums every day. When he was beaten, he screamed and abused his father, stepmother, her teacher Mahmood – whom he called her lover – and even the innocent Angelina. Hira's family life was badly disturbed. When they had guests, she was always apprehensive about how the wayward Nathu would behave and what he might tell the outsiders about her and the family. The Jesuit brothers in school tried counselling Nathu at Hewitt Sahib's behest. They even got him to swear on the Bible that he'd respect his parents. But at home, Nathu was like a man possessed. The only person to whom he listened was his uncle, Martin Master. When Nathu was locked up in his room for breaking things, it was Martin who arrived to open the lock and let him out.

It was discovered much later that actually it was Hira's sweet-talking brother Martin Master who was responsible for driving a wedge between father and son and for spreading false rumours about Mahmood and Hira's relationship. The man whom Hewitt Sahib trusted totally was the one responsible for brainwashing his nephew against his parents and for getting him addicted to the liquor and cannabis that were to kill him when he was only twenty-five.

Martin Master had been eyeing the Sahib's palatial house for a long time and tried to cause a rift between his sister and the Sahib. He got his greedy father to support his plan to try and mess up the land records since he handled all the papers. But Hewitt was no fool, and kept account of every cent in his coffers.

After many failed attempts, finally, Martin found in the short-tempered Nathaniel the perfect weapon. He set out to increase the tensions between the father and the addict son to such an extent that, one day, the son told his father that he was going to live with

Martin Master. Martin told Hewitt Sahib he had no problem; both were his homes. The Sahib also agreed since he was annoyed with the dusky, ill-mannered and rebellious son from his first wife. That is how Nathaniel went to live in Martin Master's house, and on the pretext of looking after Nathaniel, Martin Master got his salary tripled, well above the wages paid to Hira's tutor, Mahmood Baksh.

Years later, when Nathu was around sixteen and Baby Angelina around twelve, Hewitt Sahib, who was camping in the Bhilangana valley on his inspection rounds, went missing. The coolies said that he was last seen near the Bhilangana river, hunting tigers. The river was in spate, and it had been raining heavily. Hewitt's badly mangled corpse was found almost a week later near Haridwar. Some said that he had been shot before being thrown into the river, otherwise he was an expert swimmer. Some said that he had been attacked by a man-eating tiger and may have lost his footing and fallen into the river. Others said that maybe he was disturbed by the escalating tensions at home, and on discovering Martin's true intentions, had just lost it and jumped into the river.

Who knows?

Whatever may have been the case, Hewitt's death was just as dramatic as his life. It took about a year for everything to come under Martin's control. After that, there was hardly anyone who remembered that Hewitt Sahib had even existed. It was only the Baadi songs that remembered Hewitt Sahib and Gulab–Hiruli. Hewitt Sahib's grave was still fresh when Martin made a quick trip to Calcutta with all his property papers. He had forged Hewitt's signatures and managed to get all his property, money, even Hewitt Sahib's pension fund transferred in Nathu's name with himself as the sole guardian of Sahib's minor son. Soon after, Nathu and Martin and other members of the Baadi family moved into Hira's house. In a few days, the Baadi family, guided by Martin Master, had taken over the entire estate and told Hira that she would have to pay them a good price or the family would sell her off to someone. 'You can go wherever you can find shelter with your daughter if you want to avoid that,' she was told.

A community panchayat was called at Hira's request. Hira's wily father told the panches that he, in his old age, couldn't bear the expenses of the now-converted and, therefore, alien mother, and her daughter's English education. He also said that the house was now in the name of Hira's aunt's son, Nathaniel, who was actually not the son of the Englishman but of a Baadi man. Gulab had already been pregnant when she had returned to her maiden home, he said.

Again, who knows? All stories from the area appear amid swirling mists, you see.

What everyone knew well was that Nathu did not get along with his stepmother. If Hira stayed here and her blue-green-eyed daughter Camellia Angelina kept attending the English school, it was possible that, sooner or later, the missionaries would appropriate the property and the Baadis would end up looking like fools. Which is why the panchayat decided to take every aspect into consideration before arriving at a decision.

Before their next hearing, the panchayat elders visited Hewitt's mansion and were awed by it. It is said that they sat on the Sahib's chairs and ate a lot of meat and drank a lot of alcohol at the table, and returned to declare Nathaniel as Hewitt's successor and to nominate Nathua Baadi and Martin Master as his guardians. Hira was given a month's notice to come to a decision. After all, finding a suitor for a beautiful widow, especially when she had a beautiful daughter as well, would not take too much time.

Spoilt by Hewitt's love and care, Hira declared that she, the wife of a tiger, would never stoop to living with jackals. After such an insulting insinuation, the Baadis' panchayat declared that they had made their decision. How could a woman run a property without the support of her kinsmen? It would have been a different had she had a son. How could a widow, the mother of a girl, claim property? 'If you want to have the airs of a rich Englishwoman, go to the plains where there are many missions. Stay there. We'll think that you have cut your ties with us,' Hira was told.

Beyond this, local sources can't say much. What I have managed to gather from the grapevine is that Hira then took her daughter along, and with Mahmood Baksh's help, all three moved to a city somewhere in the plains.

As for Hewitt Sahib's English officer friends, they had always been angry with him for raising his native wife to the level of an Englishwoman. Who says that the caste system is practised only by Indians?

Hira and Baby Angelina's story brings us to this point and then stops. Hoping to meet you again for a joyous occasion.

Many greetings.

Yours truly,
Lala Paramlal Shah

Dear ones,

Forwarding you Tapish Sahib's mail. Our Bi Allarakkhi is no more. May God bring peace to that weary soul.

Vidya

Rampur

Greetings to Mohtarma Vidya Behen from Makhdoom Alam Khan 'Tapish'.

It is with a heavy heart that I inform you that, after your departure, Mohtarma Bi Allarakkhi could not recover, and despite treatment, she passed away last Friday. May Allah grant that pure soul a passage to heaven.

I also regret to tell you that her only daughter, Haidari Begum, and granddaughter, Amaal Jaan, could not meet her while she lived. They could not find a flight from America to India to arrive before she breathed her last. By the time they reached the kothi, Bi Allarakkhi was gone. The next day, after burning incense at Bi Allarakkhi and Ammajani's graves, they left. When she was at death's door, I asked Allarakkhi Bi if she had any last wishes or messages, to which she simply said that all the secrets of her singing lay in the spinal cord of all ragas – the Merukhand. Tell Haidari, she said, that she should not stop doing riyaz along the Merukhand path; that will keep her musical spine straight. She must also not allow her daughter Amaal to stop practising.

Aah yeh banda-e-garib, aap se lau lagaaye kyun?
Aa na sake jo waqt par, waqt se yaad aaye kyun?

Oh why has this beggarly heart moored itself to you?
From hour to hour, why recall one who could never make
it on time?

Everything was over by the time Haidari Begum and Amaal Jaan reached. When I conveyed Bi's last message to her, Haidari embraced her mother's tombstone, and stroking her grave, kept crying softly for a while. That was Allah's will perhaps.

What was my own relationship with Bi?

I had not answered when you had asked. What could have I said? I have not been able to fathom whether I was drawn to her or her voice. Nobody did or could make a place in Bi's heart after the death of Haidari's father, Moti Pandit. I just want to repeat the truth through one of Bi's favourite khayals in Raga Desi:

Saanchi kahat hain Sadarang, ye nadi naav sanjog,
kaun kisike aave jaave, daana paani kismet laave,
yahi kahat sab log.

Says the poet Sadarang, the only eternal connection
is between the boat and the river,
who comes, who goes, the food we eat, the water we drink
– is all kismet, so say folks.

I have said a little, but you can draw your own conclusions from it.

In the letter you had sent after reaching Delhi, you had requested Bi Allarakkhi that if she had any information about her friend, Hira Bai, she pass it on to you.

As you know, Bi did not talk much, and she was easily hurt. And in all these years, I have not been able to talk to her about much other than her professional work. But a few days before her demise, Bi had summoned me and said that she wanted to dictate whatever she remembered about Hira Bai for your book. For the next two days, she slowly told me many things in her earthy voice: about the culture of her times, and Hira Bai. I was instructed that, through this note to you, I reveal all that she could not speak about when you met her last. I am sending you the information because one never knows when I, too, might receive my final summons.

She also requested that I send the pages to you in Delhi as they are, so that they are in front of you, and whenever you write the book about that era, this information can also be included in it, if you so wish. It will bring her a lot of peace if that happens.

You will be happy to know that I forwarded your address to the America-bound Haidari too. I also told her that it was Bi's wish that if she had any information about Benares and Sherkothi, that she should send it to you. She will send you all the information by letter or email at her convenience. She said that Amaal is the most educated in her family. If Amaal were to agree, she would ask her to write everything down and send the notes by email or post from America.

Haidari is also an introvert like Bi Allarakkhi, but I told her how freely Bi had spoken with you. And that she had an unshakeable faith that only you had the gift to turn her memories into a chronological narrative. Which is why it is our duty to share every bit of information that we have with you. Bi Allarakkhi's unhappy soul might find some peace in it.

I had also asked my grandson Nawaz to send Bi Haidari's email ID to you. He is the only one in the family who knows about computers.

He also has a good command over English by Allah's grace, at least much better than I do. But this generation cannot be trusted in these matters. For me, everything seems to have lost meaning after Bi's death. I am also counting my days, immersed in memories. Like Bi Sahiba, it will bring me a great deal of happiness too, should this information be honoured with a relevant placement in your book.

May Allah bless you with a long life.

Teri khoobi, teri izzat, tera iqbal doona ho,
tu auron ke liye duniya mein neki ka namoona ho.

May your talents, your reputation, your prosperity double,
may you become an example of virtue to others in this world.

Your well-wisher,
Makhdoom Alam Khan 'Tapish'.

***Makhzaan-e-ulfat-e-Hira Bai*, as dictated by Bi Allarakkhi, penned down by Makhdoom Alam Khan 'Tapish':**

Jal rahein hain e daag-e-dil turbat pe jaane ke liye,
roshni kam ho rahi hai neend aane ke liye.

My spirit and heart are craving the last journey,
the light, too, is dimming, so I can sleep.

My mother Husna Bai, whom I lovingly called Ammajani, was a renowned and prosperous tawaif in Benares, and was the student of the well-known sarangi player, Ustad Aashiq Ali Khan Sahib. She had made a name for herself for various kinds of classical and semi-classical singing ranging from khayal, tappa, tarana to the light-hearted thumri, chaiti and kajari. Benares in her time was famous not only for its scholars of Sanskrit but also its classical composers, musicians and dancers. Almost every ambitious exponent of these art forms came to Benares to hone and display their expertise and to pray to the holy river Ganga-ji. In our times, musicians, musicologists, old and moneyed patrons, and well-known shayars and Bhakha poets, all visited the houses of tawaifs regularly. Most of these performers were rich, and owned much land and many houses in the area.

The two gems of mehfils in those years were my Ammajani and her friend Hira Bai. The biggest reason for their success was that they had humbly and rigorously trained under some of the greatest and most exacting music gurus of the time. There were a number of famous musicians living in Benares, some of the nation's best: singers such as Masooman, Badi Maina Bai, Nokhi Bai, Dallu Jaan, Champa Bai, and rich cognoscenti such as Babu Harichandra, Janab Sherbahadur, aka Bacchu Babu, and the Maharaja of Kashi, Prabhunarayan Ju. Gopal Mandir's Channu-ji, Misir-ji and Bade Ramdas-ji were some of the notable Dhrupad gurus. The sitar maestro Aashiq Ali, too, had earned immense name among the experts. His patron was one major zamindar, a Pandey from Ahrora. Tabla virtuosos included Baldev Sahay, and on the tappa-thumri scene, there were the unforgettable Ganpat Rao and Taj Miyan. Their voices shone like torches across the Ganga.

You can also ask Radhaprasad-ji, the grandson of Raibahadur Vikram Singh-ji, for information. From the time of Radhaprasad's great-grandfather, they had been hoarding a vast collection of compositions by the past generation of musicians. If they have not been thrown away in ignorance, they can still be obtained. I only remember a few years in Benares, because I was only fourteen when Ammajani left Benares and moved to Sherkothi.

It was very painful for me to leave Benares. I was born there, grew up there, made friends there, and started studying music there.

But call it destiny: There was a king, the owner of a big estate, Kalika Prasad Singh Ju. Ammajani fell madly in love with him and agreed to leave Benares and move to the faraway Ruhelkhand to live with him. Maharaj Ju left no stone unturned in caring for her, but who can stop the heart from wandering? Any time anyone mentioned Benares, Ammajani would go quiet and misty-eyed.

Actually, after coming to this side of the Ganga, Ammajani grew very lonely, and it became difficult for her to pass the time when Maharaja Ju would not come home for days. So, she sought his permission to visit nearby places occasionally to watch plays that the travelling theatre companies would put up, of course, only in the company of trusted old chaperons. Ammajani had become fond of theatre after moving here, and sadly, it was theatre that would destroy her later.

The travelling theatre companies were mostly owned by Parsi seths. They spoke Gujarati among themselves, but were savvy traders conversant in several other Indian languages. They had gauged that in the north, Hindustani was the language spoken commonly among people. So, they had plays written for the stage by renowned ustads of Urdu, like Agha Hashr Kashmiri, and writers of Bhakha, like Betab. These were shown in different cities as ticketed performances and drew large audiences. The plays were mostly musicals, with sonorous scores especially prepared by classical musicians. The booklets of these songs were sold at all major melas. Given the vast revenues that these plays earned them, the seths accorded deep respect to the professional singer-actors and their ustads. They were retained on good salaries and the theatre company took good care of their boarding and lodging. Seats for the stars were always reserved in first-class compartments when they would be travelling by train.

One of the biggest companies of the time was one Moonlight Theatre Company. It had come to our town. It seems like only yesterday when Ammajani had gone to watch their play

Bharat Milaap. The heroine in the lead role in that play was Patience Kapoor. A very beautiful Anglo-Indian girl, she was pale-skinned, blonde, with merry blue eyes like a deep ocean. Ammajani told us that there were three beautiful Anglo-Indian sisters in Calcutta, and Patience Memsahib was one of them. One of her relatives, Amelia Cooper, had become the English tutor to the Raja of Charna's estate and his mistress, Jamila Bai, also a singer and courtesan. Amelia Cooper, Ammajani and Jamila Bai became good friends. It was Amelia and Jamila Bai who had my Ammajani addicted to Parsi company theatre. The three friends made sure they saw every play in their town or in the neighbouring cities. So, they had gotten the tickets of this play *Bharat Milaap* for all three of them.

The three friends wanted to watch this play especially because Kajjan, the daughter of the other famous bai of Benares, Sharifa Jaan, was appearing in a bit role as Sita in it for the very first time. She, too, had blue-green eyes like a cat's, so she was called Kajjan, but her real name was Champakali. Even Bi Sharifa had sent word to Ammajani that if the play came to her city, she had to watch it as her friend's daughter was in it.

Little did we know about the trouble this trip to the theatre was going to trigger! But who can avoid the inevitable?

Maharaj Ju wife's brother, his Saale Sarkar, who was well known as one with a roving eye, sat in the seat next to Maharaj Ju's. He himself hailed from a big talukdar family of an area near Bundelkhand, but worked closely with Maharaj Ju as his right-hand man. He was so enamoured by the blue-green eyes of the delicate Kajjan that he got a letter, written for him by Maharaj Ju, delivered to her mother, Bi Sharifa, standing guard over her precious daughter in the wings, asking that she should meet him immediately after the play.

Bi Sharifa was in a dilemma. She knew what the summons meant. But her girl was an innocent fifteen-year-old. How could she just send her into the arms of this man? But everyone at the court also knew about the Saale Sarkar's vile temper. He was known to be a two-faced devil. On occasion, he would ask for Husna Bai to visit Maharaj Ju's palace fully aware that Maharani Ju would have her thrashed with shoes. It was common knowledge that there was many a quarrel within the homes of the rich at the time in which people could be maimed or even killed, and no one raised an eyebrow! Nobody could be trusted. It was known all through the city that the brother-in-law used to drink with the king, but he also used to fill the queen's ears against him. Big homes have big secrets. Who would risk trouble by saying anything about their affairs and fights?

Maharani Ju was just as eccentric as her brother. She was the daughter of a rich landowning family from the haughty Bundelkhand region after all. She could drink two bottles of liquor in one go. Various kinds of heady alcohol were sent to her from there: wine brewed from pomegranates, prunes, raisins or chillies and ginger. Then, she listened to ballads about her brave ancestors to the accompaniment of a tambourine late into the night. She was an insomniac and would sleep only after taking a full dose of morphine. Anyway ... the silly stories just keep tumbling out once you get started.

So, I was talking about the theatre. Who knew that this cursed play, *Bharat Milaap*, would lead to the separation of Ammajani and Maharaj Ju, after which all the music in her life would evaporate.

After some haggling, Bi Sharifa overcame her anger and fear and sent her daughter Kajjan to Maharaj Ju's Saale Sarkar. Being a tawaif's daughter, she did not have to worry about preserving her virtue. So Kajjan lived with Saale Sarkar for eight years as his concubine. Ammajani told me that, in that time, he covered Kajjan and her mother in gold. But she was a prostitute's daughter after all, and prostitutes are not known to be very discreet. One day, Kajjan confided to her patron and lover that, when she had received his letter, her mother had consulted the other bai in Sherkothi. And she, Husna Bai, had advised her Ammijaan against sending Kajjan to him. At that point, it was Kajjan who had insisted, and so her mother had agreed.

The Saale Sarkar, brother-in-law to a maharaja, took this as a great insult and made sure that Husna Bai was separated from her mentor and lover. He used black magic to achieve this, Ammajani said. First, one of the women he had planted in Sherkothi hid the lucky cloak that the Baba of the Kalika Mandir by whose blessings Maharaj Ju was believed to have been born had given him when he turned twenty, and after that, it was easy to have him killed him off by arranging a car accident.

Now, let's leave all these sordid tales of royal intrigue aside, and talk about Ammajani's closest friend Hira Bai. I have heard that she had come to Benares from somewhere in a town tucked away in the Himalayan forests after the Mutiny, with her extremely beautiful daughter, Angelina. In those days, Benares was the land of all the famous musicians and their patrons, and many talented dancers and singers had made a name for themselves there. Hira Bai was a truly gifted singer from a family of singers. She was around twenty-seven or twenty-eight when she arrived in Benares. But in those days, tawaifs started making their mark by the age of fifteen. Many wondered why a talented singer such as her had not come to Benares until then. Who had she been trained by? But this was to remain a mystery.

The mother and daughter revealed very little about their early life. One could tell from their conversations in English, though, that they were both educated and hailed from a respectable family, and after falling on hard times, they had been forced to enter this world of professional singers. The dais and kutnis, who go from one house to another to offer massages and treat feminine issues, are known to be able to extract anyone's secrets. But they could only find out that Hira Bai had lived as an English officer's wife for many years somewhere in the hills and had arrived here after the master's death. Only Allah knows the truth.

In those days, many young Englishmen from the Company would marry many beautiful Indian women out of sheer loneliness. Being away from their families in a foreign land where they had come only to earn money, many took to keeping harems of sub-wives. They used to call them 'bibi', and usually made a cottage on the grounds of their houses available to them and the bibis' various hangers-on and children. These small cottages were known as 'bibi ghar'. There are many such old, rundown bibi ghars on the premises of big houses in the old city. Only a handful remember why they were given that name. Anyway!

About the native wives, I have heard that their British masters used to pay them around forty silver coins with the Queen's face on them as allowance every month. Food for them was sent from the main house, and if the sahib was generous, the native wife and children were even provided with a few servants. At social events, the bibis did not mingle with the Englishmen and their English wives. Only Englishwomen were considered capable of conducting themselves properly in genteel society. The sahibs had not come here to live forever and would return after having amassed a considerable amount of money. Under such circumstances, their poor bibis would be forced to live on the streets. Very few officers provided their Indian wives and children with a roof over their heads or pensions for life.

As soon as a bibi was known to have been disowned, pimps would start circling her, and under their guidance, most of these bibis would end up in areas such as Dalmandi or Hiramandi.

In Benares, we had heard whispers that Hira Bai's husband was actually a rich senior English officer. He had done an official survey and then made a lot of money from the forests. And he had married her. But one day, when the Sahib died while hunting, the usual happened. Her greedy maiden family turned against her, declared her stepson as the Sahib's successor, threw Hira Bai and Baby Angelina out of the house and took control of it. The English officer friends of the Sahib had been uneasy with the high status he had accorded his Indian wife, and her pleas to them for help went unheard. They cleared all the money and gold from the Sahib's accounts and turned their eyes away from the helpless widow. Finally, like many destitute wives, Hira Bai, and her daughter, Angelina, were also brought to Benares by a well-wisher.

Hira Bai was an extremely beautiful woman. Well-built, pale-skinned, with curly hair. She stood tall and had sharp features with a slightly hooked nose and intoxicating hazel eyes. She was a head-turner all right. She was obviously well-educated but did not speak much. Her voice was naturally melodious. Having lived long with an Englishman who helped her move around in high society, she had a good grasp over English and also spoke Urdu very well. Which is why, as soon as she arrived, she became hot property and made a name for herself in the region's mehfils.

Her closest friend, my Ammajani, Husna Bai, was the complete opposite. She was talkative and lively. She spoke and laughed easily, and was even invited to places far away from Benares to sing her famous thumris, kajaris and chaitis in that deep, sonorous voice of hers. She had learned on the job mostly, but she had a good memory and could remember everything she had read. Actually, she was passionate about reading. Even if Ammajani saw a loose page lying on the side of the road, she would pick it up to read. If the paper wrapped around the groceries the cook brought had the name of a poet, she would not rest until she had emptied it of the wares and read it.

Ammajani bonded with Hira Bai over shayari, printed books, and singing at kajari duels.

My Ammajani was not mean-spirited and selfish like other tawaifs. Even before they became close friends, unlike others in Dalmandi, she never mocked Hira Bai because of the difference in her diction or her mannerisms. Later, not only did she teach Hira Bai the Banarasi Purabiya dialect, but also explained to her the intricacies of the various styles of thumri singing and the magical monsoon kajaris from Mirzapur and Benares. She also gave Hira Bai useful tips on proper conduct in Hindustani mehfils and what attire to wear when performing. For her part, Ammajani also got a working knowledge of English from Hira Bai, and even learned from her a few English songs written in praise of the British Queen and the wives of viceroys. For being able to sing in a foreign tongue, Hira Bai received many compliments from sahibs who attended these mehfils.

I have heard that, after making a name for herself, Hira Bai's daughter, Anjali Bai, recorded a few of those songs for a recording company in Calcutta. Anjali was a precocious child. Unlike me, the ups and downs in her early life had taught her to be careful in speech and rather calculating and sharp about money matters. She was also very proud of her beauty. May Khuda not allow me to lie, both mother and daughter were adept at gauging which way the wind was blowing. It is because we did not understand the value of this trendspotting, which could make our art more saleable, that Ammajani and I lagged behind them and lost out on much.

Even after we moved to Sherkothi, from her visiting ustads and accompanists, Ammajani would hear regularly about the mother and daughter's special attitude, costumes and jewellery, and the fee Hira Bai and Anjali Bai exacted for their presence in mehfils. Ammajani used to say that, in the beginning, Hira and Anjali had started paying attention to Indian costumes only at her behest. Otherwise, when they first came, the mother and daughter mostly wore dresses in pale pastel hues that made them look like

Sufis in mehfils that sparkled with all the colours of the rainbow and more. To give them credit, the duo was grateful to Ammajani for her advice.

While we lived in Benares and went to visit them with Ammajani, Hira Bai and Anjali always welcomed us warmly. And if I ever requested them to sing or teach me a few English songs, they did so without any hesitation. Unlike other tawaifs, the mother and daughter were not mean but generous in sharing with us whatever they possessed. I also learned from them a few Pahadi songs which were sung in Himalayan villages in the month of Chait, like our chaiti when the Hindu new year begins.

The opening of a bandish, which I don't remember fully, was '*Yo aayo Chaita ka mahina*' (Here comes the month of Chait). We have heard how fertile the month of Chait is from the chaitis and dadras from our region. So, the song described how, during Chait, a girl in the hills, unable to visit her parents like others, touches the braid her mother had plaited and remembers the tinkling of the bells tied around the cows in her maiden home.

Tears would roll down Hira Bai's cheeks while singing this song, and Ammajani, who would be listening to her, kept her company by shedding a few tears herself. Hira Bai sang this song at Chait baithaks without tablas and sarangis, like sozkhwani during Muharram. And even people who did not understand the words would start crying, so powerful was her voice. It is true that the month of Chait brings the blooms out. It makes the limbs heavy, brings back old memories. Ammajani used to say, '*Chait maas utpatiya ho Rama*' (Ah, this wicked month of Chait).

Nobody cares for the tears of singers. We would start weeping as soon as we remembered things we could never talk about. Music gave us relief.

It is said that, after tasting the sweetness of Hira Bai's voice, the Mishra brothers from Kashi desired to become her students, to learn semi-classical singing. The ganda-bandhai, the formal ceremony of tying a holy thread in acceptance of new disciples, took place, and she started with teaching them khayal, and then moved on to the lighter tappa and thumri. The Mishra brothers were later invited to the court of Nepal's Maharaja. It is also said that, at an annual event that lasted some forty days, the two brothers performed multiple times and received five lakh rupees as reward from the Maharaja of Kashi. Five lakh in those times would be equal to a few crore now. Haaye! Ammajani had hoped that she would get me trained under them, but the two never returned from the court of the Nepalese king.

Training them had made Hira Bai an even better singer. When a famous Banarasi singer, Ustad Bashir Khan, heard her sing a Bageshri bandish, '*Maalin laai chun-chun kaliyan*' (The gardener-woman has brought a few choice buds), he became besotted with her, and later took advantage of his proximity to her. And then he opened up his jealously guarded treasures of not just rare old khayals, but also dhrupads and tappas set to music by the mad lover, Miyan Shori. Later, Khan Sahib also shifted to Calcutta. In those days, Nawab Wajid Ali Shah used to hold many brilliant gatherings of singers and ustads in Matiya Burj where the British had banished him just before the Mutiny. '*Khush raho ahle vatan, hum toh safar kartey hain*,' he had recited. Be happy my people of Lucknow, we leave on a long journey.

Haaye! This wretched heart holds so many memories! Even now, every bandish sparks a memory. Last night, when I heard the bandish '*Bhor bhayi milan bhailava*' (Early in the morning, love just happened...) in Raga Jaunpuri, it reminded me of how a particular Marathi guru of Ammajani had risked the ire of the impoverished Muslim ustads by starting her training with this bandish.

Bhau Buva he was called. He came from a poor Brahmin family in Maharashtra. He had always had a sweet voice, but all his father's money went into making ends meet. It was when he joined a travelling Marathi natak company with his elder brother that he could move from city to city, singing and acting in female roles in plays before his voice broke.

Around that time, his company put up a new play in Indore, where the court singer Bundu Ali Khan Sahib noticed the melodious voice of the boy playing the role of Ram's wicked mother, Kaikeyi. So what if he was dark-skinned? His voice was like that of a flute. Khan Sahib summoned him at once, and somehow managing to get the holy ganda tied, took him in as a disciple. Having suffered many a hardship, the boy fell down at the feet of Bundu Ali Khan Sahib who had been trained in the gharana style and only offered training to children belonging to his gharana. The charm of Bundu Ali Khan's deep and sombre voice was such that even the most established tabla and sarangi players were in awe of him. He drove audiences crazy by opening a song only by humming the same notes repeatedly like some magical mantra. Ammajani's sarangi player, who had coincidentally the same name as the great singer, had played with him in the past. He always touched his ears and said that if anyone had inherited the gift of the ustad's gharana, it wasn't his sons or sons-in-law but this Brahmin pandit's child, Bhau Buva.

Lallan Miyan also told us that, when the talented ustad saw that the child's pockets were empty at the time of the ganda-bandhai ceremony, he handed him a copper coin and said, 'This I shall consider to be your formal guru dakshina. Hand me this with a flower, and now, from this day onwards, you are formally declared both my son and my disciple. All the knowledge that I have with me, will now be handed to you.'

Thanks to his ustad's blessings, the one-time heroine of Marathi plays who could barely manage to fill his stomach singing '*Jo mam nayan chakor indu*' (Darling, you are to my eyes what the moon is to an enamoured chakor bird), became a rich star singer of his times.

So rigorous was the guru's training that, within just the three months the company was in the city, he taught Bhau Buva any number of ragas. Afterwards, Bhau left the company's job and focused on his singing career. Later called Pandit-ji, Bhau Buva used to laugh and say at mehfils that his training was far from run-of-the-mill. As a sign of his total deference to his guru, despite being a Brahmin, he would take on his palm the phlegm his guru spat out while clearing his throat, treating it as a kind of benediction. A few times, when the ustad wished to eat meat, he even volunteered to go and buy mutton, and accepted being slapped by him in a full mehfil without moving a muscle. Finally, the guru was so happy with him that he chiselled Bhau Buva into a perfect diamond.

Like many other tawaifs, Hira and Ammajani also tried their special ways on Bhau Buva to get him to accept them as his formal disciples and teach them some more rare ragas, but he was a man steadfast in his celibacy. I was told that, each time, he would fold his hands and say, 'I have been wedded to my music forever, sister, and am incapable of loving anyone else. I am sorry I can go no further.'

It is by trading many such stories under a full moon or even during the moonless daytime that we singers carry on with our nomadic lives. How else could we continue our journey?

Today there is singing and dancing everywhere, but it is almost rare to have a row of devoted connoisseurs of music sitting in front of singers. It is for them that we stopped to narrate interesting reflections on music, anecdotes and old memories, and then picked up the thread of the raga once again. The young – when they do – listen to music on their laptops privately. They shut out the idea of sitting in live gatherings or mehfils. That is dry, desiccated music to us. What kind of music receives no appreciative wahs from listeners? Which musical baithak can be complete without pieces of gossip and anecdotes? Music today just lands on the ears of youngsters like Nawaz Miyan who say they love music but don't understand what live music is all about. They can never experience the beauty of those moments when music, the musicians and the audience become one – like a clay lamp with several wicks that gently come together and become one, and after that, all you see is the glow.

Arre, how can a musician or ragas find peace if people listen to music at any hour they fancy. Last year, two boys had stuffed two plastic pegs into their ears to listen to music while crossing railway tracks and could not tell when the engine sounded its whistle; so they got cut into pieces on the tracks. Everyone's trapped within themselves through their mobiles.

Tapish Sahib told me that I had made him reticent like myself and recited a couplet:

Paavas aaya jaan ke, bhayi kokila maun,
ab toh dadur boli hain, hamahi sunego kaun?

As the monsoon rains arrive, and frogs begin to croak,
the koel falls silent thinking she will not be heard any more.

Days go by without any conversation, and I don't know who to talk to without moving my tongue and about what.

A few days ago, an English newspaper wanted an article on classical music. They said they wished to come and talk to me about old styles of singing. Come along, we too want to know what your generation, which listens to music through so many wires, machines and OTT channels, thinks about Hindustani music. But when the foolish journalist started dividing up our musical traditions into Hindu and Muslim but repeatedly said how Ganga-Jamuni tehzeeb still survives, he sounded exactly like politicians on TV. At this point, I offered him my salaam and called Billu to show him the door. Can one first ask the singers their religion, count the votes from his religion, and calculate both to arrive at the current value of their sur? Does he know the story where once, when Ustad Rahmat Khan, while resting behind a pillar in a Hindu temple, was listening to music, and at one point, without looking at the face of the singer, he shook his head in appreciation and said, 'Subhan Allah, bhai wah, so good!' Then Ustad Sahib asked his disciples, 'Who is the singer?' Someone whispered back, 'He is a pandit.' Ustad Sahib said, 'Pure sur belongs to neither a pandit nor an ustad. It rises from the depths of the singer's bone marrow.' For us singers, notes follow neither caste nor lines between nations. A singer who has become one with the light of music, will therefore wander day and night in search of that one true note. Forever moving and not putting down roots anywhere – this is a state of grace like that of a fakir.

Kashi was the dargah of all artiste fakirs at that time, and all the talented people coming from all over in the court of Ganga-ji found the support of one or the other tawaif during their days of struggle. If someone managed to find a place within a famous bai Sahiba's house, then sooner or later, he could turn lucky and get the chance to exhibit his skills at a mehfil. And if he did well, from there would begin the long line of invitations to big mehfils for him. Which is why, contrary to what people think these days, a real bai was not sought after just for physical gratification. These bais had absorbed the training of countless generations. Your generation might not even know this, but embellishments like the meend, the gamak, the murki and the khatka came from vocal music and were introduced lovingly into the repertoire of shehnai, sitar and veena players. Performances which make you go 'Wah! Wah!' today owe a lot to these female vocalists of Dalmandi.

Bais carried a lot of weight with the moneyed families of rajas and zamindars of the time. And aspiring young artistes used to pray for a bai's patronage so that they could perhaps get a lucky break with her blessings and get invited to sing or play at a big mehfil. That is what happened with Ustad Bashir Khan. He was recommended by Hira Bai and began doing the rounds. Soon he was getting invitations for performing at the mehfils of many rich families in Calcutta. But he was a thankless one, that man. As soon as he earned some fame in Benares, he shifted to Calcutta without telling anyone. He knew that once he was granted the vaseeka, the monthly stipend, he would enter the court, and thereafter, his name would be formally adorned with the prefix of 'Ustad' or 'Pandit'. Irony was, whereas the bais who helped sustain those ustads and pandits during their lean days even hawked their own talent to push the fortunes of their beloved young protégés, bais remained bais for life, and the thankless males whom they promoted flaunted the honorifics of 'ustad' or 'pandit' and just upped and left them without so much as a by-your-leave!

May Allah bless those who made available for these female patrons of artistes the grand platform of All India Radio. To propitiate some social workers and political leaders who were hostile to these women of easy virtue, those who were opening new gates for these professionals went ahead and appended honorifics like 'begum' or 'devi' to their names. May Allah bless the Minister Sahib with a place in heaven who shushed the political leaders and always treated us tawaifs with respect during those lean days.

The tawaifs did not disappoint their patrons. They sang so well on the radio that, soon, all of India was listening to their voices! Despite that, at mehfils, some guests who had suddenly become rich after Partition would occasionally try to misbehave with the tawaifs. But for women like Hira Bai, there was no turning back. So they just kept broadcasting and cutting discs. In one of those discs, Bi Sahiba sums it all up in a bandish in Raga Gaud Sarang: '*Mann re, apan son saancho rahiye*' (Oh my heart, stay true to yourself).

Ah, as I think back on the Benares of my time, the first thing to come to mind are its winding lanes. Those narrow, serpentine lanes were the veins of the city. They kept getting narrower as they moved away from the sides of the grand palaces built by the rajas and zamindars along Ganga-ji. The lanes had shops on either side, selling saris, utensils, household items, sweets and, of course, Banarasi paan. You could be sure that everyone crossing the alleys was masticating rolled-up paans in their mouths. When they talked to each other, they'd simply turn up their chins so that the saliva would not trickle down their freshly laundered and starched kurtas. The ghats of Ganga-ji had a charm of their own. As soon as winter would set in, rafts would assemble on the river waters, and soon that would become a platform for female singers with voices as invigorating as the gentle purvaiya breezes. Then many other well-known musicians and their appreciative patrons would pour in and a unique mehfil would begin. One patron had made a small pamphlet in which he listed, in rhyming couplets, all the famous female singers of Benares. The pamphlet was titled *Besva Stotra* and sold a number of copies on publication. Hira Bai, too, owned a copy.

When Hira Bai and Ammajani were at the peak of their careers and their friendship had deepened, it seemed as if someone cast an evil eye on them. The reason for things souring was a handsome Punjabi sitar player, a Pathan, Manawar Khan Sahib. He arrived in Benares, and promoted by the court of the Raja of Benares, was soon giving concerts that exhibited a remarkable musical ear and skill to match. After Khan Sahib found a place in the court, his family, too, moved to Benares. Manawar Sahib had a fifteen-year-old son, Tajuddin, who was tall, well-built, well-dressed, and a bit of a rake. The alley he crossed would be filled with the smell of the expensive perfumes he fancied. He had a very sweet voice. His bosom pal, Ikram, was then working at Ammajani's house. At a mehfil, many famous artistes and tawaifs including Hira Bai sat to listen to Tajuddin. As soon as the singing was over, the hall resounded with wah-wahs from every corner. Everyone from Suggan Bai to Aashiq Ali Khan acknowledged him as a new young talent and, after that, a group of tawaifs almost kidnapped the handsome boy. Under their enthusiastic tutelage, Taju Miyan learned not just various stylistic embellishments to use in his singing but also mastered the intricacies of courtly behaviour. His father had a regular stipend to his name, he himself was young and unmarried, and there were no pressing demands on his time. So Miyan Tajuddin practised a lot and was soon winning over every mehfil and bai's heart. The resultant competition soon turned the bais of Dalmandi against one another and filled the atmosphere with a certain tension.

Oh Bibi, we professional singing women have an age-old tradition that makes us care more for our own well-being, not chase matters of the heart. A real courtesan will harden her heart while honing her skills, and the minute there is any danger to her earnings, she can turn unyielding like wood. That's it. As soon as Tajuddin started gaining fame, his female admirers stopped his freebies. If he knocked at the doors of a kotha asking to be taught a certain bandish, instead of the mistress welcoming him at the door, a dai or durban would be sent to tell him that the bai-ji had a headache and could not see him. Taju Miyan had been regularly visiting our house too. Ammajani told me that Hira Bai had been soft on the young boy who had struck a friendship with young Anjali, saying it was not good to mistreat him or simply ignore him after having showered him with praises. What was his fault? Just that he was handsome in addition to being a good singer and was making a lot of money and fame at mehfils? Ammajani had reacted strongly to this. She said to Hira Bai, 'Don't get me started, Bi. If your daughter has fallen for him, should we also consider him our son-in-law? We do not share our stale rice even with God. You should be careful, Bi, or soon your daughter and you will regret it.'

This encounter froze their deep and warm relationship of many years. We did not meet each other for many days after this. When we did, there was always something rankling in the mind.

So, as I had said earlier, the face of the country was changing, so how could the city of Benares remain unchanged? There were changes everywhere. We started hearing names like Gandhi Baba and Pandit Motilal at our mehfils. A few rich men started wearing khadi kurtas and caps. There was a bai called Surasti among us who had made a lot of name for herself singing khayal, thumri and tappa. She joined the Swadeshi movement in that wave and started singing patriotic songs at Congress meetings. Our Vidyadhari Bai went to meet Bapu-ji. The two of them started a club called the Tawaif Fund, which used to donate regularly to the Hind Swaraj Fund.

While this was happening, we, the tawaifs, continued living the same hard lives deeply scarred by the big war. Dig a well every day for drawing water, as they say. That was us.

This one year, Hira Bai sang a kajari song composed by the famous Piremghan Babu of Benares at the famous monsoon kajari-singing contest of Kashi and Mirzapur: '*Sir pe sahi odhe re odhniyan khelein kajari, hilimilike sab jhoola sang, jhoolein sabhi sakhi prem bhari*' (Their heads covered just so, girls with their hearts brimming with love, on swings, singing kajari songs with friends).

By now, the relationship between Ammajani and Hira Bai had soured further because of the battle for one rich jeweller's attentions. Babu-ji belonged to an established family of jewellers in Benares. And when his angry mother saw the growing intimacy between Hira Bai and him, she left with her daughter-in-law on a long pilgrimage. This became a topic of much discussion among the local tawaifs. How could Ammajani bear this? At the next Budhwa Mangal mela, when barges turned into platforms for night-long musical performances, Ammajani also sang '*Kahan gayo mero Holi ko khelya, sipahi Rustam Ali baanko sipayya?*' (Where has he gone, my fellow Holi player, the handsome soldier, Rustam Ali?) in the memory of an old frequent visitor of Dalmandi. The composition turned many eyes red.

That year, Ammajani discovered that Maharaj Ju had come to the big Budhwa Mangal mela to listen to music. Maharaj Ju, that is, Kalika Prasad Singh Ju Sahib, was the fifth son of the king of the famous clan of Pancha in Champanagar. His mother was from a princely family in Bihar. Those days, performing black magic on people to control or destroy them was quite common in the eastern states like Bihar. The same black magic was thought to be the cause of the death of Maharaj Ju's older brother, who passed away young and suddenly from acute diarrhoea. Maharaj Ju was born after the brother's death, it was believed, with the blessings of a priest of a Kali temple near Asansol. The priest had been a guru to his mother, who was mourning her firstborn. The guru told her she'd soon have another child, and miraculously, she found herself pregnant soon afterwards. By way of thanksgiving to the priest of the Kali temple, the newborn was given the name Kalika Prasad. For three years, the young Kalika Prasad was not allowed to go beyond the second floor of the palace for fear of his life. Come Diwali, a special puja was performed for his well-being at that temple.

When Kalika Prasad Ju was around twenty, the priest gave him a special cloak and told him to always keep it with him, which Maharaj Ju did, whether he was in the state or outside. It is said that on the day he had the fatal car accident, he did not have it with him. One of the palace maids, a paid informant of his enemy, had hidden it. Otherwise, sixty is not such an advanced age to lose one's life when a car merely bumps into a tree.

Maharaj Ju was very fond of music. His father, too, was fond of it, but he did not understand its intricacies the way the son did. Maharaj Ju himself also played the clarinet and absolutely loved collecting newly released gramophone records. He always advised me to sing with my soul, not just my voice. Every spring, he performed the Saraswati puja in Sherkothi for the goddess of all arts. On that day, he would wear a string of jasmines around his wrist, put another one around Ammajani's neck, and make her place a string of jasmines each on each instrument. If a great performer was giving a recital and the urge to have a glass of wine overcame him, he'd cover his face while drinking so that the musician was not offended.

It is heard that the Baba of the Kalika Mandir had told Maharaj Ju's mother that, before he was born, young Kalika Prasad had been learning music from the gandharvas of Nagaloka. He may have missed a beat and so arrived on earth by way of punishment. Had he not missed it, he may not have been born a mortal.

Anyway, so after the baithak on Budhwa Mangal on Ganga-ji, Ammajani and Maharaj Ju fell in love. So deep was their love that she left everything in Kashi behind her and agreed to move westwards to settle in faraway Ruhelkhand. When we moved into Sherkothi, all our ties with Kashi snapped. Hira Bai met Ammajani a few times in mehfils, but as they say, a string of pearls once broken cannot become whole again. A knot remains.

But the shrewd Hira Bai did not overlook her friend's sage advice about her daughter and the young rake Tajuddin. She began to act tough about her daughter's growing proximity to Taju Miyan. What Ammajani had told her might have been a bitter pill to swallow, but in her heart, she knew it was the truth.

This was a delicate time in her life as a courtesan when she could detect, before others did, a certain faltering in her pristine voice. She started making preparations for the formal elaborate auctioning of her daughter's virginity, her nath-utarai, wherein the highest bidder could spend a whole night with Anjali Bai and, as a token of her becoming a full-fledged bai, remove a little gold nath she had been wearing in her nose. How could Anjali's intimacy with a mere sitar player's son be tolerated at such a critical juncture, when bids for her were being invited from the rich and prominent in the land?

Finally, Taju Miyan was forced to move out and was supposed to have settled somewhere near Dhaka. But after that, we heard that Hira Bai suddenly postponed Anjali Bai's nath-utarai and moved to Calcutta overnight with her. No one knew why.

For the record, Hira Bai said that Calcutta was now not just the seat of political power of the British but also the real cultural capital.

In Calcutta, mother and daughter managed to put behind their differences and come closer, and as expected, almost a year later, Anjali Bai's first performance was held with much fanfare on the property of a Bihari zamindar. Anjali's skill was, at the same time, being constantly honed by the biggest gurus in Calcutta. As Hira Bai had hoped, in her first public performance, her daughter won such acclaim that soon she was being talked about as 'the voice' from Bombay to Mysore. Anjali Bai's name now became synonymous with the style of singing from East India, one that had originated in Benares. Hearing of her success, Ammajani would suggest that, while the old critics and connoisseurs were around, why shouldn't we experiment with the traditional style like Hira and Anjali and present it to new connoisseurs at the record companies with new themes and vocal embellishments? But I did not agree.

For us, sur is God, I told her. And adding frills to it to earn more money and name seemed petty and disrespectful to me. Couldn't she, too, see how Anjali Bai was manipulating our spiritual music in various languages to appeal to the tastes of the English, Marathi, Gujarati and Parsi seths with lots of cash but no finely tuned ear for music? In my opinion, margi sangeet or classical music is not for everyone. Our duty is to make people aware of the difficult but real soul of margi music. To start cooking it with all kinds of spicy ingredients would not bring out its authentic flavours. We cannot treat music as instant noodles. If we also get swept with everyone, we run the risk of making the public forget what real music is.

I was aware, as is every tawaif from Dalmandi to Hiramandi who betrays her lovers, that she must steer clear of love and romance. She is the sole breadwinner of the family, be she thirteen or thirty. To act arrogantly like an ustad or put on the airs of a married woman can prove costly. Youth is short-lived, and if not planned for well in advance, a prostitute and a wrestler's old age can end in grief.

Anjali, who had seen difficult times at a very young age, had realized that she had to do whatever it would take to protect her rights as a performer and invest her money well. The world might call it a woman's animal nature, but everyone needs food, clothes, house, jewellery, music at every age, don't they? Be it a tawaif or a babu or their wives. Which is why tawaifs, who mostly had no father or brother to help and protect them, prepared their daughters for the trade even if their hearts wept. And to that end, I agree with what Hira Bai did. Taju could have proven to be an obstacle to her daughter's rise as a high earner.

This is reflected in the few letters Hira Bai wrote to Ammajani from Benares. She clearly resented that she had to send her daughter who had studied in an English school into the midst of dissolute rich men for money. But what were her options? Even earlier she would sing the tragic thumri that bemoans the loss of virginity: '*Ehi thaiyyan motiya hirano ho Rama…*' (We have to lose our pearl in this place, O Rama). She'd tell Ammajani that all of us prostitutes have to lose the pearl, and once lost, it can never be found again. May Allah give her soul peace. She was a good woman after all.

While getting all this written in these last hours of my life, I am also hoping that if it finds its way into your book, maybe the good readers will find a few drops of sympathy for the tawaifs of bygone days who sacrificed their blood, sweat and youth but never compromised on their music. Had it not been for them, Bibi, truth be told, the art of many of today's ustads and gurus would not have been able to reach their high points given the abject poverty they were surrounded with.

But will this generation of listeners, who merely download their music with the click of a button and listen to it by plugging their ears against the world, be bothered to gaze into the inner darkness of the lives of bais?

Is gardish-e-ifraak se fooley na faley hum,
subza ronde sa ugti gayin paavon ke taley hum.

A vagabond at the hands of constant partings, we bore neither flowers nor fruits,
like grasses we grew, only to be trampled underfoot.

Everyone enjoys the rain. But how many pause to consider how and where the clouds gather and why they rain? And how many those showers drenched? The women of Ammajani and Hira Bai's times were like showers of joyous music that constantly enriched the music scene, keeping it lush and green, year after year. Thanks to them, the music they fed remains in our midst, so a scholar like you, after getting a glimpse of its riches, comes all the way from Delhi to this little hamlet.

I found just one letter from Hira Bai in Ammajani's trunk, which I am sending along with this draft. May Allah again show the entire world the beauty of these forgotten voices, which had gathered yesterday only to disperse like spent clouds.

Thus, the end.

The letter from Hira Bai to Husna Bai

Calcutta

My dear sister Husna Jaan,

Soon after Taju Miyan left, Angelina and I left Benares for Calcutta. We were like bees who had been smoked out of the garden. The journey of almost four hundred and fifty miles to the city of Calcutta, that we undertook with a heavy heart, brought us to a rented house near Nakhoda mosque in the Chitpur area of Bada Bazaar. And my Angelina and I are slowly learning to live in Calcutta. It seems the city does have connoisseurs who can tell the difference between us deredar tawaifs, with a family lineage running into centuries, and those cheap low-caste chuneywaalis and kanchaniya singers who mostly screech in the name of singing and sell their bodies. So, even if the atmosphere here does not change, hopefully there will be no lack of musical opportunities, food or steady allowances from major patrons. As God wills.

Since we got here, Anjali who has always been a frail girl, has been beset by some ailments. She sits lost in her dreamworld, not eating well. At the mention of fish, she feels nauseated.

How can I fault her for this? She was born an Englishman's daughter and was raised as one. An Anglo-Indian woman had been hired just to teach her to use cutlery. Who knew she'd end up the daughter of a tawaif?

When I was pregnant with her, I was confident that, since everyone had been hoping for a boy, God would bless me with a son. Instead, I gave birth to a girl. But her father was overjoyed. He adored her beautiful face and blue eyes that he said she had inherited from his side of the family. Reassured by his fondness for our girl, I kept her close to my bosom, and we raised her with a lot of love, making sure she lacked for nothing even if it meant that

I had to go hungry. That has probably spoilt her somewhat and made her petulant and self-centred. Her father used to say that she looked exactly like his mother and that he would send her to England for her education. That Angelina Baby would make us proud by studying there. But her father died, and then she had to leave her childhood home.

Angelina felt lost for days after that. She would keep asking where her father was. Didn't want to eat this or wear that. She would throw things and burst into tears, and then try to hit me with her tiny fists and ask why I had brought her here, to take her back home.

What could a poor mother who was struggling to establish herself as a courtesan in Benares tell this little child? Home? For our home, I had been betrayed by my own people who grabbed everything Eddie had left behind, and then we were simply discarded. After that, my priorities in life underwent a change. The only thing I cared for now was survival and earning my own money to keep my head high. We would not have made it had your daughter Allarakkhi and you not pulled us out of the distrust, fear and rage we had within us when we arrived in Benares, where my teacher made away with whatever little I had managed to bring and disappeared.

It was disheartening that, just when my Angelina was getting somewhat adjusted to her changed circumstances, all of you moved away to Sherkothi.

I was afraid that the altercation that we had before you left may yet break her heart, so I did not see you as often as I wanted. Everyone says that having a talented and beautiful daughter like Anjali has the potential to make my old age comfortable. But truth be told, who could be a more pitiable sample of a mother than me?

You had been right when you said that the daughter of a randi has no right to fall head over heels in love with people like

Tajuddin. But you also know that our heart isn't ours to give or snatch away again and again. All we have left is talent, and by that we must live until the day we die.

Tajuddin not only took my daughter's heart with him but ceased all communication, and after that experience, something within her turned into a block of ice. Now the situation is such that Anjali has come to hate and mistrust not only her mother but also all men. Every time she sees me getting ready for mehfils, she cuts into my heart with her poisonous quips. 'Wah, Bai-ji! You've worn a splendid outfit! Who would say that you are the mother of such a big girl! Good. Nobody will bother me today.'

In such moments, I feel like tearing off my outfit and putting on rags. Then I remember how necessary it is for a performing woman's survival in a world where men control the money, the mehfils and even the courts. It isn't that Anjali does not accompany me. Her youth and talent light up all mehfils. But she continues to consider me an enemy. She picks faults in everything I do and drives me to tears after every mehfil. The theme is the same: Why do you drag me everywhere like a pup? I cry every night and wonder if this is my own daughter saying such things.

Seene mein ho gaya dil-e-naummeed khoon,
dekha toh kya suna bhi na aisa sufaid khoon.

The blood that courses through my heart, lies drained of all hope,
never seen, nor even heard of blood, this white, and as cold.

Anyway! A small heart will always be lost in trifles. May the One above protect us all.

I try to convince Anjali as often as I can that a parent's love will remain even if the earth shifts from its axis. Look at Badshah-e-Awadh Jaan-e-Alam, I tell her. He has been forcefully locked up in Matiya Burj. But the incarceration hasn't dented his love for music and the fine things of life. Great people do not let quirks of fate put out their spirits. A few days before leaving his beloved Lucknow, on Holi, Jaan-e-Alam dressed up and sang the popular bandish in Raga Tilak Kamod: '*Neer bharan kaise jaaun sakhi?*' (How shall I go to fill water, dear friend?).

But Anjali shrugs it off saying, so what? He is a Badshah. Even if an elephant dies, it is worth over one lakh rupees they say, don't they? What are we? Mere tawaifs. If our lover dies, we wouldn't know which dark lane his body may be rotting in.

How can one respond to this? I am hoping that time will heal and fade Tajuddin's memories.

We recently got an invitation to Matiya Burj from the same emperor who had splurged untold wealth on music, musicals and dance performances in Awadh. Let me close my chapter of personal woes and tell you about that memorable grand mehfil.

When I arrived, they treated us very well because we were from their region. Then, after the few formalities, the music began to flow. Both Anjali and I were amazed to see the erstwhile Badshah of Awadh begin the mehfil by singing two lovely pieces composed by the renowned tawaif, Tahira Bibi. The first one began with, '*Jab chhod chaley Lucknow*' (When we left Lucknow), and then he sang his own famous lines: '*Babul, mora naihar chhooto jaaye*' (Father, I am forced to leave my natal home behind).

We now faced a dilemma, since we ourselves had also thought of and rehearsed these very bandishes for this mehfil. Anyway, we asked for God's blessings and sang two of Jaan-e-Alam's other beautiful creations: the first one was that famous Dadra, '*Dilbar mera gayo kaunse des, is nagari mein aan pado andes*' (Where has my beloved gone? I am forever looking over my shoulder in this dark city). And then we presented the thumri in Raga Khamaj: '*Ram kaise paar utrey, kya karun, kuch ban nahi aata*' (I cannot figure out how to reach the other side, O Lord; how do I cross this river?).

I poured all my own grief into these songs. Anjali accompanied me ably. When we finished singing, we found that there were tears in Jaan-e-Alam's large eyes. He announced that we were being appointed royal singers in his durbar at Matiya Burj. Then he showered us with money, clothes and gold. He also expressed great affection for my dear Anjali and himself put a string of pearls around her neck by way of blessing. I was ecstatic.

And listen! The famous virtuoso of the Natwari style of Kathak dance from Handiya tehsil in Prayag, one Pandit Kisunlal was at the same mehfil. He was ordered to accept Anjali Bai as his formal disciple after tying the sacred thread on her wrist. What else could I ask for? You were right when you said that God always ensures our well-being. Maybe my darling daughter's heart will find some solace by getting attached to such great teachers in this city where we are new. I know your gentle heart has thawed towards me by now. Please be happy for me and bless my Anjali.

I hope your daughter and you are living a peaceful and comfortable life. Do write to me a few lines when you find the time:

Ek haal mein insaan ki basar ho nahi sakti,
ab rang tabiyat ke badal jaayein toh achcha.

One's fortunes can't always stay the same,
it would be good for the colours of life to change.

Your adopted sister,
Hira

An incomplete letter written by Bi Sahiba to Hira Bai

Sherkothi

Zila Rampur

Jaaneman, Rahat-e-Jaan, my beloved sister and friend, I teared up on receiving your letter after such a long time. I followed Maharaj Ju to Sherkothi and left Benares behind, but the thought of my teary-eyed friends and cohort bidding me farewell makes me hiccup still. After reaching Rampur, Allarakkhi and I moved into the house of a Makhdoom Alam Khan 'Tapish' Sahib, a dependent of Maharaj Ju's. We spent all of the month of Rajab at his house. Then, we moved to the new house. My daughter fell very sick after coming here. She recovered after many prayers and treatments. But she remains slightly dull, and nothing has been hidden from you. Whenever I try to take her out, she looks at me with an expression of betrayal and runs back into her room. Our old maid, Shubraatan, is convinced she has been possessed by some djinn.

Maharaj Ju keeps visiting, and on his orders, I am no longer going to mehfils. Now I must sing only for him. He is a little eccentric. Allah knows that I run away from even the whiff of a confrontation. My mentor is a man of few words. He doesn't say anything, but I sense that he fears that some of my clients from Benares might try to reach out to us. He probably also fears the effect loneliness might have on a tawaif's daughter who has had to leave all her friends and playmates behind. But he has only seen the great care with which women in palaces are raised. He wouldn't know about the lives of young girls living in the lanes and bylanes of Dalmandi on whom every passer-by claims to have a right. He has told me many a time to teach my daughter to cover her head the right way. Why does she not know how to talk and walk daintily, he said once. The girl at the same time seems to be beset with some unspoken and strange anxiety. What do I say, I am really in a fix like you, sister. Maharaj Ju has been kind enough to continue the girl's training in music. When I see her being taught by renowned musicians, I thank Allah that the gift that's been carried in our blood across ages will remain protected for another generation.

Delhi

Dear brothers,

I have conveyed all the information I have managed to gather from Ranikhet and Allahabad to Sukumar Chacha. I have even received his quick response by post. (Radha Dada was right that Chacha's invitation will not come via email but by post.) In his small handwriting, using an old favourite pen, he has written that my findings about tawaifs like Hira Bai, Anjali Bai, Husna and Allarakkhi have resolved many of the mysteries that had been bothering him. So, he is now assured of my interest and research capabilities in music and wants me to quickly pay him a visit and take all the material (including a few old, rare photographs) he has been collecting with great care for years. Then, after having given all his material to a trusted chronicler, he too will be able to die in peace like Allarakkhi, he tells me.

I'll need some money for travel and lodging in Kolkata. Please transfer whatever you think is right into my account. You know I don't need any luxuries. Just enough to live in a neat and clean place in an unfamiliar city for a week, and for commuting to Sukumar Chacha's house every day by tram, metro or bus. Also, if Radha Dada can send Putul Di's address. I had only met her as a child. And even then, I had been awestruck by her storytelling and knowledge about music. It would be lovely to meet her again and remember old times.

Vidya

~

Seattle

Dear Vidya,

I'll ask Krishnan to transfer the money. I also spoke to Radha about this. His earnest request is that instead of a hotel, you live in Putul's (aka Madhobilata) house in South Kolkata. Putul's house is fairly big, and after Professor Sahib's death, she has been left alone there with memories, three dogs and her book-lover husband's library of over a thousand books. Her house is also close to Sukumar Chacha's.

You know how Radha is. He immediately called up Putul and informed me that she'd be happy to revive the generational bonds of friendship between our families. I am attaching her address, email, mobile number. She has already been informed that you will be staying with her, and she is quite delighted. Now all you have to do is, when you find the time, send her your date of arrival and your flight timings.

With love,
Dada

PS: I can't stop myself from sharing this old letter from Radha based on his discussions with Chacha and interactions with music gurus running gurukuls in the West. You'll also be able to gauge our Chacha's quirky ways from this. He seems to think that, in India, we have been forcing Western fusion music upon our musical traditions and, ultimately, this may sound the death knell for the future of Indian music. This is how driven Chacha feels by a few overenthusiastic buffoons presenting Indian classical music to Western audiences like some exotic circus. And this, to Chacha, is just not on! Maybe, depending on his mood, you can also discuss this delicate issue with Chacha, and can then add that as an addendum to your book?

The old letter from Radha

This time when I went to New York for a publishing seminar, I discovered that Chacha and Chachi were staying at their elder son's house for the summer. I had wrapped up all my work-related obligations and was happily squatting at a friend's empty flat to accomplish some sightseeing. I was delighted to know that Chacha was here, and we could spend some happy hours together. After all, Chacha is also a rich old man and must be looking for a companion such as me.

So I went to meet him. He hugged me lovingly and we sat chatting for long. Chachi's innocent happiness cheered me further. According to her, Chacha and I were just made for each other to do addabaazi in New York!

I had no interest in talking to their son, Shantul, or his live-in partner. Poor Chachi has been spending her time suffering their gibberish English chatter, dragging her rheumatic body to write long letters to her other hippy son, Bantul, while cooking fish kalia for Shantul with special fish bought from Bangladeshi shops.

It didn't sit well with her that, while she busied herself with cooking for her son, writing letters to the other, and cleaning up, Chacha should have been sitting quietly on his own after son and daughter-in-law left for work in the morning. He, Chachi told me, would quarrel with her just to have something to do.

So I was ordered that, whenever possible, I should catch the first bus in the morning for a breakfast of luchi and aloo posto and then take Chacha for a walk in the park or for a cultural tour.

Who would not accept this loving offer? Even I was tired of eating pasta, burgers and hot dogs. So, for the next two weeks, I'd pick up Sukumar Chacha's box of Pan Bahar and necessary instruments, and follow him around the lanes of New York. Poor Shantul, who was under tremendous work stress, also felt very guilty about having almost abandoned his parents and he, too, welcomed this move. When he went on and on thanking me profusely, I lost my cool and shut him up with a few choice Hindi abuses. Arre sala, Chacha and Chachi have been my chacha and chachi from even before he was born!

Even so, the poor guy would hustle tickets for interesting exhibitions or events whenever he could. Once, he got an invite to a musical event on Fifth Avenue, organized by one of his Indian banker friends. Chacha and I had tired of the bad or very bad Indian musical events but were surprised to know that this particular event was going to be kickstarted by the renowned music guru Shri Samarkant, aka Pranmani. I checked with Chacha that this was the same Samarkant Maharaj of Goduliya who swung both ways, if you know what I mean. He was known as the lover of a proud beauty, one Sakina Bai, but among musicians and music lovers, he was also whispered to be the 'Begum Samru' of a rich raja of some estate. A Bai and a Maharaja – the man was made for gossip lovers!

As usual, Chacha was bang on. From the beginning, people in the world of music were aware that Guru Pranmani was known to play for both the teams in matters of the heart. Men found in him the tenderness of a woman, while tawaifs were mad about his gentle manliness and subtly flirtatious nature. This helped him professionally. When young and struggling, a well-established tawaif of the time, Sakina Bai, had offered this coy and effeminate lad a place to stay in her kotha, thereby relieving him of financial worries.

According to Chacha, the talented Samarkant acquired at the bai-ji's kotha not just a deep understanding of semi-classical music but also the art of spending money lavishly and living well. A rich prince, who was a patron of the kotha, fell for the well-dressed, coquettish singer wrapped in a halo of attar. Who could compare the luxuries of a palace to the comforts of a kotha? So Samarkant, as soon as he found a better benefactor, left Sakina Bai and went to live with the Raja Sahib. Chacha heard from a few jealous tawaifs that the romantic Raja Sahib had rechristened Samarkant as Samru. This name – Begum Samru – stuck to him.

But when Indira Gandhi ran her scissors on privy purses, many old princes lost their regular incomes and singers their rich patrons. Moreover, the English-speaking brown sahibs, who were deeply influenced by their Edwardian predecessors, frowned on all bai-jis as fallen women and shunned their kothas.

Woe upon these sahibs! It was the age of the great wars and black markets. A bad time for established tawaifs from Lucknow to Benares and Calcutta to Patna. Soon, there were cobwebs hanging from the walls of many kothas of these once famous bais. The lanes that were once bustling with people now lay desolate. And wherever you went, you found tabla players and sarangi players, who lived off the bai-jis and mehfils, on the verge of starvation.

It is said that when all hope is lost, it is God who lends a hand. So, in came Western recording companies as saviours of starving musicians. Chacha's father became the Hindu sahib who'd guide the cheroot-smoking officers of the recording companies from Germany and Britain. He helped open several Indian recording companies to give them a local base. That started a new era.

Vidya can find a wealth of rare information on this era from the papers in Chacha's house. But to return to the tale of Samarkant, aka Begum Samru.

Singers like him were by now used to minting big money. Since the Indian scene offered less and less, by the sixties they began looking westward. The brown sahibs' midnight's children were being serenaded by the Beatles. And hard rock and acid rock were replacing qawwali and rap.

The Beatles's was a short-lived affair with India and its musical instruments. Recently, I heard that the historic three-reed harmonium that George Harrison had bought in Benares with great fanfare was sold by the auction company Sotheby's for just three hundred dollars. That, too, not because the buyer understood the value of the instrument, but because it was the sacred hand-me-down of a white Beatles singer.

Samarkant had always been able to tell which way the wind was blowing, and he shaped his music as per the changing times. He first correlated Indian classical music with spirituality and yoga, and then packed a few foreigners and took them to Goa where numerous international singers held pop concerts. One such rich rockstar fell so deeply in love with Samru that he got him a green card. After reaching America, he tried his hand at many things, and then, very cleverly, created a successful tonic with his many virtues. For his American benefactors, his music was like an exotic orchid, and for NRIs like Shantul, who had left behind their motherland and parents without a second thought to become millionaires, he became a respected representative of the musical heritage of the Hindus.

It was after reaching Los Angeles, the fabled haven of fresh talent and bisexuals, that Samarkant first became Pranmani and then, slowly, thanks to his PR skills, became the highest authority on Hindustani music. He started a successful gurukul in LA and became the apple of rich New York-based NRIs' eyes. He would visit New York three to four times a year to bless his old students. It was said that Samarkant-ji no longer visited India because of his allergy to tropical humidity and dust, which troubled his chest and throat.

When we arrived at his mehfil that evening, he gawped when he saw Chacha and then lunged towards him and touched his feet as further proof of his traditional humility. Then in his American English, he started explaining to the onlookers what an iconic critic of old-style gharana music was in their midst that day. He introduced Chacha as one from the old-world elites of India who had inherited the love of and insights into classical music from his learned forefathers. Chacha's house in Benares was like a temple for old musicians, he said. Finally, Chacha grew wary and whispered, 'Now stop all this natak, Begum Samru, let's hear some music!'

But now that Chacha's forefathers and inheritance had been mentioned, the Lalwanis, Khannas, Kumars, Charatamals and their mothers started clapping for him. A few well-endowed ladies waddled up and requested him to sit in one of the front-row seats meant for the major critics. I looked apprehensively at Sukumar Chacha's taut face and a kind of mischievous look beginning to flash in his sharp eyes. I then prayed to Ma Kali to offer her protection to Samru.

The room was very cold as the Americans seem to like extra-cooled rooms. Shivering in that ice-cold room, I wondered: How many singers and musicians from India land up in New York kissing the corner of the self-anointed Guru Maharaj Samarkant-ji's flowing dress with its Kashmiri embroidery? All to solicit a few programmes organized by cash-rich organizations run by rich NRIs.

Chacha whispered that he was reminded of Raja-ji when he saw Samarkant's half-closed eyes scanning his listeners shrewdly. In the past, when he was struggling to move up, the dust of the lanes and bylanes of Benares did not bother him. Nor was he fazed by some amused whispers doing the rounds in the area about his mysterious relationship with his new royal benefactor. Once he had reached where he wished to be, Samarkant wasted no time in leaving Benares and following another rich socialite to Delhi. His latest mentor was married to a prominent man with business interests everywhere. And from there, it was Go Goa Gone.

Nobody knows when the wronged Sakina Bai, who had faced many hardships in silence to support a young Samarkant and his talent, left Benares. Some say she became a sanyasini and moved to the Himalayas, and still others that she took jal samadhi in the Ganga. A few boys from the city who had moved to Bombay claim that they have caught glimpses of her there, but nobody has any proof. When in his earliest avatar, Samarkant sang, his eyes were always locked with those of Sakina Bai. By now he had arrived internationally, and his eyes glinted with a certain shrewdness not unlike a businessman's. He now flecked his English speeches with Sanskritized Hindi and wore long gowns and ethnic shawls in the manner of Hindu sanyasis.

That evening, one of his female disciples, weighed down by false studied airs, was accompanying him at the event. She sang off-key and one could not sense in her a disciple-like devotion and deference for her guru as she sat, almost cheek to cheek with him, laughing, making eyes at him. Finally, it was when she winked at him while singing a certain thumri about love, that Chacha's face began to look thunderous, and I knew big trouble was brewing for her.

And it did not take too long. After the guru brought his brief recital to a close, he announced that his disciple would present the next item. She was introduced as a famous new international talent, Vidushi Shobhana Kusumarkar, singer and music scholar. The disciple in turn made a great show of touching her guru's feet and fiddling with an iTanpura on her iPad. Then, placing her hand on her heart, she coyly asked her guru and Chacha, 'Am I allowed to begin, sirs?' and then began singing a Hori composition in Raga Khamaj about a very young wife cavorting and playing Holi, while complaining to her husband's sister that he was messing with her:

Hori khelat moson nai re nai re
Ka kahon nanadi anokhe piya so
Barjori kar mori bahiyan gahat hai
Apni kahat aru kachu na sunat hai
Aaj laaj mori gai re gai re...

Her notes kept slipping out of her grasp but, again and again, she cast long, coy glances at her guru, who had a certain smile playing upon his wet, pink mouth. Suddenly Chacha, who had been sitting quietly next to me, lost it. 'Lahaul bila quvvat, yaar! What is happening here? Is this a song or a parody? Please stop this drama!' he thundered.

The singer stood up a little shaken, and was soon replaced by another young disciple, a drummer with blond dreadlocks.

At this point, Chacha ordered, 'Chalo!' and we left.

I heard recently that Guru-ji passed away following an acute attack of asthma. His chautha was performed for days on social media. His ashes are still doing the rounds in cyberspace in urns.

Such is life, brother! Even the ashes of musicians are now immersed in cyberspace.

Yours truly,
Radha

~

Kolkata

May God bless you, our Kalyaniyasu Vidya,

Radha Dada had already informed me over the phone about your plan to visit Kolkata. I have heard so much about all of you from Sukumar Dadamoni over the years. And my husband, who used to visit Allahabad quite often for work, never tired of praising your mother's warm hospitality. Radha Dada has also told me in great detail about the trouble you have undergone to collect rare information about old singers and musicians from all sorts of faraway small towns.

Growing up, both Dada and I heard and spoke to so many illustrious musicians, but instead of writing books to bring their divine gifts to light for the next generation, neither one of us has ever even discussed them between us at length. We have just been busy carrying out daily chores. Unlike Sukumar Chacha, we did not even share all our memories about music with each other. All we ever shared were anecdotes, gossip, and a good laugh. And now, those alleyways and the people who lived and loved and exchanged music are all gone. I often wonder how long even Ma Ganga will survive in this city, its jostling crowds and pollution?

When I think about the mehfils, the singing and music back there in my father's home, it feels like a long-forgotten dream here in Calcutta. When I came here after getting married, my mother-in-law had made a long face and subtly warned me, saying that at their home, it was only the menfolk who talked about music, not us women. And even the men had to step outside to listen to the kind of music played at mehfils. She did not tolerate mehfils and closed-door baithaks in her home like the people in Lucknow and Benares. I had heard her out, smirking behind my veil. Radha Dada had made this match after having thoroughly researched my would-be-groom's interest in music. I was married to him only after Dada was sure he would be my viaduct into music and see to it that I kept up my interest. So long as he was alive, I attended many mehfils with him in the city. When we were younger, we would sneak out of the backdoor, and later, became bold enough to leave by the main door. My mother-in-law, in the way of old-fashioned mothers-in-law, knew it was better not to fuss. So she, God rest her soul, very graciously ignored us. She was sensible.

See Vidya, when you leave the place you were born in, grew up playing and chatting with childhood friends in, a profound sense of loneliness can take root in a young woman's heart. Husband and children will fill this particular vacuum only for a few years.

And when the children leave, and then the husband, you soon lose track of time. It becomes immaterial to you, as a lonesome widow, which season it is outside your window, what date it is in the calendar upon the wall, and before you know it, the loneliness within you merges with the vast loneliness outside. Do trees remember the leaves from the season past? Let them fall, the tree says perhaps, and just stands silently! That's how I am.

It will do me a world of good to listen once again to conversations about music and artistes from the bygone era, between a scholar such as you and Sukumar Chacha. It will be like a greening rain falling on this desiccated tree. I will also be able to meet Sukumar Chacha. We met often while his wife, Chachi, and my husband, the Professor Sahib, were alive. But since their passing, I haven't met Sukumar Chacha, only spoken over the phone to give him my pranam and good wishes on festive days. He must be miffed with me. But maybe he realizes what an old bandish in Raga Alhaiya Bilaval puts so movingly about the likes of us: '*Na morey paayein na pankh, na ur bal, na kahu sudh ko liveyya…*' (Neither my feet nor wings nor my listless heart has the strength to fly. And there's no one left to ask about my well-being, leave it be). I have digressed again.

You'll find our driver Hariram at the airport. He will be holding a placard with your name on it. I would have come to receive you, but the traffic is terrible, and I am allergic to dust and have difficulty breathing with the smoke fumes on the roads. I step out very rarely because of that. My knees have also begun to trouble me a lot; maybe it is my weight. Radha Dada says that this is what happens when you put a truck on a Maruti's frame.

Anyway, you don't need to be terrorized by my maladies. But if your flight gets delayed for some reason, do give me a call. If I were to make a local call, these rotten airport people would either not answer it or, even if they were to answer it, they'd give mostly incorrect information.

And yes, this is your house. Live here for as long as you please.

With love,
Madhobilata

~

Kolkata

Dear brothers,

Thanks to Putul Di, I have managed to reach her home very easily. The flight was late, but the driver Hariram was present at the right time and place with a placard saying, 'Bidda Debi'. He is as talkative as us. He updated me on his mistress's health and also enquired about my credentials. He spoke about his late master with a lot of respect and talked about the care with which he treated his wife. 'Aha! Poor thing has withered away,' he said. 'She only has three dogs for company, and she treats them like her children. It will be good for her to go out with you to Banerjee Sahib's house. Sahib is very jolly. But he has also weakened and become trapped in the house after Boudi's death.'

Old servants become confidants of the aged. Which is why Hariram-ji was aware of not just Sukumar Chacha and Putul Di's dogs' moods but also the reason for my arrival, my itinerary. My monosyllabic responses did not dampen his curious enthusiasm. 'What is the point of life without marriage?' he asked me bluntly. It wasn't possible for me to get angry at this question of his because it had that mix of affection and confusion that is so Indian.

When I gave my usual reply of 'I have so much to read and write that there's no time for all that', Hariram might not have bought the excuse, but he did not challenge it either. All he said was that when Professor Sahib was alive, many people from the country and abroad stayed at the house to study. Many musical events happened on Basant Panchami, Holi and Teej. Many Bengali and non-Bengali ustads and pandits came to be a part of them. There was plenty of food and drink and singing and dancing. When the mehfils carried into the nights, Professor Sahib would tease his non-Bengali friends' failed attempts at speaking in Bangla.

By the time I reached home, I understood the foundation of the easy companionship between Professor Sahib and Sukumar Chacha.

Putul Di does not step out of her room often, but she dragged her ailing body with great difficulty to the veranda when she heard the car stop and, before she took me inside, hugged me warmly. My luggage was brought into my room at the same time, and after I had washed my face, I was marched off right away to Putul Di's huge, old-fashioned room. She sat on her large, creaking bed in the middle of the room like a queen. I sat in the chair next to it. Soon, a tray laden with sweets and water arrived. Then, after taking Didi's permission, I went to have a proper bath. 'Lunch will be at one, Ma,' she said. 'Rest until then. You must be tired after the long flight.'

When I came out, it was noon. Putul Di looked worried. I learned that Sukumar Chacha had slipped and fallen in the bathroom in the morning and had hurt his back. Thankfully, nothing had broken, but this meant we would be able to meet him only tomorrow.

'No worries, we'll go tomorrow,' I said. 'We can perhaps catch up with each other in the meanwhile?' Putul Di looked pleased.

Truth be told, my mind, which usually shies away from feminine gossip sessions with heads resting on pillows side by side, was a little alarmed. But I had to provide some compensation for such exemplary hospitality.

Rest, once I return.

Love,
Vidya.

Kolkata

Dear brothers,

At night, the longing to meet Sukumar Chacha, in the morning, the indescribable joy of eating the gorgeous traditional Bengali 'ranna' from Putul Di's kitchen.

I could only eat sparingly out of the nervousness over the impending meeting with Chacha. Putul Di laughed. 'Don't be so scared. His bark is worse than his bite. He has a big heart. If anyone is going to the gallows today, it will be me. "Where were you all these days? I do not wish to talk to you any more!" Now eat.'

While feeding me her fluffy luchis, Putul Di was reminded of her dadi's grand haveli in Lucknow that housed antiques imported from all over the world. People of such fine tastes they were – she said – from food to music.

Her dada-ji, Kunwar Sahib, was a well-known lawyer and had resolved innumerable complicated court cases for the noblemen from neighbouring princely states and members of the large nawabi family of Lucknow. His clients kept showering him with gifts as a sign of their gratitude all his life – cut-glass vases and chandeliers from Venice, ancient chinaware from Britain, to silverware and jewellery from Delhi, Calcutta, even Mexico.

I listened to Putul Di, mesmerized. 'I still remember listening to Kali Babu's baritone as he chatted with Dada-ji in the garden hemmed by freshly watered mehendi bushes in the summers of my childhood. I'd go straight on to his lap and come in contact with his soft, pillowy pot belly. His head, bedecked with salt-and-pepper curly hair, would bob in concert with Kunwar Sahib's white head in time to some old or new bandish. Unlike Kali Babu's booming laughter, Kunwar Sahib's was restrained, like that of those hailing from the feudal families of Uttar Pradesh. His smile usually remained restricted between the two ends of his moustache. When Kali Babu laughed, it was with his entire being. The aroma of the paan in his mouth would waft out and his nostrils would jiggle, and drops of kattha and supari from his mouth would fall on his silk kurta and make it polka-dotted by the time the gathering was over. Oh Vidya, his huge pot belly would shake so much that, seated on his lap, it would seem like one were in a moving train!

'When the conversation would move to the different kinds of new mehfils and ragas, it seemed like a child had found a new toy. Every performance would be broken down to pieces and analysed closely by the friends to see how this trickster of a raga was showing such exciting results when sung by so and so. Those two friends never let any piece of music they heard and any major mehfil go unless they had it fully deconstructed. What was a singer thinking while singing a particular raga and whether the influence of his guru and gharana was reflected in the style of singing, was his little deviation noticed, why would a particular ustad insert prayer words in a bandish...

'The kind of heated discussions they used to have on such topics cannot be rivalled even by television panels these days.

'If a major issue could not be untangled, then our Nanhe Cha, that is Pramod Bihari, was sent for. The man was the biggest thesaurus in family mehfils. Nanhe Cha was famous for his unique memory of all things musical and various memorable mehfils. Among the cognoscenti, he was referred to as "Khalifa", the presiding arbiter.

'"Yaar Nanhe, please tell us whether that year Lucknow's Seth Vadilal had scolded Motibai for messing up Raga Ramkali or was it her alap of Lalita Gauri?"'

'Nanhe Cha would, by force of habit, first tap the tip of his nose with a finger and give a diplomatic response to cool the heated atmosphere a little. For example: "Bhai, everyone knows about Vadilal-ji. He is one of those people who lifts weights and drinks ginger tea first thing in the morning. He was angry already at that time, and then to add to it, he learned from Khadim Hussain Sahib that Motibai had omitted singing the slow-moving Bada khayal in Raga Ramkali at his house. He had had two large pegs in the front room and lost his cool. But brothers, such things will happen at mehfils occasionally. For instance, there was a heated altercation over whether the Raga Darbari Inayat had played at his house three years ago was better than the one he had played at Khan Sahib's last year or not.'

'"Yaar, just tell us, was the distortion of the asthayi, which Vadilal blew his top over, connected to aberrations he had detected in the singing style?"

'When these questions flew thick and fast, Nanhe Cha would defer delivering a clear verdict until tempers calmed. Many a time, the discussion would stretch late into the night. As the lamps started getting lit, my aunts, Shammo, Dammo or Kammo, whoever was at hand, would come out of the kitchen to direct the army of servants to serve plates of vegetarian and non-vegetarian food to the gathering. Food would be served, and if the discussion was still on, after a while, my mother would shyly say from behind the bamboo blinds, "Please take a bite now or the food will get cold."

'Know this, Vidya, that in those days, the first bites would be taken only after repeated requests from the hosts, and just then, Dadi would say that the cold puris were probably not tasting good, so fresh puris or missi rotis should be served to the guests.

'We should leave now,' is how Putul Di finished the story and the meal. 'Traffic is bad everywhere, and Chacha is as punctual as the English. Let's go, shall we?'

Then, as the car began to move, it was time to be briefed about Sukumar Chacha.

It was many years ago that his father, Kalisadhan Banerjee, left his house in Calcutta's Gora Bazaar and moved to Lucknow to teach at Lucknow University. Later, he chose to settle there. So Chacha was born, raised and educated far away from Calcutta in Lucknow.

'If you go to the university there today, you will see more and more tents of provincial armed constabulary with their striped underwear drying in the sun. Once glorious, the dusty campus and the redbrick rooms of the Sociology Department where his father taught look derelict now.'

During the days of Chacha's father, their beloved Lucknow was a veritable spot of pilgrimage for art and scholarship next only to Calcutta. And the university symbolized its spirit. One of its towering intellectuals, Kali Babu, had carried along the Calcutta traditions of passionately organized musical sessions and friendly and prolonged addabaazi. Within a few years, his house, surrounded by fragrant henna shrubs, became the regular haunt of all men of taste in the city. It was at this point that he struck a lifelong friendship with Putul Di's grandfather, Bade Sarkar.

Bade Sarkar was both a renowned lawyer and art lover. Music brought him so close to Kali Babu that the two friends met every day. In a few years, there wasn't one musician who, after arriving in the city, would not put in a request to be allowed to perform at either of their homes. Managing to get an invitation to their baithaks was a cause for celebration among both vocalists and players of various traditional instruments.

Kali Babu is still remembered among those in the know across the city for his grasp on not just the social sciences and economics but also classical music. Students of Kali Babu, the music expert and professor of social economics, command respect wherever they go.

'In his personal life, Kali Babu stayed away from worldly preoccupations, like Ustad Allauddin Khan of Maihar who also lived like a detached fakir. My father and Sukumar have visited their ancestral house in Calcutta's Gora Bazaar several times. But by then, the Banerjee family was living elsewhere and would only go there for Kali Pujo. 'While Kali Babu was still alive, Sukumar Chacha, who called himself the epitome of Lucknow's tehzeeb, decided to follow in his uncles' footsteps to Bombay. Soon, he joined some British-owned company as an officer. The father feared that if his son spent too much time with the "sahib log" in Bombay, his ties to his own roots might be called into question.

'But though Chacha worked in Bombay for many years, his ties to his roots remained strong. By the time he retired, both husband and wife decided to forego what was left of Lucknow and the poor university campus and moved to their long-abandoned home in Calcutta.

'This house, where we are going to meet Chacha today, came up due to Kali Babu's far-sighted father-in-law, who was an engineer, and a worldly wise one at that. As the father of Kali Babu's wife Haribala Devi, he was rather wary of his brilliant but dreamy son-in-law's bent of mind. His name was Rathindranath, but he was known as Ranga Babu. Ranga Babu, who was smart enough to keep the English officers happy, and worried as he was about his guileless son-in-law's extravagant ways with money and the future of his daughter and grandson, got busy planning a house for them. Being a pragmatic man, rather than scold his son-in-law he acted in an extremely protective and generous way towards him. He managed to convince Kali Babu to sell his land in the village and helped him buy one in the city. As he had expected, while Kali Babu stayed immersed in his books, daughter and father would visit the site periodically with their umbrellas to supervise the construction of the beautiful new house. Things were inexpensive then, and Ranga Babu kept a tight leash on the contractor. Today, cunning builders are busy transforming those beautiful old houses in Calcutta into ugly, gigantic apartment complexes. Chacha's enormous house must also be on their radar. But they wouldn't dare to raise the matter of selling the house while Chacha is still alive.

'The city around us is really undergoing great change. So many old houses are disappearing, so many historical buildings being replaced by shopping malls and apartments. Piles of rubble have erased pedestrian pathways, so our traffic crawls like ants, but we humans tend to accept change.' Putul Di sighed the satisfied sigh of a master storyteller who had painted a perfect backdrop for my meeting with the fabled Sukumar Chacha, son of Kali Babu, amid the roar of buses, the clanging of bells and the clouds of dust.

It was at this point that I decided to request Putul Di to tell me other interesting stories from her childhood that she could remember, and just mail them to me as and when she could.

Putul Di blushed. 'Arre, why Vidya? I am just a housewife, merely an avid listener of music. What insights will an expert like you gain from the narratives of a simple homemaker?'

But I was stubborn. I knew she'd relent if I kept repeating my request.

Our car stopped at the porch of the famous house in Gora Bazaar built by Ranga Babu for his loving daughter, his dreamer of a son-in-law, and the apple of his eye, his grandson.

The huge house was separated from the road by an iron gate and looked like an old dog dozing in the sun. The gardens in the front had numerous large trees: coconut, custard apple, mango, and varieties of lemon, lime and guava. The trees, like the porch, were covered with fine dust.

Putul Di had to wipe her fingers after having stroked some half-dried bushes. She tut-tutted and told me how Lotika Chachi had lovingly planted this vegetation when they had first moved to Kolkata from Bombay after retirement. With one son and daughter-in-law living outside India and another son somewhere along the Goan coast, Chacha's wife knew that, when not travelling, they'd mostly be living here by themselves. So Chachi had planted flowers that were low-maintenance, like crepe jasmine, red hibiscus, jasmine, arum. The jackfruit and champa trees, one of each, right outside the gate had been planted by Chachi soon after shifting to Kolkata. There were probably just four flowers on the champa tree, but their fragrance seemed to fill up the old home. Radha Dada had been right when he wrote to her about the house behind the garden – that without the homemaker, this house was turning into a haunted house like Miss Havisham's.

The first room we stepped into had a green brass doorknob shaped like a lion's face. It was worn down and looked grimy. It led visitors into the drawing room. The room was not ostentatious but filled with furniture and things bought by someone with great taste. There was a silver bowl on the table. Putul Di told me that Chachi, who loved aromatic flowers, always kept the room filled with fresh mogra and harsingar buds. But now it looked absolutely empty, sad, and covered in dust and cobwebs like the doorknob. Maybe nobody sat in this room any more. Who'd believe that there was a time when the friendly Chacha, with Putul Di's husband and many of Kolkata's other music lovers, used to liven up this room with their laughter and long conversations on music and musicians as they munched on various delicacies cooked by Chachi?

There was a huge open courtyard outside the drawing room. On one side of it, a flight of steps led us to the first floor. The veranda upstairs was right above another one below, but it was surrounded by railings. Chachi and her friends would come out to sit here in the afternoons to dry their hair, gossip about relatives and discuss the newly arrived daughters-in-law and their mothers-in-law stressing over the boumas' airs. This was where high-level talks were held on new varieties of saris and jewellery designs.

As we climbed upstairs slowly, Putul Di continued her commentary. 'Chachi was suspicious that her husband would pretend to sleep in the adjoining room just to be able to eavesdrop on women's conversations.

'Chacha was very fond of sleeping, especially in the afternoon. He used to call it "bhaat ghoom" or the sweet sleep that follows a full meal of rice and curries. He would go lie on the enormous four-poster bed made of Burmese teak in his bedroom. His mother had brought this superbly crafted bed with her ample dowry, and it had taken twelve people to bring it up piecemeal.'

We now entered Chacha's bedroom.

Radha Dada had described his famed bed in graphic detail to me before this meeting. Its legs had exquisite lions' feet complete with claws carved on them. The detailed work on the headboard cried out for my attention: the top was Burmese bamboo followed by a teakwood frame displaying a trail of elephants in the centre of the headboard. Around the bed stood four teak almirahs with Belgian mirrors studded to the door frame. The knobs were Belgian cut glass.

Sukumar Chacha lay on the four-poster bed, on four thick pillows, supported by two huge bolsters on either side. His now-immobile feet lay hidden under a green hand-embroidered sheet. With a weakened body, a wrinkled but intelligent face, slightly proudly flared nostrils, thin lips, and big eyes which still shone with a yen for life, Chacha said he had been waiting for us forever. Entering and being given a seat in Sukumar Chacha's room brought to me the same excitement, fear and hesitation as entering the sanctum sanctorum of a grand, ancient temple with the presiding priest offering us a seat.

Chacha smiled. 'What's this sudden burst of light? Aah! The appearance of two beautiful ladies in this old man's house! And look at this cranky old man who will not even get up to welcome you or blare a conch shell to herald your arrival. Please forgive me, goddesses! Sit! Please sit comfortably against the cushion. And please no touching of the feet here. I stopped letting people touch my feet a long time ago.

'And Putulmoni, so at last you remembered Chacha today? Ah yes, now she'll say that her driver disappeared at the moment, like the elusive seventh note in Ali Akbar Khan's playing of Raga Maluha Kedar.

'So you are Vidya Sundari, Paritosh Babu's daughter, eh? Did you know that your nana, the late Ambadutt Tripathi-ji, was my assistant headmaster? A dhoti tied high, a half-sleeved sadri, a smoking pipe in the mouth and a moustache like Marshal Timoshenko's. He was highly well-versed in music and was a strict disciplinarian. When the time came to get his beautiful daughter – your mother – married, the old man searched and finally chose for her someone quite similar to himself, minus the music: a reserved man who spoke in monosyllables, laughed seldom, and always wore khadi like him. Legend has it that, mourning the loss of one nubile, supremely gifted girl they all carried a torch for, many of Lucknow's young men wrote laments like, "Aha, the daughter from Lucknow as delicate as a jasmine bud taken away by Tripathi's vegetarian Gandhian student, Paritosh Shukla!" The laments reminded one of a marsiya by Lucknow's great marsiya writer, Anees: "Alas, Hassan, we were not there for you." The men even wore a black band around their arms for three days!

'Heh heh, don't look shocked and don't mind your chacha. This chacha is all bark and no bite. Just that I remembered your mother's face when I saw you, and old memories swirled in my mind.

'Come, Ma. Sit.

'Arre, sala Jogen! Send some tea and snacks. My daughter has come after ages. When she goes back, she'll say that her male chauvinist, old chacha is breaking all boundaries of gender justice and served her tea with no snacks.'

We sat down. A few minutes later, tea arrived in expensive but dirty and chipped cups, and on an old silver tray, a few sweets. Everyone got busy for a while. Then the cups were put down and Chacha started speaking of the school in Dhaka where his maternal grandfather lived.

'A white half pant for drills and a tulle shirt, and white socks on our feet and white sport shoes with laces – that was the uniform, and I was given exactly two pairs. I'd put the tiffin box under my arm and jump into the rickshaw. I was sent to different kinds of schools for many years. Different kinds of education. Three hours of English for us Bengalis meant reading and writing, and we first taught our children essay writing. Then came arithmetic, science, social science, and lastly, music. Which is why a dratted Bengali boy starts wearing glasses at sixteen before he has even become an adult, and by seventeen, he is nursing stomach ulcers.

'Dadu had advised mother, you have but one son, your mother-in-law and you will baby him and spoil him. Educate him a lot away from home. Feed him simple, pure vegetarian food, and get only two pairs of simple uniforms in a year, two khaki half pants, two white and two printed full shirts – no more than that. His own sons, meaning my uncles, were raised along the same lines. One was now a big officer in an English-owned company in Bombay and the other a civil servant. He told mother it would do me good to stay with them for some time. So I was sent to Bombay to live with my uncle and study there.

'You might see them as tall tales now, but nobody did anything in half measures those days. So Dadu immediately bought cloth material worth two annas per yard for two khaki pants and four shirts, which he got stitched by the tailor Hakim Ali on Dida's Pfaff sewing machine and she handed them to Ma. Thus, my fate was sealed.

'Do you want more tea? How can one cup be enough? Arre, sala Jogen, go, get some fresh tea.

'So, I listened to a lot of music all night long in Bombay, and then in Lucknow, and Calcutta when I went there for Pujo. There used be a continuous seventy-two-hour music festival at Bhatkhande College where Radha and Putul's and my families would camp with the singers, carrying paan boxes and thermos flasks of tea. When your nana came, we would respectfully seat him with the older generation in the front, far away from our talkative group.

'In 1936, Manjhey Khan Sahib of the Jaipur-Atrauli gharana came to perform. Lucknow's moody spectators ignored him because he took his own time to delineate a raga. After some cruel taunts from us, he refused to sing a thumri. Why should I lie? We contributed to his humiliation. We did not appreciate his music because we were too full of our Lucknowi style. As he sang, we just sat with long faces. We knew this always puts a performer off, even if taunts will not. We heard later that Khan Sahib got very angry and left for Bombay the very next day. Agreed that we ragged him a bit much, but even one of our talented Lucknow musicians was wronged in Bombay. He wasn't just a good teacher but also a good singer. But Bombay's Marathi-Brahmin-centric music politics came in the way there. Otherwise, didn't he win everyone over sometimes by singing ragas such as Purva, Purya, Sohni and Sanjhgiri one after the other at our mehfils? The poor man was just unlucky. He remained a struggler. But later, we all realized that it was he who left behind an entire generation of superior singers trained by him on a half-empty stomach. By the time Akashvani, etc., were created, he was only requested to help them select good singers, since his own singing voice had deteriorated. Even then, he helped create an excellent grading system for the radio to help them select good singers with a good knowledge of ragas.

'How much does this generation remember him? Not at all. But the grading system he helped create is still in use. Game-playing still goes on, though. One major sarod player was very keen on getting an A grade for his son who was an average sarodiya. To boost his case, he even brought a letter signed by a few MPs and a minister, but his request was turned down. It was the seventies, and people were still fearless when it came to protecting their national treasures. The Bengali station director at the All India Radio was an honest and brave old-school officer. He told the irate father bluntly, either the Minister Sahib should send him a proper file with a formal order to scrap the old grading system or accept the results of the grading committee which, as he knew well, had some renowned scholars on its board. He wrote: "Under the present system, the young man merits no more than low B category", and handed the application back to the father.

'Politicians still had some shame in those days. Also, musicians. The matter subsided quietly. No more was said.

'There's a funny story about the earliest Akashvani auditions. Initially, the heads of the gharanas started a virtual non-cooperation movement against the new and scientifically sound system for their grading as performing musicians. They said they were against being judged by some small-time Bengali-Marathi jury members. They stayed off for many days when called for auditioning. But the jury members held their peace. Finally, the musicians relented. One by one, they came, gave their performance, and were duly graded and allowed in. With each recital they found they had drawn acclaim nationally and even internationally. And of course, the royalties they were paid were also substantial. Most of the heads of musical gharanas may have been experts in their own fields, but it dawned on the officials that many of them were totally illiterate. They knew almost nothing about the classical texts on music and could not explain logically how and why they sang just so. For example, why was it that they played their Raga Multani in the evening and Raga Todi in the evening? When asked probing questions about the time cycles set for various ragas that were sung at different hours of the day, they'd begin to waver and break into a sweat. When asked what the basic difference between Multani and Todi is, one of them replied, "They are both perfect in their own place, janab."

'Vidya, my dear girl, you've satisfied my curiosity regarding Anjali Bai and Hira Bai, and for that, this old man is forever indebted to you. I feel no shame in telling you that my dead father and many music lovers of his generations were huge fans of Anjali Bai. My mother knew about this obsession and did not like it one bit. She had tried to destroy the many rare pictures and letters of those tawaifs that my father had collected, albeit unsuccessfully. As soon as I got wind of it, I got all that material collected by one of my trusted spies and took it in my possession. Now, that material, which has been waiting for the right claimant, will be sent to you. I am getting it all dug out and sorted properly. As soon as that is done, I'll get all the files and photos sent to you.

'I might not be alive like the heads of the gharanas by the time your book is ready for release, but this old man will die reassured that he handed over all he had to a diligent writer and researcher before dying.

'May you live long. As they say in Bengal, visit again.'

By the time Putul Di and I got up to leave, Chacha, who had spoken for so long, looked as though, all of a sudden, his strength and need to talk had died. He called out to his attendant with abuses and weakly ordered him to cover his legs properly.

Putul Di kept wiping away her tears on the way back. There was nothing left to say.

That's all.
Vidya.

~

Kolkata

Dear Vidya,

When you asked me to write whatever I could about my childhood memories related to music and musicians, I did not realize, as I agreed, how hard writing, especially about one's own experiences, can be. Where do you draw the line?

It is often said that one should always write the honest truth. But can one withstand facing the bitter truth about one's own life first? Ever since I was a child, I have known that people appreciate honest writing only up to the point it reveals dark truths about those they dislike. The moment the light falls on their own lives, even if they have been flaunting their relationship with the writer in the outside world, they are quick to point out that the writer is dead wrong. They say the writer has taken liberties and created some imaginary characters very different from the actual members of the family.

Anyway! I am sure, being a writer, you must have already been through all this. Despite that you've chosen to keep writing, and I must congratulate you for your bravery. I don't need to tell you what I now realize: there is no judge more unforgiving and stern than the truth emanating out of a writer's pen.

Sukumar Chacha is known to keep his word, and as per his promise, he will get all the stuff sent to you soon enough. How can my humble piece compare to his rare treasures? But I feel strangely relieved after having written it all down. Of course, I jostled with many old memories to write honestly about what I recollect of my big family and the stories about its real but often complicated relationships with the world of music.

But then I thought I owe it to the world. These simple tales of human love and hate, passion and malice, might add a few unknown intimate details to the work of great scholars.

Compared to you, I am a bit of a coward. So if possible, please use these stories cautiously, and it might be a good idea also to keep my name out of the introduction and acknowledgements.

Many apologies for my terrible handwriting. I still prefer to write letters in long hand. I have not been able to familiarize myself with the blasted computer despite it sitting in the house for so many years. Whenever Radha Dada comes visiting, he brings along several expensive apps and tries to convince me to use the internet by showing me how it can be used in many different languages. But when I actually sat down to write, I could only do it with my husband's favourite pen. I could gather the courage to put down those hidden histories only after picking up this familiar pen.

I am neither an academic with a scientific mind like my husband's, nor a creative writer like you. I was good at studies, but like many women my age, my life after marriage revolved around familial responsibilities with my husband at the centre of it all. It is difficult to tell how much of my life was created by my own volition and how much of it was shaped by unseen pressures. But I am not bitter about the past any more. I am writing because of your repeated encouragement, knowing well that, learned as you are, you might find this piece somewhat puerile. But even so, I write this to shed some old burdens and feel light.

When he saw me struggling to deal with my past, my generous husband used to tease me. He said, you may be hiding many bittersweet memories, but look at it this way: how many people can get the opportunity to spend their formative years at the holy confluence of literature, music and art? But I still find it difficult to decide whether it is a blessing or a curse for old and moneyed families to spend half their time enjoying and appreciating high art and then step out of mehfils to chase money and power.

Let me begin my story with Dada-ji's house, which was witness to all the important events of the early years of my hero, Radha Dada, and me.

You, too, might have your own memories of that house, but you had visited it only after Dada-ji's death when that grand house had become rather rundown. While Dada-ji was alive, the unspoken but permanent tensions between my parents and the gossipy daughters of the house feeding them remained hidden. After his death, there were many awful fights and ugly disputes over inheritance and property. It was because of all that drama that Radha Dada ultimately left the city and moved far away on the pretext of running a publishing house he founded. Now, he only visits Kolkata and its outskirts for work, not Lucknow. Why, he asks, when I raise the topic, and something in his eyes tells me to leave things be, and I shut up.

After grabbing what they could, my father's brothers sold off their shares of the property to outsiders and broke all contact with us. One after another, they were gone. And their sisters, our buas, who had witnessed and vociferously taken sides, have also passed on by now. The only person left behind was my mother, surrounded by the ghosts of the past. She now found herself surrounded by the families of two strangers and wondered who she could rely on.

We grew up with a deep and abiding love for art and beauty as our tonic. The family name, the money and property remained for us a mixed blessing at best.

Radha Dada and I discovered that relatives might have been affectionate and rich, but after all their small talk and niceties, something would be spoken politely and yet it would clearly reveal a deep dislike, laced with malice, especially about our family's ties with the world of music. By an unspoken decree within our family, their opinions, if not rejected outright, were ignored. But the one person who paid a high price for this relentless internal battle was my simple, uncomplicated mother. She was a good homemaker, but she failed to meet the raised bar our arrogant family had set for its members when it came to music. It wasn't just her lack of beauty but also her lack of interest in music and art that created a permanent wall between her and the rest of the family.

Radha Dada was older, and in trying to protect me and make a life for himself outside his family's influence, he soon started feeling suffocated. True, he had friends like your brother Sanjeev and some others, and spent a considerable amount of time with them, but a certain dejection born out of the snobbery and bitterness within our large family gripped him tight. It reached a point where despite Amma and I persuading him hard, he still would not get married. Parents of many good girls showed interest, but Dada shied away. However, he made sure our mother never lacked for anything. But what went on deep within him, no one could see. To this day, only music perhaps can traverse its depths.

Radha Dada has a sharp intelligence and defiant temperament woven into his DNA. This is why he finally moved away from the family business altogether to start a publishing house in Lucknow, which is still very successful.

But money can't buy everything.

In life, only a few relationships will, after they are formed, grow, and many of them will die. Most times, logic has no role in it. Partly because he remained introverted and partly because our mother, Amma, preferred silence to letting out her emotions, a steady bridge of communication could never get built between Dada and her. Later, Amma came to share a deep bond with my husband who belonged neither to their community nor was given to talking much. As a man of few words himself, he perhaps sensed Amma's unspoken fears and anxiety for her future after Dada's departure better than me. He realized that, as she aged and grew frailer, she could not go on like this. And finally, on his advice, I asked Amma to move in here with us during her last days. I now realize that her last days with us were indeed full of a quiet joy.

Often, what we consider bad luck turns out be an opportunity. When Amma did not need to have a caregiver with her at all times, she began opening up for the first time in her life. It was then that I started parsing out details about her personal life, little by little, and heard her complaining about her past, while I rubbed oil on her knees. I noticed in my mother an intelligent mind with many sharp insights about what had been happening around her, even as she remained written off as a plain housewife with no knowledge of or taste in the arts. This soft-spoken woman, who ate very little, knew all about the inner workings of the joint family and had a tremendous understanding about the real personalities of its many members.

Amma also shared with me many interesting stories about the musicians invited to perform at the musical events in our house over the course of several generations. Only a sensitive and silent observer could have seen this ever-evolving play of life and art within the four walls of her father-in-law Bade Sarkar's house. In braiding my own memories with Amma's, I realize that just like the Jaipur-Atrauli gharana singers, well known for blending ragas seamlessly, we too create a picture of a large family where various people will suddenly reveal entirely different facets of themselves than what is known of them. This has revealed a lot to me. Recounting each story, I have discovered many new and rare facets of our life together in my grandfather's house.

In the shared memories of a mother and daughter, irrespective of whether they are or are not close, a few notes, a few experiences are always similar. Take my letter as an example of a mixed raga. And if some notes do not sound right or remain unclear, then use your expertise as a writer to address them. I give you that right.

I had once asked Amma hesitatingly, 'Babu-ji and his siblings kept you at a distance all your life. How did you still manage to look after them so well?'

I still remember Amma's soft, shy smile. 'You don't have to learn to love your own, Bitiya. After all, didn't they put up with an unmusical woman with no talent until the end? It's all our karma!'

Let's return to those major family events. When I was a child, be it preparing for a musical event or a wedding, the blueprint of everything was drawn out in the dining hall of our big joint family. And there's no two ways about the fact that the king of that realm was my dada-ji, the renowned barrister, Rai Bahadur Kunwar Shardul Vikram Singh or Bade Sarkar.

We would pick up our spoons and start eating our breakfast only when Bade Sarkar did. He took his time. He first shook open his starched napkin while looking lovingly at the fifty or so family members seated around him with his sharp eyes. It was only after that that he'd take the first mouthful. Dada-ji kept tabs on us all. Every member's place at the table and routine was predetermined. If someone was not present, their whereabouts would be questioned immediately. Where has he gone so early in the morning? Why? For what reason?

Bade Sarkar was so sharp that it was unimaginable to mislead him with a wrong answer. He knew every member's age, likes and dislikes, their basic nature, and had all the information about the marital lives of all his children. Despite his stern exterior, he was caring. He was also very careful about the rights of his poorer relatives, especially daughters-in-law, such as my mother, who lived lives estranged from their husbands and their perennially scared children.

My father, Anantvijay Singh, was always distant with us throughout our childhood. His inconsolable disappointment with his second wife, our plain and timid mother, had a profound impact on Radha Dada and my minds, even if it may not always have been obvious. As in most large joint families in those days, our father's estrangement from his second wife and his deep disgruntlement with his children were not a secret. But familial loyalties prevented the members from flaunting these tales outside. Out of pity, father's brothers kept trying to make things easier for us in their own ways and, of course, Dada-ji and they were like our sun and moons.

It is said that if God creates weakness, in his own way, he compensates for it too. So while Amma was just a silent cog in the machines that ran the household and kept the mundane things going, her two children, compared to the other children, revealed a far better understanding of and interest in music. To underline this fact, every morning at the breakfast table, Dada-ji would smile and ask one or the other of us general-knowledge questions about music and other subjects and was quick to congratulate us if he liked our answers. This would light up our entire day. Others can choose to agree or disagree, but for me, the entire universe revolved around Dada-ji and his sons.

Dada-ji's face was generally serious, but he cracked a big smile while praising us. The day he looked worried, not just us but every male in the family would also get anxious. A series of complaints would be made at once, husbands would look at their wives questioningly as if it were their fault. The scared mothers would cover their faces and look at their children with stern eyes for no reason and the children would try every moment not to giggle or say anything at this time of trouble, which might break Dada-ji's concentration, causing something untoward to happen.

The family was large. And the garrulous relatives would keep talking about random things all day. At these gossip sessions, our hapless mother would become the easy target of ridicule. According to my father's pampered sisters, our loquacious buas, their mother and our grandmother, could not cope with the infertility and death of her son Anantu's (our father) beautiful first wife. After that, probably just to keep the family line going, our father was married off to 'this one', despite the obvious lack of compatibility. Bade Sarkar never remarried after his wife died in old age despite the insistence of friends, but he got Amma married to our father upon the advice of a friend. It was a quick matchmaking, and my mother entered the house even while her husband, Bade Sarkar's son, was deep in mourning over his beloved first wife.

Because of this history, people would say about our mother, 'She could come here only because of that. Otherwise, had her mother-in-law been alive…' It is a tradition in Indian families to leave halfway the mention of anything that could emotionally hurt a woman. Even so, the way it is spoken about, the meaning is never hidden from anyone, especially the intended audience.

Those were times when this happened in many homes.

Our Babu-ji had turned into the frosty eldest son after the death of his first wife. Since she had died childless, there was a mounting pressure on him to keep the family line going. When our Amma was married into the family soon after the ritual mourning period of Babu-ji's first wife's death, Dada-ji is said to have just handed over the keys of the house to her and said, 'Now this house and its reputation are in your hands.'

No one gave a thought to how someone should have looked after the new young bride in her initial days at least! Amma was naturally shy, and she was further overwhelmed by the splendour of her marital home. She came from a modest home and did not ask or say anything. She did not even think that she needed the family's support to be able to bond with her husband who was already desolate. Or at least that is what she said.

Like I said before, those times were those times!

A strict mother-in-law, stubborn sisters-in-law, the husband's petulant and cheeky younger brothers, their wives – all followed every move of the new bride in most homes. There are so many musical compositions listing the terrors of a young bride too, no? Well, for our Amma, these were not characters appearing in thumris or dadras but real humans. And she had to deal with them all.

Other than the three sons at home, Dada-ji had three proud, beautiful daughters who had been married young into affluent families. They must have found their marital homes lacking in some way compared to their maiden home, with its old money and generational patronage of music and art, which is why they kept visiting it throughout the year on some pretext or another.

The eldest sister, Shammo, was the most audacious. She was respectfully referred to as Shammo Bibi. Her skin was milky white, her forehead was broad, and beneath it she sported a parrot-like hooked nose. Her teeth protruded somewhat, but she used to get a dimple on her cheek when she laughed. She pampered her voluptuous but well-toned body, one that would be considered sexy today, with expensive saris and make-up. She had great taste even in jewellery. Which is why it was considered a must to have her imprint on the making and distribution of every piece of jewellery in the house.

Nobody could beat our Shammo Bua in her courtly ways and singing all night at women's get-togethers during weddings.

The one after her was Kammo Bibi, the most attractive of the sisters with her wheatish complexion and well-etched nose and eyes, and was she short-tempered! I was very scared of her. She did not get along well with her marital family and contractor husband who was rich but oh-so uncouth. On top of that, despite many Western medicine treatments and jhaad-phoonk, she could never bear a child. Maybe that was the reason for her deep dislike for our fertile mother. Nature had tried to compensate by giving her a fairly decent voice. Her family and she were very proud of that, and we have heard many a time that she had a rare collection of black diaries full of traditional songs that are sung at weddings in her beautiful handwriting. As soon as the family got together, Kammo Bibi and her diaries would be summoned.

The only role Amma had to play in these family meetings was of serving tea and snacks. So, there would be one song sung for her at all these ladies' gatherings:

> *Aji kali kallo ke sau-sau mijaaz, kalo rang khoob hi khile.*
>
> Oh this dark-skinned one thinks no end of herself, her dark skin really glows.

When Bua would start singing, the three sisters would roll their eyes at Amma and join her. This sent the other women into peals of laughter.

As I have said, those times were just those times.

Neither enmity nor friendship was expressed overtly. But many nasty asides were made jokingly all the time. When something seemed to hit its target and the audiences clapped merrily, fistfuls of currency were circled around the heads of singers as if to ward off the evil eye, and then distributed among the servants.

> *Gori lugiyan bachchon ko tarsein, kallo ki paltan taiyyar ki kalo rang...*
>
> The fair-skinned wives long to have children, while the dark one has gone on to produce an army...

It was at these mehfils that unmentionable discriminations based on colour, race and caste emerged out in the open. Other hidden histories were also brought to the fore through folk music: the misdeeds of the domineering mother-in-law and her daughters, the uncaring husband with a roving eye. If the marital home was described as hell, the maiden home was painted as though it were a many-splendoured heaven. The fair-skinned women longed for everything – sweets, children, jewellery – but these would all go to the talentless, dark-skinned, low-caste – Dom and Chamar – women.

Amma dispassionately served tea, sweets and snacks to everyone, kept a straight face and her bent head covered.

The childless Kammo Bua visited her marital home only rarely. Maybe her female relatives there made similar songs about her, I wondered. Whatever the reason, she spent most of her time at our haveli where everyone respected her opinion. She was given the biggest, most comfortable room in the house and nobody could cross the LoC of her doorstep without her permission. Her husband – the rich and crude contractor – only visited for major family functions. He was short, his voice was a little nasal, and his face pockmarked. He walked with a slight stoop. But he spoke in very polite tones to his in-laws and was very fond of good food. He was from the western plains and disliked the yellow arhar, masoor and moong dals that we loved. Each time he visited, Amma would make a special black urad dal just for him with a lot of ghee, for which he praised her a lot. Bua disagreed with him on nearly everything, including his preference for black urad dal. It was as if a wall had come up between the couple as soon as Bua had clapped eyes on her husband-to-be, and that just stayed between them.

It was probably as a compensation by her maiden family that Kammo Bua had been given the biggest, airiest room in the house where our father used to live with his first wife. After her death, Babu-ji had left that room full of memories and shifted to the one with an adjoining library next to it. We could never enter that room without Amma's permission.

After our birth, Amma always slept with her children. When he grew up, Radha Dada moved to another airy room on the second floor. He spent most of his time in the college or with friends like your brother Sanjeev. He respected your music-loving mother a lot, and was scared of your stern professor father just as Sanjeev was.

We could go into Kammo Bua's room when she stayed there. We could visit her only if summoned, and would listen quietly to whatever Kammo Bibi had to say with our hands clasped. If she did not ask us to sit, we would keep standing respectfully. There was no question of playing with the window drapes or touching any of her things. Kammo Bua's big, proud eyes and sharp lips were just like our father's, and just like him, she rarely smiled at us. Like Babu-ji, the corners of her lips were always turned down in disdain in our presence. Her fingers were long, supple and beautiful. It had been understood from their shape that she'd become an artist when she grew up. So, Kammo Bibi had been taught watercolours by a renowned painting teacher of the time. There was a music teacher too. But the highest aim was to have her married to a suitable man. So, even this training in art was meant not to hone her talents but to increase her value in the marriage market, nothing more. All this continued until her wedding, but after that, 'The End'!

When Kammo Bibi got angry after seeing her newly married groom, her watercolours and tanpura and harmonium were hidden away for a while and taken out only slowly. Our Kammo Bua only performed at family functions. She had painted numerous pictures of beautiful girls offering flowers to the Buddha or crying at his feet, which were hung in many different rooms. While putting up these pictures, she would become either sad or angry.

Sometimes she would say to me, 'Not just painting, I could sing classical music better than many scholars such as you. But in our days, everyone would have been against their girl performing on the stage like a bai. You are lucky that times have changed. Our generation actually landed in a dilemma. If Rabindra sangeet had passed muster on Akashvani, then I should have become an A-grade singer. But that was not to be. Anyway,' I was told, 'since you are no great beauty like your mother, maybe music might redeem you.'

My mother, while chewing her supari, would hear about it from my angered mumblings and say, 'What's the point, my child? After all, Kammo Bibi is so unlucky.'

Our youngest bua, Dammo, was beautiful and fun-loving. Her cheeks would dimple beautifully when she laughed. Her glowing complexion and sharp features were like Babu-ji's, but just like her young brother, she had a yen for fun and was affectionate like Bade Sarkar. Her voice, too, was very melodious. It was said that her music-loving husband once heard her singing a bandish in Raga Chandni Kedar at a wedding and fell for her so badly that he immediately sent a marriage proposal. She was the only one in the family allowed to sing outside at baithaks in the city without a care.

Whenever she returned to her maiden home, we got to hear our sombre father's laughter. Dammo Bua was the only one who could enter the study without permission, while neither Amma nor we, nor even a bird, could venture inside without his say-so.

She remembered thousands of spicy anecdotes related to the musical gharanas, ustads, singers and mehfils. She would share them with Babu-ji for hours and laugh loudly at the juicy bits. Her tall husband was a senior government officer and visited his in-laws sometimes. A true art and music lover, he was always welcomed in a grand way. Special mehfils would be organized in his honour.

We would wait for the visits of Dammo Bua's husband for another reason: he loved children. He always took Radha Dada and me to the big Gymkhana Club in the city for kebabs and lemon sodas whenever he'd come over. In the era of the British, membership was restricted only to a few officers and the big affluent families. Kammo Bua's application to the club had been rejected twice, and each of those times, she had found fault with the servants and screamed at them for no reason.

'Poor Jijji!' Dammo Bua would say, and leave a lot unsaid that would resonate for a long time like a tanpura's reverberations.

There was another reason behind Dammo Bua and her husband's special affections towards us. According to them, we might not have inherited the beauty of our father, but both at school and in music classes, we had proven ourselves as worthy young torchbearers for the family.

Babu-ji's dear departed first wife was the only granddaughter of one of Kammo Bua's husband's fellow officers and was apparently also one of Dammo Bua's closest friends. When Babu-ji saw her dancing at a wedding function like a spinning top, he fell in love with her tiny waist and urged Foofa to plead his case and propose that she marry him. When Bua saw her parents hesitate due to some predictions made by some foolish astrologer, she insisted that they ignore the prophecies and, finally, got the frail beauty married to their darling brother. But the forecast the astrologers had made of her early death that, truth be told, had also scared our Dadi, came true. Soon, within four to six months, a dreaded disease took hold of her. When, despite multiple treatments, she did not recover, it was decided that she be taken abroad. But she passed away before that.

After this incident, Dada-ji selected a bride not on the basis of beauty or a love for the arts, but on the basis of health. That is how, in one of the buas' words, a 'talentless bride with uneven teeth and a thick waist' became our father's second wife and our mother. On the very first day, Babu-ji had gotten angry with her on account of her lack in the beauty department and he could never let go of this displeasure. But before he died at the young age of fifty-six, the ugly wife he so disliked had ensured the longevity of his family line by making him the father of two children.

We also had a Manjhle Chacha, the middle of the three brothers, a renowned scientist who, at the beginning of his career, had left the country with his wife and children to work far away from home. Thereafter, they would visit us only during the summer vacations or Durga Pujo. It's funny that I do not even know his real name but remember him only as my 'Manjhle Chacha' or 'Scientist Chacha'. Next to the unconditional love we got from Dada-ji, it was Scientist Chacha's. Radha Dada and I would get excited as soon as we would hear that Chacha and his family had arrived. We knew that Chacha and Chachi would summon us as soon as they'd freshen up. Then would begin the magical event of them taking out presents – always appropriate to our ages and interests – from their big trunk for everyone in the family.

Our Manjhle Chacha was sensitive and understood our pain. Which is probably why, no matter how busy he was, he would take us out and buy us extra presents, listen to me sing and Radha Dada recite poems, and praise us, kiss our foreheads and give us a silver coin each as reward. The year we got a medal or trophy, we got a gold coin.

How I wished he'd stay here and the buas would leave – I told Radha Dada many times. Dada remained quiet. He understood domestic politics better than me.

The youngest in the family and very dear to all of us children was our fun-loving chacha, Pramod Bihari, who on account of being the youngest, was always called Nanhe Chacha, and sometimes Nanhe Cha. He was a supreme art lover and was the life of mehfils in not only the city but the entire region. He was acutely familiar with many bai-jis and jaans, and we had heard whispers of many hush-hush relationships. There was only one lack in his life: children. His wife, Manjari, was childless. But unlike our buas, she was always affectionate towards us. Radha Dada detected a certain sly pity even in her love because, every now and then, in her gossip sessions with the buas, she would take pleasure in contributing to the famous stories about Babu-ji's dislike towards us.

The buas used to treat Manjari Chachi with respect. One reason behind this was that she had come from a very affluent family with a hefty dowry, and the other was that she had a very sweet voice. She would be called to sing banni songs at wedding processions and garis at wedding banquets, and when she picked up the notes of a Chait song at a high note, or sang the opening of a banna, a song lauding the young bridegroom, the faces of the family members would shine with pride. Even the menfolk appreciated her singing. Manjari Chachi also had a treasure trove of folk and semi-classical songs, which she did not let anyone other than Kammo Bibi see. She could memorize a tune by listening to it just once. She was also a small-time writer of shayari and had penned innumerable sehras for many grooms in our family, which were printed in gold on red paper and distributed among the grooms' parties. That was the fashion those days.

Her husband, our Nanhe Chacha, was also a great ashukavi – an excellent creator of limericks, which he'd come up with spontaneously. I remember many rhyming couplets or dohas written by him on our family members. The doha on Kammo Bua went thus:

Kammo tum ghunni bahut, khaat adhik ho paan,
jaat nahi sasural ko, baat let nahi maan.

Kammo, you're silent and wily, you eat too much paan,
just won't go to your in-laws' nor listen to anyone.

On Dammo Bua:

Shammo ki tum huye bahin, o' Dammo naam kahaaye,
padhti nahi, gavat firat, upar neeche dhaaye.

You are Shammo's sister, known by the name Dammo,
you don't study, you keep on singing, and up and down
you go.

He would tease Radha Dada:

Radha tum itne bade dhodhak bhaye sayaan,
paaye kachu bhi akkil aayi nahi, fakat karat ho maan.

Radha, you great big toad, you are growing fast,
you have no common sense, yet you're arrogant to the last.

In this huge family, being the eldest son of the eldest son, Radha Dada enjoyed a special position. But I was the spare daughter of the eldest son's very healthy but talentless wife who had been grudgingly accepted. So my father's family was in two minds about me until the time I gained their acceptance on grounds of my intelligence and naturally sweet voice. Nanhe Cha had then written about me:

Saraswati ki hai bahin, Putulia naam kahaaye,
padhti bohot, bolti tanik, gayan naam kamaaye.

Goddess Saraswati's sister, she is our Putulia,
studies hard, hardly talks, sings her way to glory.

It wasn't that Amma and I did not understand the barbs hidden in the constant quips from family members, ones like, 'If not her beauty, at least her brains will ensure that she gets somewhere.' But we had gotten so used to living in the midst of criticism that even this much was sufficient.

Amma always remained the outsider in this circle of familial laughter and poetry. But nothing in the house could happen without her intervention. She silently took charge of the house's kitchen, gardens and accounts, without any complaints. The servants worked only under her supervision, and she was asked about everything in this house. When which festival or baithak would be organized and how; what would be the things needed and how many people would be eating and staying; which ustad or pandit would be accommodated in which room in accordance with their beliefs, and what kind of food would be cooked for them in which kitchen; for whom would English alcohol or local toddy need to be procured surreptitiously and where would it have to be kept – all these decisions were made by Amma silently over the years.

I would always make a face at her in displeasure, but slowly, over time, I realized that Amma could not find the time to do anything special for Radha Dada and me in the midst of all this coming and going. Even then, she took care of all our needs.

Amma's helplessness deepened despite being married into such a wealthy family because of our father who handled all the family's finances. He always acted stingy when it came to Amma. When the old Maharaj would come and ask for something or Munshi Chailbihari whispered that a certain bai-ji had been insisting since midnight that she be dropped to the station only in Bade Sarkar's car – then the budget would be increased without even being asked. But when Amma went to ask for our school fees or money for our uniforms, standing hesitantly, coughing at the doorstep of his study, our father would, at times, make her wait like a beggar. Then he'd yell at her, calling her a spendthrift. This was one of the favourite dramas Kammo Bua and he enacted often. Amma knew it would be a bad day for her if Kammo Bibi happened to be in the study. She would have to listen to her comments as well: 'Are thorns growing out of your children's bodies, Bhabhi? It was just last month that we bought socks and clothes for them?'

'Ji, they are growing taller, they are at such an age where they are outgrowing their clothes and shoes fast,' Amma would say.

'Look at this growth spurt. This is not in our family. It has been brought over. As they say, "While in a leader of men, it's the head that's big, it's the feet in the serfs."' And Kammo Bua would drive the knife in harder: 'What is that couplet? "It's no use being tall like a date palm; you give no shade to the traveller and your few fruits are out of reach,"' she would finish with a cruel laugh.

It never troubled anyone to gift an expensive pashmina shawl to a pandit or ustad from Jalandhar, or give a cheque of fifty thousand to a bai or jaan for her mujra performance. No one batted an eyelid when it came to sending the old Rolls-Royce to pick up Khan Sahib from the station. But any talk of expenditure on our school education brought out the beast in them.

We would get anxious whenever we heard Kammo Bua's fake, irritable voice as she would step out of Babu-ji's study. Her dainty nostrils would shrink at the sight of our ugly mother as though she had seen a frog.

'Just look,' she would say loudly. 'Haaye, our brother is as good-looking as the moon; his first wife was so pretty too. The second one looks like she has been picked from a kasbah like Kayamganj. So what if she has a clear complexion, you'll lose sleep if you look at that bulbous nose at night. She can cook well, they say, but can she ever hold a bloody tune? That day when Pandit Bhatkhande had come home, she was serving him food. Babu-ji said lovingly that he is a renowned singer, so she lowered her head and said that writing and reading were fine ways of spending time. His morsel stayed in his hand.

'Our brother grew up listening to the best ustads and singers. Haaye, this is why the light seems to have gone out of him.'

Our father was a magician with the Urdu language. He would hit my mother with such flowery words that Amma could not even complain. Let me narrate an incident. It was the wedding of one of Dada-ji's prominent music-loving zamindar clients, and two major singers were set to sing on the day of the boubhaat. When Dada-ji's old man Friday, Ramtahal, came and said that Bade Sarkar has said that the entire family is invited, so everyone must go, Dada and I started jumping excitedly. A wedding and a musical contest between two singers – wow!

We got ready in our party clothes well in advance and sat waiting for the car in the bamboo chairs kept in the veranda. Amma wore a big diamond brooch made in the Western style and a heavy Banarasi sari that smelt of sandalwood, which the poor thing had probably only worn a couple of times after her wedding. She had filled the parting in her hair with sindoor and put on two thick pearl bangles along with multicoloured glass bangles on her wrists. I kept running my cheeks against the silkiness of her sari for a long time and savouring that mild perfume!

'Why don't you dress up like this every day?' I said and stopped. How could Amma wear such an expensive sari? Our Babu-ji was a friendly social butterfly. It was said that mehfils blossomed only when he arrived, but he always left Amma behind at home when he went for these events. He would be accompanied sometimes by Kammo Bibi, sometimes by Radha Dada, and on rare occasions, me, because my ordinary-looking face had been compensated for by my having a somewhat melodious voice. Babu-ji's musician friends who had heard me sing bhajans at the baithaks at home had come to the conclusion that I could become an excellent singer with good training in music.

By then, many brilliant women from respectable families such as Bengal's Naina Devi, Sadhana Bose and Dipali Talukdar and Maharashtra's Durga Khote had earned a reputation by singing at Harivallabh or Akashvani Sangeet Sammelans. And singing for the radio was not a matter of shame but a roadway to fame. Which is why, maybe, after several years, this blessed event had arrived when we got the green signal to take our mother along with Radha Dada and me. But soon enough, we were proven wrong about Amma.

Babu-ji's Impala arrived at the porch at the decided time, and we started to climb into it. 'Come?' Radha Dada said to mother. But poor mother, with her veil on her head, stood waiting for her husband's permission. She understood him better than Dada or I did. I was shifting to a side to make space for Amma when Babu-ji stopped her with just a glance and shook his head. Amma bent her head and stood a little apart, utterly humiliated. As he continued to seat the rest of the family members in the car with care, my father's face showed no signs of any regret.

Ramtahal-ji shut the door and started the car. I still remember the wounded look on Amma's face as she was left behind by her renowned clansmen and their wives, a small and insignificant presence on the porch. When I think back to it, it feels as if I have swallowed tobacco juices instead of spitting them out. Had I not been afraid of Babu-ji's anger or Kammo Bua's razor-sharp tongue, I would have opened the door and jumped out. Dada, as always, maintained an expressionless face, but I knew how he felt.

It was at that moment that I decided that I did not have to become a singer to make these people happy. I knew our family had long been hoping that I would become a renowned performer of classical music, which would add to the family's reputation as grand patrons of the traditional arts. When musical soirées and baithaks were held in our house annually, I was encouraged to perform in them. No event at our home was considered complete without music and dance performances. First, there would be the performances, and those would then be followed by lavish feasting and drinking. Every member of the house was handed a pre-planned role at all these events. By the time I was ten, I was considered a good singer and a decent family representative for welcoming the musician guests to these gatherings. Dada-ji decided that, along with the elders, I too would meet up with the musicians invited, at the station. It was a huge honour, and I continued in this role until I got married.

These special assignments helped me meet some of the most distinguished musicians and musicologists, of whom Khan Sahib of Patiala was the most flamboyant. I had become a big admirer after listening to his deep baritone voice on the records, and when I discovered that he was invited for the year's baithak, I was hugely excited. I dressed in my prettiest red velvet frock and matching red shoes. I had even got my nanny Laxmibai to tie red silk ribbons on my long braids.

The car had arrived at the porch on time, and with Munshi Chailbihari-ji and Nanhe Cha as supervisors, we took off to pick up the great Khan Sahib. But what was this? The person who got off the train, unlike the picture I had of him in my mind, was a wheezing fat man with a flabby body and a thick moustache above his pursed lips. He kept chewing paan and spitting into the paandaan one of his disciples held out to him from time to time. He addressed us in a Hindi laced with Punjabi, and yelled in the midst of the bustling, noisy station that the smoke of the trains was suffocating him. He abused one of his disciples as he grabbed the walking stick he was carrying for the maestro, and requested Munshi-ji to arrange for warm water at home so that he could wash out the fumes from his throat. He also said that all food served to him must be cooked in pure ghee. 'Please don't include any dal from the Hindu kitchen or vegetarian dish in my meals, understood?' He should also be taken to the pandal where he'd perform right after his bath and meal, he said. 'Shall we go now, sirs?' It was clear he was a star.

In my shock and dismay, the words of welcome I had memorized while leaving home remained unsaid. Nanhe Cha was more used to such stars and handled the situation with ease. 'Everything will be taken care of, sir. We are here to serve you. Please honour us and come,' he said.

The journey back home was spent in silence. It must have been eight in the evening when Khan Sahib entered the grand guest bathroom next door with a huge towel slung across his shoulder and we, uncle and niece, waited in the drawing room for him. Chailbihari was in the kitchen, busy ensuring that Khan Sahib got piping hot food as soon as he got out of his bath.

Suddenly, a scared-looking disciple came out of the bedroom and said, 'A big problem, sir! The special Mysore Sandal soap that Ustad does not bathe without is not in the bathroom. And as the cautious Ustad Sahib says, if he does not wash away the grime and soot on his body soon, when he sits in the mehfil and sings the first note "sa", it may not emerge shining like a pearl.'

Not for nothing was Chailbihari called Chanakya by our family. First, he stepped inside to placate an angry Khan Sahib and reassured him that the soap would be acquired and made available even if the earth's axis would have to be tilted.

Then, as he came out, he sent one of his men to Lala Jagatdayal's shop in Sadar, clicking his fingers and adding, 'Bhaiyyu, you go and come back just so! Got me?' Luckily, the soap Khan Sahib had been deprived of was brought in on time and presented respectfully to him for his beauty bath.

Then came the meal. As per his request, all the food had been cooked in desi ghee and was pure non-vegetarian. Salan, biryani and kebabs floating in ghee.

As I saw the ustad salivating and tearing into the meat, I wondered how this carnivore could do justice to the tender nuances of pure classical music. But as ever, Nanhe Cha knew better. He kept serving him food with devotion and praising him. When the meal got over, a big box of paan was brought in, and then, masticating the fragrant leaves slowly, Khan Sahib made a grand entry into the pandal erected outside for the event.

He accepted everyone's wishes. Then, he sat down with his disciples and began fine-tuning their tanpuras. Once he found everything up to the mark, he closed his eyes and began to caress the surmandal lying on his enormous lap ever so gently with his plump fingers. When sa-pa-sa began to reverberate in the air, Khan Sahib opened his mouth and the purest note emerged.

After that, it was as though his entire being was suffused with a kind of divine light. The audience witnessing this miracle was as if in a trance.

People remembered Khan Sahib's recital at the haveli for a long time, we talked about it for days.

I heard that, after Partition, Khan Sahib moved to Pakistan. But unable to adjust to the new muhajir life there, he passed away within a year or so. Babu-ji did not eat the day he received the news. A week before his death, Khan Sahib had sent a letter to our father in which he had included some rare combinations of notes for Merukhand riyaz handed down to him by his guru, and said that while religion might have divided us and thrust us in different countries, in his dreams, Ma Ganga continued to call out to him from our side. Ever since he arrived in Pakistan, his mind was not at rest and his notes also disenchanted and in disarray. Could Bade Sarkar Sahib please talk to Pandit Jawaharlal Nehru and arrange for his return?

By the time arrangements could be made, Khan Sahib passed away. On hearing the news, Chailbihari-ji burst into tears and accompanied Babu-ji for the special namaz organized in the ustad's memory.

A case exactly opposite to that of Khan Sahib's was sarangi player Guddan Khan's. He was of the firm opinion that it would have been better for ustads to have stayed back than move to the other side after Partition to live like neglected paupers. 'How do I, a musician, leave my own doorstep?' he asked Nanhe Cha and Chailbihari-ji with innocent dismay. 'Arre, am I a tomcat that will go wherever the cream is?'

Guddan Khan Sahib had a fragile body, glasses hanging by a thread, a crooked butterfly moustache, and he sported either a cap or a turban on his head, and wore an achkan over narrow

Lucknowi pyjamas. His instrument was a part of his body. Once, on a bright day with the dappled sunshine of early spring, he treated Radha Dada and me, seated amidst the flowers, to the divine beauty of a combination of ragas Basant and Bahar for an hour. I have never heard such sweet music since.

When we heard that the ustad had taken ill, Radha Dada and I were sent to enquire after his health. We were shocked to see the dire circumstances in which that divine musical genius lay dying. His humble house could be approached only through a maze of lanes spattered with mud and goat droppings. We entered a courtyard through doors with curtains made from sacks upon them and an open dirty sewer next to them. There, in two to three tiny rooms, lived his wives and many children and relatives, all appearing half-starved. Guddan Miyan was on a dirty bed with a chequered quilt, coughing lifelessly. The smoke from the stove kept wafting towards him without him seemingly realizing it. Everyone was worried about what would happen to them if Khan Sahib died.

We did not know where to sit.

When Radha Dada asked, 'How are you, Ustad-ji?' the ustad smiled like a child and, suppressing the cough, said, 'Now it is time to go, Radhe Babu. But habit dies hard. I keep trying to practise the Merukhand on my fingers, now that my sarangi is not on my shoulder. I now think that, for a better understanding of how ascending and descending notes work in different ragas, one should practise them in many permutations, many combinations. Sometimes, the raga might just reveal a new face to the musician! Now look, when I played the Maluha Kedar yesterday, its pure nikhad did not appear. It had shifted shape. Fine, that's also all right. Maybe it will come out fine some other day. The note nikhad seems to be somewhat cross with me these days.' Then he smiled again like an innocent child.

A wife's nasal whine emerged from behind the curtains: 'Khan Sahib is the only earning member in the family; may Allah mend his health soon. There is no other grown-up in the family, and he has several children. We can manage to arrange food only sometimes. Now, if our esteemed guests can help in some way, otherwise...' the rest of her speech turned incoherent as she wept.

We were quiet for a time. What could we have said?

We put the envelope sent by Babu-ji under Ustad-ji's pillow and asked permission to leave. He kept staring at us for a while in reply, and then whispered something as though he were speaking to himself. We bent down to listen. 'Be it a king or a fakir, only someone with the right temperament can sing and play music. If you play music with understanding, even the notes will begin to behave differently.'

That was our last meeting with the maestro.

Young journalists these days keep criticizing the systems of the old zamindars. I agree with them. But even the manner in which corporates who have turned into patrons of music function, raises many questions. Even then, whatever I have seen and experienced of this world makes me conclude that the older generation treated music as something sacred and followed the right rituals before learning. All the institutions that represent music now only try to control the notes or display them in a way that is insulting to our music. Radha Dada was telling me that a tyre-seller in Ludhiana has been in the news as a new patron of musical gatherings in the capital. He dresses in expensive clothes and is armed with state-of-the-art sound systems. Curious, when he went there, he found that the tyre-seller made the audiences squirm with embarrassment by giving an hour-long speech in English about India's musical traditions and the role of patrons like him in salvaging it for them. All the while, the singers and musicians waited in the wings. Social scientists say that music is a flowing stream – the water might change, but the landscape and the appearance of the water remain the same. But even those have started changing in our lifetime. Who would have thought that the NRI children of Sukumar Chacha or our homes would not be organizing mehfils in Kolkata and Lucknow? Instead, they'd hold fusion festivals in New York, Chicago, Goa and Manipur, and present a few small compositions as one of the flavours? And that their English friends from Kolkata to California or Kentucky would fill the chillums of ustads and have their fill of Indian classical music through music videos uploaded on YouTube? That our major artistes would be on the roads outside Parliament clamouring to get a Padma Shri from politicians and would be performing in front of drunk guests at the weddings of the children of these politicians?

What can our media, with their almost unknown credentials in this field, write about all this? These new critics arrive invariably late at mehfils and ask around about what has been sung or played, and then leave for their office after half an hour where they google the artiste's profile and then write their piece praising the performance by Ustad or Pandit or Vidushi So-and-So! The artiste is happy, and so are they. But I simply cannot participate in such happiness!

I end on this frustrated note.

Let me know well in advance about your next trip. I enjoyed talking to you so much that I am eagerly waiting for you to come back again.

Yours,
Putul Di

Chiranjeev Vidya Rani,

I am glad that we finally met. These days, I see an increasing lack of seriousness among the audiences. The capacity for serious scholarly work is shrinking among musicologists too. God bless you. This old man was so delighted to see you with my favourite niece that day. You may have felt I spoke a lot. But, as I might have told you before of a piece of advice given by a renowned been player to his disciples about listening very carefully to an old musician and an old Brahmin, even though they may well be past their prime: 'Because you never know when you might suddenly find a precious pearl hidden in those rambling words!' he'd say.

The way you regularly shared all your findings with Radha, Sanjeev and me all through your travels convinced me that, at long last, here is someone who should inherit my personal treasures of classical music and great performers. As per our ancient Indian tradition maintained in gurukuls, while assessing a disciple's suitability, the guru first asks about the family and parentage. But that day when you entered my house like a kalbaisakhi storm, to me you at once brought into the room your late mother's beauty, your brother's aura of intelligence, and your father's scholarship. My heart shushed my mind and whispered, 'Old man, today's the day for you to hand over your treasures.' I am forthwith arranging to forward to you all my diaries with my stray jottings, anecdotes, written and oral, along with letters exchanged with various friends and photographs collected over the years. A tech-savvy but rather foolish nephew of mine will help send you those.

After living a full life packed with different kinds of experiences, I find satisfaction in knowing that I am leaving this world of music to daughters of Saraswati, not Adam's sons. I did not expect Radha and Sanjeev to make use of my treasures, but I trust that with the help of all these you will be able to recreate a lost era and its music and go on to produce what will also be a readable and informative book.

While going through my precious collection, I feel a churning within me like any other artiste feels before unlocking and sharing his creations. My inherent selfishness and managerial training have shaped my long innings as a boxwallah music lover. This mind, like Krishna's prudent wife Rukmini, is trying to hold me back even now. But with age, a wife's iron hold on her husband loosens up. This, I feel, is the hour of generous sharing. Very few ustads and gurus have been fortunate like me to have found a mind worthy of their life's wisdom.

Had every dying guru found someone like you at the right time to hand over their knowledge to, the fate of our music would have been different. As things stand, all that remains of my generation's knowledge is scattered in bits and pieces. But this old man can now hope that your pen will be able to connect most of the dots, match the pictures to words, and present a somewhat clear picture to the generations to come.

It is only recently that your extremely shy brother, Sanjeev, slowly opened up to me. He confided that your father, who died young, remained, despite his deep scholarship, stiffly opposed to women from good families, including your mother, publicly presenting classical music that had been so closely associated with tawaifs. He told me how once, when your mother, who wished he rose above his prejudices, had played for him a record she'd brought from her natal home of Kesarbai's eternal Raga Bhairavi bandish '*Jaat kahan ho?*' (Where are you off to?), your father only said that it was for the best if this kind of singing stayed restricted to deredar tawaifs. That they could go on sitting with their paan-chewing sarangi and tabla players as they regaled men in the audience with gestures and expressions no good woman should have demonstrated.

Maybe there was a valid reason for his stance. Big politicians and officers might have started getting invited for the inaugurations of big music festivals, but most middle-class patrons found these musicians unsophisticated. In mehfils now, men consider themselves above reproach when they look lustily at singers as they perform. Several times when they have come out with 'wah, wah' at a totally unsuitable moment, my hands have itched to hold them by their ears and throw them out of the hall.

From what I knew, your mother's family, especially your nana, the late Pandit Ambadutt Tripathi, might have been traditional, but he was no Edwardian conservative. He was also a man of few words like your father, but unlike him, Tripathi Chacha was an uncomplicated man who loved music deeply. Among friends in mehfils, he was considered the master of one-liners. He would argue through the night with toughies like Putul's grandfather or my father. They both acknowledged his scholarship based on ancient works on music dating back centuries. He was open to the idea of getting the talented women in his family to train under Muslim ustads. On the other hand, we were told that in the family of his son-in-law, your father, no one had even been a bathroom singer.

It is possible that this last bit was just a rumour spread by the admirers of your beautiful mother, the learned professor's daughter. She was a lady entirely out of their league, for whose husband they harboured much envy and malice. According to my informants, many of these admirers used to visit your nana, to allegedly sort out some academic problems, but in reality, it was to catch a glimpse of the elusive Miss Tripathi. So whatever be the truth, for years these admirers blamed your harsh father for breaking many a heart by marrying such a beautiful and talented woman and depriving the world of music of a star.

At this stage of my life, I agree with your father on one count. Music lovers have been getting more and more frivolous over the years. The nature of musical events has changed, not just in Delhi, Kolkata and Mumbai, but also in New York and California. Those old, rich patrons exist no more. The well-heeled who inaugurate or organize or promote classical music events are mostly uncouth, penny-pinching corporate honchos, or salesmen promoting a product. The source of their wealth could be located in dealing in products ranging from chewing tobacco to internationally branded sweets and namkeens, hotels or restaurants. When they got a little money and an expensive music system, they thought they were expert patrons and walked around with a puffed chest, dropping the names of bestselling musicians as though they owned them.

Just recently, a major politician arrived an hour and a half late to inaugurate a music event. A scared voice announced on the mic that he had been stuck in a very important meeting, had just left and would be arriving soon. Old men like us kept waiting to hear the senior musician. We weren't sure how long she would keep singing. The self-respecting singer finally issued an ultimatum that if 'dear sir' did not make an appearance within half an hour, she would leave with her musicians. Maybe it was our good fortune or something else, the minister arrived within ten minutes of that announcement. The curtains were raised immediately, the minister smiled with his fake teeth and issued a fake apology, but the learned singer had lost interest. She sang disinterestedly. The usual glow was missing. She sang her gharana's popular song, '*Nevar bajo re*', but even that sounded listless.

I am told the new trend is throwing parties with kebabs and alcohol at farmhouses and five-star hotels. The conversations, as expected, peter out before long. And fat men in ill-fitting suits are soon exchanging political gossip while the musicians play on.

Radha and Putul's mother was also one such woman who had a huge collection of stories about the musicians who played at their house and their music. But she wilted under the antagonism of her husband and in-laws. You should talk to Putul about her. Mothers tell their daughters many secrets on their deathbeds that they haven't told anyone. My departed wife became like a rain-filled cloud full of things unsaid because she did not have a daughter to confide in. So, you should ask Putul to write too. You might find something worthwhile in her notings.

I have come to the conclusion that one of the major tragedies of independent India is the silencing of women such as Radha and Putul's mother. Hindustani music has lost out on countless singers and experts because they chose to stay quietly with their 'genteel families', either because of their upbringing or out of the fear of confrontation.

As far as our families' history, geography and sociology are concerned, Putul must have told you all about them with feminine trust, or will tell you. So be it. Even if it hurts your feelings, I hope that with the honesty of a true artiste, you will find a quiet niche for these bitter truths somewhere in your book.

My father Kali Babu, true to his name, was dark-complexioned. But unlike his dark son, his father, my Dada-ji, had a pale and clear complexion, what the Bengalis call '*khoob phorsha rong*', and was known in his village as Gora Babu. The family was from Jessore, where they owned a mud house and lived on a pension of seventy-five rupees. But Gora Babu, who was an expert on kirtan and haveli sangeet, was well respected. Ma told me that he took a boat every evening across the Ganga to Dhaka to listen to bhakti sangeet. The boatmen would not stop ferrying until Gora Babu had returned to this side. If it was raining, they'd say, 'How can we dock the boat? Gora Babu has not come back yet.'

But music and devotion cannot support a family. After completing their school education, his brilliant sons looked towards their ambitious mother when it came to higher education. At this point, their grandmother, Dadi, arranged for money from her maiden home on the sly and sent my father and his brothers to a relative's house in Rajshahi to study. Later, the most meritorious of them, Kali Babu, would receive a scholarship and arrive in Calcutta.

Kali Babu was a bright student academically, but he was also devoted to music. In addition to history and philosophy, he had received training in dhrupad and kirtan in his younger days from his father. Later, he also learned khayal singing that was fast overtaking dhrupad in popularity. He became a disciple of a renowned ustad from a royal family, and a few years later, emerged as an expert in both music and philosophy.

Apart from being an art and music lover, one of Kali Babu's biggest virtues was that he was a natural raconteur. His biggest hobby and stressbuster was running long debates on music and art. His other virtue was that he was multilingual and would make even serious academic debates on music extremely interesting with his flowing narratives. Even knowledgeable men such as Putul's dada-ji, Bade Sarkar, and your nana, would happily get drawn into his discussions which were a mix of Hindi, Urdu and Bangla. In these debates, people like Radha's father and uncle and I, who were there to fill our elders' hookahs, would also get the opportunity to hear the theories of these intellectuals without asking.

My mother's brother had shifted to Bombay. Fortunately, despite working for a British company, unlike my bourgeois nana, he was a boxwallah Bengali babu who loved classical and semi-classical music. For this very reason, I used to run off to his house during my school summer vacations. This is how I was introduced to Bombay's ticketed mehfils organized for the middle classes that were just starting out at the time, in addition to the classical Lucknow-Calcutta music. Actually, by the thirties, the Company had departed, and the Crown had gained a strong foothold. The British king had already received this island of Mumba Devi (now known as Mumbai) as dowry, and so now factories came up in the new Kalyug, and zamindars from Calcutta and north-eastern India began counting their pennies after the capital shifted out of Calcutta to Delhi.

By the time I went to Bombay, this grand city had become the citadel of the Hindustani middle class who were moneyed, English-educated, and uncaring of caste prejudices and religious biases. Here, there were neither Hindu pandits nor Muslim mullahs. This affluent city that could bring together all communities with a great generosity of spirit also came under the radar of singers and artistes. A huge contingent of singers faced with sudden penury in their usual haunts – in the princely courts in Awadh and Calcutta and Bihar – were desperate to escape poverty.

At the same time, the temple dancers and musicians, the devadasis from South India, some of whom had enjoyed royal patronage, also decided to migrate to Bombay. All of them were given shelter in the new boom town by the new rich Gujarati merchants and Gujarati-speaking Parsi traders.

The first to migrate from the north were some major ustads from the Agra gharana. I got along well with them because I spoke Hindi. They were survivors, and soon created a space in classical music circles by their ability to converse in Gujarati and Marathi. The city was also home to Parsi-Hindustani-language travelling companies and films, and saw new avenues opening up. In those days, musicians of the various gharanas were related. When the Agra musicians saw these opportunities, they sent messages to their sons-in-law, nephews, etc., that there is a lot of scope, come. Many ustads from the gharanas in Rampur, Sahaswan and Gwalior had noticed the decline of the local nawabs and kings. So, they too decided that a change of scene would be good and turned towards this metropolis. Even I got rich here!

In this city, time has always seemed to run fast. And money was flowing like a vast river. Soon, to ensure year-long earnings, some big ustads began to create little waterways to irrigate their fields. The kind of mehfils where lakhs would be spent and in which one could hear and present songs for hours in peace had gone away. Now, there were new kinds of successful and rich Parsis, Gujarati banias, and a few Maharashtrian Brahmins who had opened big companies in collaboration with the English. There were new rail lines being put across the country to transport goods, and ships, too, were being built to carry goods outside India. These contractors were rolling in money because, in exchange for a few favours, they got huge contracts and trucks full of workers at a nominal rate from the east. Then came the war. And in that era, many locals struck gold by merely tending to the hookahs of the English.

Then what! The smart ustads and bais from the gharanas had sensed the nature of this boom time by the twenties and let go of their pride and started adapting their music to the liking of their new patrons. A few were successful, while others faded into obscurity. Those who were successful did not restrict their performances to the mehfils of others, and after earning some money, they started renting halls and holding ticketed mehfils themselves.

The rich continued to hold mehfils, but only at the houses of a select few, where merchants, renowned lawyers, doctors were all present. Some of the ustads who had been receiving salaries began doing additional gigs to add to their income. And why wouldn't they? Because of their pride in their gharanas and musical traditions, they stuck to old ways. Most had many wives and dozens of children. Then there were the disciples, musicians and useless relatives who would keep asking the ustads for money for their upkeep. So now, many big ustads and pandits started to offer tuitions to the wives and talented singer-mistresses and tawaifs of the rich, and amassed a fortune in fees. This was a way of not just making extra money; it also became a means to accessing other opportunities that sprung up as they now came increasingly into contact with English-speaking people.

One of the biggest money-making opportunities courtesy the sahibs was the establishment of recording companies. The English beat the banias at their own game. At first, they used to make a face at native singing. Then, as a few sahibs came in touch with rich native zamindars and the singers they patronized, they found they had begun to enjoy the typical atmosphere of mehfils.

Some of the romantically inclined sahibs who had left behind their memsahibs in England lost their hearts to Indian bais. A renowned singer from Bhagalpur became the wife of one of them, and in the end, moved to Britain with her husband. I heard that she had a son there, who later went on to become a chaplain.

As music lovers, right after the British came the Germans. After all, their country has always been known as the asylum of music. When a few major music experts heard music at durbars like the one in Baroda, they became patrons of the major ustads. They labelled margi music as being connected to Hinduism in a few famous newspapers. It might not have been absolutely true, but such writings created a storm as far as London, which even influenced the Indian princes who had until now preferred only Western music and a Western lifestyle. The English got one such prince to create a special department for supporting the best Indian artistes, where the Maharaja's trusted courtiers were to pull the destitute artistes out of poverty and ensure a regular salary and housing and also conduct a proper performance audit. But the ustads were not capable of handling administrative jobs. So finally, in one of the princely states, a well-known music lover, who was also a wrestler, was roped in. He was designated as the minister for the Department of Performing Arts in the state. On the request of the mother of the Raja, special preparations were also made for the training of women within the palace and, later, a school was opened for the daughters of the nobility and the new middle class. With fire and oil so close to each other, there was bound to be a scandal.

Soon, a sitar player eloped with the daughter of a sardar; a heartbroken singer committed suicide. The wrestler became strict like the British and started taking action against the wrongdoers, and in that, emerged as the first successful principal of the school and prefixed a 'Professor' to his name. After that, when his son took over the position, he called himself 'Doctor So-and-So'.

A trade is a trade, and money is important. Be it Calcutta or Bombay or Awadh. The English had also been scoping out the market. When the big sahibs of the record companies went around conducting surveys of the size of the music market, they were surprised. Every Indian seemed to be an undeclared lover of music. The vinyl discs of two young Calcutta singers sold like hot cakes. When they got the news, the other white owners of Becca, Sun Disk and HMV also jumped in to fill scores of German-made vinyls with classical music and invited notable ustads and bais of major gharanas.

Here, as usual, the male singers acted uppity. One Khan Sahib went on to say that he considered it beneath him to have his voice fill a record which had the face of a dog on it, while another ustad asked if God now would make the sacred songs of gharanas play in the warrens of the riffraff! As for us, as my son in Goa says, 'We were jacked.'

But the female singers had sensed the change in the wind and their voices were being heard everywhere in the market.

The magic of the songs of Gadag's Janki Bai, Bengal's Gauhar Jaan, Shashimukhi and Phanibala, Allahabad's Munni Jaan, Benares's Shiv Kunwar, Panipat's Miss Ameer Jaan and Agra's Malka Jaan spread everywhere. Soon these gramophones became a status symbol in affluent families such as yours and mine. And inexpensively at that. The cost of one record was anywhere between two rupees and twelve annas to three rupees and twelve annas. The highest salary in those days was six hundred rupees. Singers such as Anjali Bai sang in twenty languages and earned a huge sum. She recorded all kinds of songs – not just classical raga-based ones but also folk melodies and compositions for dance dramas in Bengali, Gujarati, Braj and Awadhi, which became bestsellers overnight.

It was the time spanned by the World Wars. When Germany was ostracized, Indian merchants came forward. Lac was needed for the vinyls. What were the Indian forests for? I have many records from my father and grandfather's generation when the first Indian record factory was set up in Beliaghata. The label was Royal, owned by Mukherjee and Mukherjee.

The Bombay of my uncles was showing the colours of UP's musical diaspora. One renowned ustad and his brother – who was so fond of flying kites that he got christened 'Fazlu Miyan Kankauvebaaz' or 'Fazlu the flyer of kites' – moved with the family into a building next to the mortuary of Harkisandas Hospital. Two or three of the popular tawaifs in the city and mistresses of the big merchants sent them a proposal attached with a substantial honorarium for taking tuitions in classical music from them. The ustads were promised a salary of five hundred rupees. Fazlu Miyan's elder brother, known as Khan Sahib, took on the bais as his students despite cursing them in private. When ustads entered merchants' houses as music tutors, they started recommending their own relatives for various jobs, just as politicians will do nowadays. Among them was a student who had been a singer for the royal family in Gujarat, who was introduced to the city's record industry, and she tasted success.

Thanks to Khan Sahib, this particular well-heeled bai who had made her way into Bombay also started seeking tutors like other bais from Agra, Calcutta and Benares. All were ambitious and wanted to record for HMV, songs in rare ragas like Nat Kamod and Suha Sughrai sung to the special beats of their own gharanas;

some even wanted to be cast in Parsi musical plays. This went on for thirty years or so. Later, the bai from Gujarat even managed to buy a big house in Matunga. When numerous major singers came to the city, they stayed with her and took loans from her if they needed to. This bai sahiba also resolved many of the domestic disputes in the city for and among the singers. You see, there were singers who had migrated to Bombay, first from Goa and Belgaum. They were followed by migrant tawaifs from Calcutta, Benares, Agra and other places. Disputes among them weren't unknown, and required mature handling, which the senior tawaifs like the Gujarati bai provided.

The theatre companies set up by Parsi merchants had also surfaced by then. The singers employed by the companies were mostly women from lower castes or tribal communities. The seths had a good understanding of the newly created working classes of Bombay who would come to theatres to enjoy folk music from back home. When they saw the money to be made in theatres, many deredar tawaifs also made their way to them.

Let me return to the focus of our research: Anjali Bai. Even in this new era, she had made her way to the top in all forms of music. She was popular everywhere, be it in recording studios or in mehfils. And she had such style!

At the appointed hour, her carriage with two beautiful horses would stop at the gate where the organizers would be standing to welcome her with folded hands. Despite her voluptuous figure, she would step down daintily. She would offer a polite salaam to people like us with just a slight nod. It would make my day! When the bai entered the hall or studio, even her sophisticated outfits and sparkling, tasteful jewellery would let everyone know that the empress of music had arrived.

I kept staring at her the first time I saw her in Calcutta. She seemed like a celestial dancer from heaven. A round face, a slightly stubborn chin, and thick eyebrows that met in the middle framing her sparkling eyes. Around her swan-like neck shone her famous naulakha necklace. I had heard that the Nawab of Rampur had gifted it to her after an excellent performance. As I watched her sail in with the beautiful necklace adorning her neck, I realized why they compare a beautiful woman's neck to that of a swan. 'Close your mouth, you fool!' my uncle had said to me.

Anjali Bai, who had declared that acting in musical dramas put up by companies was beneath her, emerged as a precious diamond in the new recording industry. Gaisberg Sahib of a record company had gone to Calcutta to scout for talent, and according to my grandfather, he was so impressed by her that he paid her the fee of three thousand rupees that she had asked for. Even the biggest ustads and famous dasis of the Bengali theatre were not being paid such a sum.

Anjali Bai had a regal air and she maintained it until her last days. She earned and spent lakhs. Perhaps because she had spent her early years in poverty, she, like her mother Hira, had a thing for rare jewellery and antiques. Next to jewels, she loved owning real estate. Anjali Bai came to own many huge buildings in Calcutta like her mother. Later, when Anjali Bai's lovers and one man claiming to be her son started a lawsuit over her property, lawyers started circling her like sharks. By then, Hira Bai was dead, and Anjali Bai was all alone. She won the case, but slowly, all her luxuries began to disappear.

I will be sending some of the documents prepared by the lawyers that I found. They reveal the story of an independent woman who earned her own living and bought over her male lovers.

The letter is getting long but I can't seem to stop myself from writing to you about my chance meeting at a ship owner's mehfil with a competitor of Anjali Bai's in her heyday. She had also been a student of Khan Sahib, who was tutor to many tawaifs. I still remember this mehfil I had attended in my youth, barely out of adolescence. I had had to beg my uncle to be taken along. By the time we reached, the small-time singers had started to perform. That was the practice at mehfils. First the younger musicians performed, and then the seniors began to come one after another. The bigger the singer, the later they would come on to the stage. Many music lovers would have to keep waiting for them until dawn.

There were two titans clashing at this baithak – one from Bengal and the other from Maharashtra – and both were students of the same ustad! Anjali Bai from Calcutta, who had even earlier received training from excellent gurus, had now been made the ustad's student thanks to the influence of a rich merchant who was her patron then. However, it was said that the ustad's favourite was the truly gifted Maharashtrian, Mundari Bai.

To keep her ustad's word, Anjali Bai had agreed to sing before Mundari Bai at this mehfil. She was no fool. She knew she would not be able to make a name here by angering her ustad. She had gleaned, too, that the ustad had an intimate relationship with Mundari Bai, which is why he wanted to prove Anjali Bai, who had more or less forced herself upon him as a student, to be the lesser singer at this mehfil. All of us knew that he had made Mundari Bai practise for twelve hours every day for this performance. But what do we say about Anjali Bai? She did not let even a line mar her face. She showed her respect for her guru; the pallu of her expensive Baluchari sari on her head, eyes downcast, she followed all the rules of the mehfil's decorum to a tee.

The tension in the mehfil kept intensifying: What and how would the two students sing? Would Bengal win our hearts or would Maharashtra?

Anyway! Finally, the moment arrived, and the curtains were raised. Dressed in the Baluchari with her signature diamond brooch (gifted to her by some raja) on it, Anjali Bai appeared with her musicians from the green room backstage. First, she entered the hall echoing with applause, and with her eyes closed, bent forward, touched the stage and then touched her head to take its blessings. Afterwards, she touched her guru's feet, gave her musicians some instructions, and then with her sharp eyes, took stock of the audience, full of the richest men in the city, and offered them her salaam. This went on for a while. Then closing her eyes once again, she sang the first note – the mandra nikhad – marking the presence of Raga Lalit, the raga sung at break of dawn. She revealed her Sufi style with every alap in the extended Jhumra taal:

> *Bhoraheen aaye jogiya morey dware, maathhe tilak lagaaye,*
> *sanwari surat, mohini murat, ang bhabhoot ramaaye*

> At dawn, at my doorstep arrived the monk, a tilak on his forehead adorning his beautiful dusky face and ashes smeared all over his body.

Such a voice and such command over the beats! That open voice singing between two medians rang out like a drum and started giving shape to that spectacular song. How could she sing the entire stanza in one breath? When she had continued for a while, I felt that I was drowning along with the others in some deep ocean of sound, holding on to Anjali Bai. For a few moments, we could not breathe. Then came the next stanza, gently guiding us back to the shore. Then, after a while came the taans, gleaming and swaying like a string of precious pearls. Each time she completed the cycle and arrived at the 'sam', I would feel like this raga could not have been sung by anyone else but her.

Anjali Bai closed with a thumri and, for a while after that, there was silence, as if none of us could believe that we had gotten to feel the divinity of surs so closely. Then, all of a sudden, we woke up, and the hall rang out with applause. Despite the curtains falling twice, we kept clapping.

When Mundari Bai came on to the stage, it was tough for us to imagine that anyone could hold the audience's interest after the spectacular performance we had already seen. Who knows? Maybe showing off her skills and establishing her superiority had been Anjali Bai's real aim, not to present the ustad's style? But Mundari Bai was also the deredar tawaif Sundari Bai's daughter, and she turned out to be a true product of her ustad's gharana that specialized in mixed ragas. When she sat on the stage, there was no anxiety or tension about her. She had a long, fair face, and wore a plain white Chanderi sari with a thin border, a string of pearls around her neck, and diamonds in her ears that twinkled now and then, which I still remember. She told the audience, 'You just heard the magic of a royal Bengali take on Lalit; now hear from Mundari Bai Punjab's Lalit in the madhya laya.'

Another round of claps. Tit for tat. She hit out with such grace!

The bai touched her hand to her chest and bowed to her ustad sitting in the front row with other students and started singing. What was this? Her Lalit alap was exactly the same sur and yet so different, but it was filled with a strange energy. The raga that Anjali Bai had sung was in a Sufi style and wore the colours of an old love. This Raga Lalit was in a new style with an opening that was in an emotional medium laya with three taals:

Bhanda yaar da jobna, duje nazar nahi aawanda

I am so deep in love with my beloved that I can't see anyone else.

She was adroit in using the madhyama, the fourth note, both as sharp and flat tones. Placed together, they brought out in the same line both a request to the beloved and also a Sufi murid's cry to her pir. Then there was a string of the gharana's special taans.

The learned audience was beyond satisfied. One raga, two openings, two forms, two ways of being sung!

After collecting all the praise, when Mundari Bai got off the stage, Anjali Bai, who was known to be extremely arrogant and competitive, embraced her, and taking off her string of priceless pearls put it around Mundari Bai's neck and kissed her forehead. See, in those days, there was competition among artistes, but they were also honestly appreciative of real talent. After Mundari Bai's Bhairavi, not just the rich men who had arrived in four-horse-driven carriages but even those who had to catch the morning's milk train to return to their faraway homes left humming both forms of the Lalit.

I heard that, before he left, Anjali Bai pleaded with Khan Sahib and also got her rich lovers to pressurize him and offer him a lakh and a quarter as monthly fee so he could come to Calcutta to train her and teach her his gharana's unique voice culture. I heard from Mundari Bai's Marathi patrons that after returning to Bombay, Khan Sahib would laughingly shower abuses on Anjali Bai and did not miss telling his students that he had knowingly taught the arrogant bai the wrong names of ragas of certain compositions because she had wanted to rob the musical wealth of his gharana just on the strength of money. 'My Mundari Bai is the real talent,' he would say. I never heard that he charged a big sum to train Mundari Bai. He maintained good relations with both her mother, Sundari Bai, and her.

This Mundari Bai's son, Alam, who later became a famous tabla player after playing it for the Beatles, moved to California, and it is rumoured that he is Khan Sahib's son. But like his father, the son also turned out to be uncaring. He earned a lot abroad, but nobody knows when Mundari Bai, who lived a life of penury in her old age, died. Some say that, like Amir Khan's Munni Begum and Bhartendu-ji's Mallika Dasi, she too went to Benares and drowned at a ghat.

May God bring peace to the souls of these abandoned generous people.

The Marathi principal of a big college was also emerging as an organizer of musical events in Bombay in those days. I attended countless excellent mehfils at his house near the traffic light. But after Partition, he started paying Hindu singers of Marathi origin a bit too much attention and would always say something vulgar like sending the Muslim gurus back to Pakistan, so I stopped visiting him. Actually, the politics of the country had entered our world of music at the time. Fools like us had not been able to sense that this political climate was trying to divide the city, and later the country, by slyly sorting music into silos of Hindu music and Muslim music.

I did not realize it even when the first riots between the Hindus and the Muslims broke out in 1929 that, in the next twenty years, this disgruntlement would catch hold of even the innocent Muslim ustads in Bhindi Bazaar who, in order to survive, had until then been catching trains to far-off places to teach music to women from respectable families. They first discarded their achkans for coats and trousers while leaving for work for the sake of steady employment. But slowly, as the fissures in society deepened, things came to such a pass that Muslim singers only arrived with Muslim musicians and Hindu singers with Hindu musicians. A circle of Urdu lovers was formed in Lakshmi Bagh; so, in response, Hindus formed a committee to organize Hindi Bhakti music.

The actual riots might have started in 1946, but the bitter foundation for ingénues such as Noor Jahan and Roshan Ara leaving for Pakistan was laid during these years that my unfortunate generation was witness to.

All this is not directly related to music, but somewhere connected to the hearts and minds, the change in the thought processes of musicians in the years that followed – that's what I believe. And maybe it is disheartening, but I mentioned all this so that it is in writing.

A few sketches, notes and photographs are yet to be sent. I'll get them scanned and send a zipped folder as soon as I can.

Be well and happy.

Your chacha.

Delhi

Dear brothers,

I was just about to forward this long letter from Sukumar Chacha when I suddenly got some amazing information linked to our subject in a letter from Ranikhet's Himmat Singh 'Nirbhay' ji.

I am attaching that as well.

Vidya.

Letter from Himmat Singh 'Nirbhay' to Vidya

Ranikhet

Most respected Vidya-ji,

Please accept my warmest regards. The reason for sending this special letter is this: Recently, I had to go to a village near Almora district in connection with an FIR filed there against me for publishing a report against the mining mafia in the village. In this remote area, a few outsiders in collusion with the panchayat pradhan have confiscated a piece of land on which they are carrying on illegal mining activities damaging the nearby farms. Their loutish workers also pose a threat to the women in the region, which had my friends in the village worried.

All these details might seem irrelevant to you, but it was while pursuing the story that I bumped into a mine worker, Jasua, while he was drinking tea at the local Golu Hotel. A few details that came out of our conversation may probably be connected to the focus of your research: the singer Hiradevi Baadi, aka Benares's Hira Bai tawaif.

Jasua told me that for the last few years, on the pretext of mining work in Terai, the kidnapping and selling of the region's women in the red-light area has also been going on. One name kept surfacing in the context, that of a pimp who would encourage poor, lonely, young women to run away from home. When I did some more digging, I was told that he is perhaps the illegitimate son of the unmarried daughter of an Englishman and a Baadi woman who left the hills for the mainland many years ago. The woman must have been rich, which is why she had managed to get her half-breed newborn sent here from Calcutta to be brought up by distant relatives whom she promised a large sum for his upkeep. This unfortunate child called Shakir could speak both Pahadi and English very fluently. But soon after turning sixteen, he ran away from home, became a notorious procurer of women in the region and lived with a wayward from his mother's village, who was his mistress. Locals tell me that Shakir has green eyes flecked with gold, like a leopard's, and he moves around with a similar gait without making a sound. He is involved in various illegal activities, and they say he earns a sizeable income from whatever his line of dirty work is. He flashes obscene amounts of money to local girls who have known nothing but poverty since they were born and married, and they soon fall into his trap, especially those tortured by stepmothers or harsh in-laws who work them in the family fields like mules.

The bastard Shakir is often seen dressed in women's clothing. Some say he changes his appearance to fool the police, but Hirua Tailor's son tells me that the spirit of a tawaif seems to live within him. And this evil spirit has told him that he might have the body of a man, but inside he'll always be a woman. The foreigners with dreadlocks, who come here to get high, gather at the Devi temple in the evening. They call him 'Darling Shakira', and he flirts with them shamelessly.

Even the villagers try to avoid that area. Why step in front of a leopard, they say. Who knows when he may decide to pounce?

It is said that this Shakir or Shakira supplies all kinds of drugs and intoxicants to these aghori foreigners, and the villagers say that he has charmed the foreigners so that they keep him hidden amongst them.

I haven't seen him until now, but from whatever I have heard, he seems to be Hira Bai's daughter Anjali Bai's son with Tajuddin.

All else is fine. Hope your writing is shaping up well.

With regards,
Himmat Singh 'Nirbhay'

Queens, New York State

Dear Vidya,

Please accept salaams from Haidari, a friend you haven't met. A couple of months ago, my daughter Amaal and I flew in from America and visited the graves of my nani, Husna Bai, and her beloved daughter and my beloved mother, Allarakkhi Bi. Amma was no more when we reached, so we could only offer our prayers at the graveside and then came back to America.

I had often pleaded with Amma that our days of struggle had ended, and in America, Amaal, my granddaughter Koel, and I are living very well by God's grace. Since your beloved Sherkothi has also been sold, what's keeping you there? Why don't you consider moving in here with us? But she kept insisting that she wanted to live out her last days in her own land, that Tapish Sahib was taking great care of her. And even though her trusted maid Shubraatan was no more, good old Ramdei was always there for her.

So, here we are, mother and daughter, who have returned from India burdened with the guilt that we were not with Bi in her last days. We also realize that we'll never be able to repay Makhdoom Alam Khan 'Tapish' Sahib for the way his family and he have taken care of my mother over the years.

These things happen as God wills.

On the eve of our return, Tapish Sahib had requested me that I should write down whatever I know about my mother's and nani's lives and the artform they revered. He said that Bi had been happy to learn about your family's old connection to Kunwar Shardul Vikram Singh's family. She admired your upbringing and the way you had so humbly come running to her for your research work instead of sending a letter or some low-ranking representative over as most people are wont to do.

Tapish Sahib's request already brought to the surface many things I thought were best forgotten. And then, I also found a mail from you waiting for me when I returned.

Finally, I have begun to hand over to Amaal whatever I know, and to remember a world fast receding in the mists of time. My daughter Amaal is better than me at working with computers.

At first, I thought I will write it all down in my own hand, but as I began to reminisce, I realized I have never kept notes or a diary. So when many memories just overwhelmed me, I simply put my pen down. Where can these anecdotes take my heart? Finally, I have asked Amaal to write it all down for me as I dictate them to her.

I have had to learn so many languages in this short life that, when I have to write anything, the first question is which language I should use. Usually, the best language to write stories in is the language of your childhood. But it will be difficult for me to express myself in the Hindustani of my childhood. I had learned the language when I was a child, but as I grew up, the English medium my school taught in and Western music together overpowered my mind and also hybridized my music. My shrewd grandmother was happy about me getting more and more anglicized. But my mother was not too pleased. She worried when she heard me hum foreign scales, but she knew by then there was not much she could have done. After that, my relations with Amma remained rather frosty.

At the boarding school in Bombay, where I was sent by Nani to get an English-medium education, we either spoke in Marathi or English. The sweet Hindustani I had grown up surrounded with in Sherkothi was almost lost in the course of my education there. Then, when I reached America, I realized that if I wished to make a living in New Jersey, the English I had learned from the Jesuit nuns in Bombay had to be adapted into American English. Here, the children of the new rich Indians and Pakistanis could learn something about their country, but for that I had to learn their language first. So, once again I hid my old language within me and adopted an American English. My job also demanded that I leave behind the Western tunes and moved more and more towards ethnic Hindustani music.

As a child, I had learned that for us professional women musicians, it is always when in Rome, do as the Romans do.

So, Amaal and I have decided that we will together write the story of those in Sherkothi in Hindustani, in the Roman script. She is familiar with the intricacies of digital communication and will record my story in the Roman script and email it to you soon. At the end of what has been dictated to her, Amaal will attach her own note in English for you. I am sorry if this causes you any inconvenience. My apologies.

As spoken by Bi Haidari and written by Amaal

As a child, at the best of times, one only hears bits of conversations between adults. The ability to join the dots to get the full picture comes much later. I grew up with my nani and my amma, and a large number of housemaids. I vaguely remember that, one fine day, when

I was around ten years old, I was told that my father, whose face I did not remember, had passed away.

Over the next two or three years, I'd learn that after spending several years in Sherkothi a little before his death, he had left to go back to his wife and children.

'Why there? Why didn't he stay here?' I had asked Nani, while giving a light pull at each of her arthritic fingers and cracking her knuckles, something she would ask me to do often to relieve her pain.

Even at that age, her fingers were delicate, and shone because of the bright diamond on one of them when Nani wrapped her dupatta around her head. As she fixed her paan, she said, 'We have a saying, that when the time comes to die, your own soil calls out to you.' It was just the love for my mother that had pulled an angel by the name of Moti Pandit here to Sherkothi. When he realized that he was going to die, he returned to be with his family.

What about us, I wanted to ask. We have seen this happen to us and ours so often that we have now lost count. I kept my questions to myself but may still have shown some emotion.

When she saw my face, Nani simply said, 'Why do you worry, my little ruby? All of us are still here with you. Now go, practise your musical scales upwards and downwards by turns, until the notes sound perfect. Only if you practise every day till a certain age will your voice obey you and traverse all three octaves at your command. Get me? Now go!'

That's all.

I was always surprised and sad that there were no photographs of my father, Moti Pandit, anywhere in Sherkothi. If there was one, like all my friends, I too would have kept it by my bedside. My father was gradually reduced to a shadowy figure in Sherkothi, one who was never discussed by anyone at home once he left us and went back to his family to die. Actually, fathers' photographs are never seen on the walls of homes of the likes of us. In our diwankhana, there were rows of pictures of grandmothers, mothers, their great gurus and ustads, other well-known singers, and even a few autographed photos of glamorous yesteryear movie stars. The pictures would be garlanded during festivals and silver dishes with flowers and burning incense placed in front of them. I used to be a talkative child, but gradually, surrounded by these rituals and unasked questions that would not go away, I grew quieter and more and more introverted.

My mother, Bi Allarakkhi, had always been a quiet type. But my nani was very talkative and also very affectionate towards me. She'd tell me anecdotes and scold me if I made a mistake while practising my scales. But I was quick to size up her moods and my importance in her eyes. The hard-headed professional side of my nani would be visible when she'd make arrangements for the participation of mother or herself in mehfils at big houses. I saw her drive a hard bargain for a fee for herself and her accompanists. Amma and Nani would haggle with the hosts inside a closed room on the first floor, where they also discussed what sort of music would be presented at the mehfil and their own outfits. Neither of them cared if I was there or standing outside listening in when these discussions happened.

I don't remember Amma ever raising her voice at me. But she never pulled me into her lap for a cuddle or a chat or showed excessive affection. It was Nani who would shout at me and throw me out if I created a ruckus in the room saying, 'For God's sake, leave us alone right now! We are working!'

Gradually, I began to feel that, though there was no obvious dearth of anything in Sherkothi, there was a certain lack of real warmth. I began dreaming of a time when I would be able to run away from the oppressive atmosphere there, go to a new place and lose myself among new friends.

The only friends I had at the kothi were our servant Shubraatan and her three daughters – Rahiman, Fahiman and Noorie. My initial years were restricted to playing with and talking to them. Shubraatan was very affectionate towards me. And on occasion, I also got some bits of information from her. It was she who told me that my amma was sad all the time after being forcibly moved from Benares to this kothi. The hearts of tawaifs, which are always duty-bound to make clients happy, don't trust anyone, not even their permanent patron. So, after moving to Sherkothi, Nani kept her daughter away from the very shadow of Maharaj Ju. One can't trust menfolk, she told Shubraatan again and again. 'Don't you remember Agra's Champa Bai, who had been forced to live out her old age alone because the Jagirdar Sahib who was her patron had suddenly lost his heart to her daughter?'

Old age is a tawaif's greatest fear. It plagues her even in her dreams. Daughters are the only support in old age. So, despite leaving mujras and mehfils after moving to Sherkothi with Maharaj Ju, Nani saw to it that her daughter's talent continued to be honed and she received the best training for mehfil performances when her time came. There was always a big, well-built watchman posted at the doorstep. No random passer-by could even think of entering our kothi's gates. The only men I have seen entering the house have been Amma's ustads or my tutors. Shubraatan said that big tawaifs lived big. '*Koi takhiya bilaar ta nahi hatin hamaar hujoor ki antey jaaye baithati?*' she'd say. That is, Ammajani was not a greedy cat that, after her mentor passed on, she'd search for another. Like I mentioned earlier, till such time that Maharaj Ju was alive, Nani never performed anywhere except for him. But she was worldly-wise enough to ensure that her daughter kept up her connection to the world of classical music and prepared for major performances in the future. These would help her in her old age.

Shubraatan told me that Amma's nath-utarai – the formal, publicly announced deflowering of a young virgin in our community against a hefty fee, after which the bidder removes her nose ring, a symbol of virginity – was done by my father, Moti Pandit.

'What a man!' Shubraatan said with awe each time she spoke of him. He was a lion-hearted man, and it was because of his generosity that I could step outside my house and talk and laugh with others. But Moti Pandit, Amma's legendary lover, was not hers forever. Once he sensed his own vulnerability, he decided to spend his last days with his lawfully wedded wife and children.

'It was after that, Bitiya, that your amma seemed to fold into herself and has remained thus,' Shubraatan would say with a sigh and tears in her eyes.

Human nature is strange. Nani had parted from Maharaj Ju by the time I was born. But she had already seen to it that regular training and our association with those lucrative mehfils continued in Sherkothi. Nani was talkative and blunt when it came to her professional concerns. 'How can we tawaifs just leave our profession,' she'd say. 'We have to take care of our own futures.' And she did, closely monitoring the hours of hard practice, learning new compositions and teaching her girls all those age-old manners observed by our kind at formal mehfils.

Compared to Nani and my amma, my voice and looks were more or less ordinary. On top of that, the training that I was getting and the comments of outsiders also bothered Nani. Her daughter's old age would depend on me after all. Nani herself never performed a mujra because she had promised her mentor Maharaj Ju that she would not. So when we got invited to any big mehfil, Nani would take Amma along. If a rich patron she respected made a special request that she too perform, Nani would fold her hands and say that warning bells of old age had begun ringing in her voice now. 'I apologize for myself, but my daughter Allarakkhi has a very sweet voice. Please be so kind as to listen to her.'

And Allarakkhi never once disappointed her listeners or her mother.

Classical music flowed in my mother's veins. A gift from nature, some would say, or maybe it was the legacy of her father's family. Her father, Nani's first lover and my nana, is said to have been a renowned ustad from the Hubli region. Nani heard him sing at a mehfil in Benares and lost her heart to him.

'It was a moonless night,' said Shubraatan, 'and Ammajani could not help losing her heart to Khan Sahib's Raga Jogiya rendered in his deep, resonant voice: "*Khevatiya saanwro paar utaaro raja*" (Oh dusky boatman, please take me with you over to the other side).'

Khan Sahib had a melancholic, Sufi-like temperament. It was said that, after his ustad had heard him singing a melodious prayer at a dargah, he brought him home and started training him formally. Allah has put music in the child's soul, he said. But after his ustad's death, Khan Sahib returned to a dargah near Hubli. From there, he, along with a few fakirs, went to Benares, where they sang at the Budhwa Mangal mela. It was at the mela that my nani met him again. My mother was born nine months later. By then, Khan Sahib, with his band of fellow fakirs, had left town. When, after a long search in numerous dargahs, he was finally located and informed about Amma's birth, it is said that he was quiet for a long time. When he ultimately spoke, he said, 'She is an Allarakkhi, Allah's child. Her voice will shower the listeners with God's grace.'

How could a fakir be wrong? Shubraatan had told me that Amma was nine, but by then everyone knew what a gem of a voice she was born with. When one of her father's students who was visiting Baroda heard her reading a noha during Muharram, he apparently broke into tears and said that, just like her father, the girl's voice too seared the heart. He returned and told Khan Sahib, Amma's father, about the girl. Khan Sahib sent someone over and got Amma, still a mere girl then, called to Bombay to perform and held a formal ganda-bandhai ceremony for her. After that, he trained her for four years so thoroughly and patiently that, by the time she was thirteen, Amma's voice was already the talk of Benares and Calcutta. He sent her back to Nani, thereafter, saying, '*Ja, jitna mere paas tha, tujhe de diya, aagey Allah tujhe bahut dega!*' (Go, what I had, I have handed you. From here on, Allah will bless you with plenty.) Amma, in an unguarded moment, once said, 'No one asked me if I wanted to go to Khan Sahib for talim, nor did Khan Sahib ask me if I wanted to stay with him and not return to Sherkothi to my mother. I was just sent back and forth.' She never spoke of this time with her father again.

As soon as Amma returned, there was a deluge of invitations to mehfils. And it was in one of the grand mehfils that she performed in, that Amma's eyes met my father Pandit Motilal Misir's, and the conversation led to a formal proposal from him for her nath-utarai. Following that, her tawaif customs and singing, everything, changed.

My father, Pandit-ji, belonged to a well-established Brahmin family, and his official name was Kripa Shankar. I heard that he looked and walked like Motilal, a colourful and famous actor of those times, with a rakishly tilted hat and a cigarette dangling from his full mouth. First, his friends started calling him Motilal, and the name stuck.

His family had been trading in attar and tobacco for generations. They were an old family and dealt in crores. How could the romance stay hidden from the clever Nani? But like I said before, she was a worldly-wise lady from a deredar gharana. When she realized that the tall and handsome Moti Babu was more interested in her daughter's singing than his father's accounts books, she started encouraging Amma to not just to meet and mingle with him, but also did not fail to talk at mehfils about how Moti Babu was kind to her daughter. She then began the conversation about nath-utarai. When it came to offering a fee, as expected, Moti Pandit paid whatever she demanded and, with great pomp, took my mother to his bed. But all this was not done in the way shown in films. The haggling was done in a very refined manner, and the rich patrons who fixed the fee of the nath-utarai of deredar tawaifs were themselves experts in music.

After their move to Sherkothi, there was a hiatus, but Nani made it clear to my father that she would work her way around Maharaj Ju's laws and help him visit the girl. My father agreed. After Maharaj Ju's death, there was no holding him back.

Moti Pandit had learned gharana music in Bombay and had a naturally melodious voice. I don't know for sure, but Shubraatan said that while Amma was being trained in Bombay, she had perhaps been meeting Moti Pandit because she looked so resplendent. But I have no way of knowing if that's true. Amma never spoke about that particular part of her life. She just carried it like a black pearl deep within her heart. This was one of the reasons for our estrangement – her extreme reluctance to talk to me about my father. What I do know for sure is, whenever he was in the mood and sang an ashtapadi by Jaya Deva's in Raga Maand, '*Kshanam adhuna narayanam anugata manusara radhe*', Nani would tell me that it was so melodious that passers-by would stop on the road to listen. I heard that Pandit-ji had gotten Amma a phonograph along with a record with a Punjabi song recorded on it: '*Daal gare mein baiyaan, main roi roi jaaniyan*' (My life, I would like to put my arms around your neck and weep on your shoulder). Amma had heard this song in a play and liked it a lot. She'd take it out of the black trunk and play it so often that the record stopped working! If Amma was nearby when the song played, her eyes would well up. She'd sit quietly, listening.

> *Gori da chitt laga Chambe diyan dhaaraan –*
> *Chambe diyan dhaaraan peyne fuhaaraan.*
> *Yaaraan de naal bahaaraan…*
>
> The fair one thinks of the rivers in Chamba –
> the rivers in Chamba, gurgling like fountains.
> Those sublime hours of joy with the beloved...

Travelling from Sherkothi to Benares to Bombay and back constantly and the high life took their toll. Moti Pandit contracted lung cancer at a young age, went back to his family, and died within months.

Sherkothi was desolate again.

Truth be told, my mother's temperament and singing were a riddle for me and remained so. By the time I came of age, Amma had become quite the loner. After her riyaz sessions in the mornings and evenings, she'd roam the gardens of Sherkothi alone, like a shadow, wrapped in silence yet restless. If I asked her anything at that time, she'd only give monosyllabic replies and quietly return to the world of music. It seemed like she had no love or anger left to give even to her child or anyone else, no attachment or desire left for anyone. Except for her singing.

Nani used to say that Khan Sahib's fakir temperament had repossessed his daughter since Moti Pandit's death.

I forgot all my resentment whenever I heard Amma sing with the anguish of losing love at a young age, the trauma and passion all put into her singing. When she sang, it would seem like a hundred lamps had lit up in the rooms. Nobody has been able to mine and use the latent emotional content in the compositions in the khayal style like her. And it was not as if she was all emotion and lacked technical proficiency – she never missed a single beat, even for a second. Almost forty years ago, she was singing Raga Shuddh Kalyan at the wedding of a seth's son. She paused teasingly on the undulating nikhad, the seventh note, for a long time, and when she reached the high shadaj, a famous Tamilian music critic sitting next to me, who barely ever had a good word to say about Hindustani music, ended up asking himself in English, 'Where has she been all my life?'

When I ask myself the same question, I now face a bitter truth. Because of my stubborn resentment towards my introverted Amma, we could only develop a very formal relationship, and that's how it stayed until the end. This was not hidden from Nani's sharp eyes. Which is why, when Nani decided to send me to Bombay to get an education in English, she knew I would not be homesick. And I wasn't.

I was merely twelve. Nani was of the opinion that the world was changing. 'The old mehfils and customs are a thing of the past, the old forts of Urdu, Brij and Awadhi are gone, and the future belongs to English. The proof of the pudding is in the eating. Look at the name Hira Bai's Anjali has made for herself by recording raga-based songs for three minutes each, and English songs in those instruments with keys? Truth be told, my Allarakkhi is far better, but nobody cares for things from her world now.

'Oh you silly girl, understand the changing tides. Your nani has not drunk the elixir of immortality. To make our daughters successful, we Sherkothi women will also have to change with the times. There should be something that will make a person turn around to give our Haidari a second look. Times are changing, Bibi. Those nightlong mehfils where we could take long alaps in peace, the long stretches and turns in beats, they are all going away. The new rich want zippy songs. They'd listen to Dhamar in Kaafi while shaving, rather than the slow-moving, majestic Darbari. The British are filling only this on the three-minute records and sending back home, and among the babus, too, these are being played on gramophones.

'Our Allarakkhi's daughter might not be as beautiful or talented as her mother, but in the coming times when she speaks on music in English, the senior officers and VIPs sitting on sofas in the front rows will praise her talent. I am of the opinion that these songs filled in lac records that are played on English machines are going to be the future. As for English, know that it will become even more valuable after the English leave. So, it will be a good idea for my granddaughter to learn the language and become familiar with Bombay.'

Initially, the recordings were only of bhajans, naat or the fun thumri and dadra songs. But as the market expanded, the margi music of the major singers also joined the fray. As always, Calcutta was the pioneer, where the British Company officers had decided to very carefully introduce records of Hindustani music to cater to the growing market. As always, the musicians and heads of the old gharanas opposed this. All of them were of the opinion that, by being recorded on the English-made records that were being played in every alleyway and warren, the hard-earned talent of the ustads and their music would be sullied. Once great singing was made available to just about anyone within the confines of their houses, then even the lowly prostitutes and pimps might start singing these compositions in every lane. A renowned ustad saw the logo of a dog on the record and started muttering prayers and threw the company's representative out of his house saying, 'Will we singers trained in the gharana style now have to sing under a label that bears the photo of a lowly animal?'

Nani had a different view. One major reason for her being drawn to the recording business was the success of Anjali Bai, the daughter of her old friend Hira Bai, whose records were available from Bombay to Calcutta. She who was her own daughter's age. What was Anjali worth? Her Allarakkhi had been born with music in her veins thanks to her gandharva father, while that thick-browed daughter of Hira Bai, Anjali, fancied herself an English madam! Nani was also convinced that the reason for Anjali Bai's fame was her attitude, one which her Allarakkhi had unfortunately cast off after her lover Moti Pandit's death. Anjali Bai might have been fair-skinned. But would she receive such accolades just for wearing some beautiful clothes or adorning herself with jewellery and singing at a mehfil with her airs? Nani would say that Hira Bai's daughter had always been cunning. She got close to whoever she thought would be good for her career at that point. 'I hear she charges three thousand rupees as fees for the recordings.' It was her melodious Allarakkhi who had the voice that deserved to be recorded. Power-packed and full of light.

Then she learned that her sarangi player Bundu Miyan's son, Wahid, was not just playing for films but also for recording companies and had become very famous. She quickly sent a letter from Sherkothi requesting Wahid to get Allarakkhi's daughter, Haidari, meaning me, admitted to a good convent school in Bombay so that her life could find a connection to that city of plenty where she could later earn a livelihood. God willing, her hermit-like daughter would also then have to visit that famous city where there is a great demand for singers in films. Once she had set her heart on something, our nani would not rest until she achieved her aim. So, I was quickly admitted, and then one day, armed with two trunks and a basket of fruits and sweets, I left Sherkothi with Bundu Khan for Bombay.

Nani passed away while I was in my final year of school. After her death, my amma was left all alone in Sherkothi with its echoing walls. The era of mujras and mehfils with famous singers and musicians ended while Nani was still alive. My amma was not particularly interested in hustling for invitations to mehfils or finding clients. Her expenses were met by selling fruits and flowers from the garden. Tapish Sahib was of great help to her in those days of change and she was grateful to him for it. Later, when I moved abroad and Sherkothi was sold, it was that gentleman who provided Amma shelter until her last days.

It is difficult to comment on the nature of the relationship between Tapish Sahib and Allarakkhi. At least, on Tapish Sahib's part, there was the total supplication a devotee has for his master, bereft of lust. The poor man found his happiness in the fact that an artiste like Allarakkhi trusted him so much.

Amma had probably hoped that I would return to her after completing my education in Bombay and take control of our family's musical legacy. But after the convent's clean, simple life, I had started hating that world full of glitter, rivalries and betrayals. I was the first one in my family to have studied English, and after getting good scores, wanted to study further. I was adamant that I wanted to stay here and do something. 'If you want,' I told Amma, 'you can buy a house here. What's left there?' We kept exchanging letters for a long time. Finally, Amma handed over the keys of Sherkothi to a few old servants and moved here with me, thinking that she'd return if she couldn't adjust.

We first rented a house in Bandra, which belonged to Nani's old acquaintance, Sharifa Jaan's granddaughter, Riffat Apa. The mother and daughter, Latifan and Riffat, lived on the ground floor, while we were on the first.

The lack of money plagued us much during that period in Bombay. Amma and I considered playback singing and started making the rounds of recording companies. Like my mother, our landlady, Latifan Khala, was also sick of the shenanigans of married men and the control their families exerted over them. And now she had also started recommending acting in Parsi theatre in addition to playback singing. She said that, if Amma liked, she could introduce her to a few Parsi seths who were looking for singers. There was both fame and money in theatre. Amma made it clear that in Bombay, like Bazid Mushtaq Hussain Khan Sahib and Kesar Bai, she would work in films only for the sake of the music. She said this to all the seths and company officers she met as well, ones who had loved her heavy and trained voice. But so far, they had only met starving singers ready to do anything to put food on their table. They were not used to dealing with deredar tawaifs who had minds of their own.

David Menezes, a relative of one of my teachers, Miss D'Costa, came to our rescue. He was an admirer of Amma and used to play the piano for silent English films at Empire Theatres. But trouble was, big studios such as Wadia Movietone, Bombay Talkies, Mohan Studio and Filmistan wanted background music. Recording companies only paid a hundred rupees as fees. And be it a sitar player or a tabla player, it was necessary for them to keep playing without any breaks. Everyone fulfilled the new demands of the new age. What we would probably call multitasking these days.

The three Shenoy brothers of Bombay, who had started one of the first recording companies in India, also lost Agra's famous ustad Faiyaz Khan Sahib from their studio around this time. Later, the head of the Kirana gharana swallowed his anger and began recording. The fees, however, remained a hundred rupees per programme. Those days, singers of the stature of Roshan Ara and Anjali Bai, who had joined early, were being paid as much as one thousand rupees as recording fees. Of them, Roshan Ara left for Pakistan with her husband. That left only Anjali Bai behind. A Baali Sahib in Jalandhar composed the music for her that she sang. Money was showered on her.

Around that time, Ghulam Haider, another celebrity in the world of radio and recording, paid Amma a visit and was very impressed by her. Thanks to him, Amma started getting a number of gigs in the industry. It was then that our financial condition reached a stage where I could continue my education.

Amma's first song was recorded for Haider Sahib, '*Haaye mujhe kahin ka na chhoda*' (Oh, my reputation is in tatters). At rehearsals, Haider Sahib would sway and tap on his cigarette tin. Look at the turns of destiny. As soon as Amma and the chain-smoking Haider Sahib became a hit duo, there was an explosion in his family. His wife started fighting with him about his relationship with this tawaif from Benares. Haider Sahib started looking stressed and sick. Finally, Amma went to his wife with folded hands and said that their relationship is only professional. If she does not like it, she can keep her husband. She had long ago tired of all the drama and worries that followed lovers and admirers.

After this, I don't know how, a very colourful and outspoken rich Punjabi man, Jatinder Chaddha, entered our lives. Before coming to Bombay, he had invested and lost a lot of money in theatre companies in Uttar Pradesh and had arrived here to try his luck in the movies. In those days, Pakistan was on everyone's mind and Riffat Apa wanted to sell her house and move to Pakistan. She asked Amma to buy her house, but we did not have that kind of money. That house was sold off, and one fine day, we moved into Jatin Babu's flat.

By now, Amma had befriended a screenwriter and a gifted shayar from Kashmir, Ghulam Mohammad Shah. She had also gotten addicted to the theatre like Nani. And this amazing storyteller was not just a shining star of the Parsi theatre but an encyclopaedia too.

His association with a young and talented artiste such as Amma soon became informal, and they started visiting each other. Jatin Babu's temper kept rising, but Amma had become so famous that acting like an asshole would only damage his reputation. When Amma and I moved out of his flat into a house, he followed us like an item from her dowry.

Jatin Babu was a very clingy person. I did not like him tagging along all the time, but kept quiet. Amma had kept her quiet distance from me through all this, and our relationship had always been strangely delicate; besides, what could have I said to her about it all? But like me, our old maid Shubraatan too did not like Jatin Babu from the beginning because of his heavy drinking and violent temper. The only thing that gave her peace was the thought that, in light of Bibi's growing closeness with the screenwriter, Jatin Babu would be sent packing soon.

But the send-off was a rather disgusting affair. 'Do you know, Bitiya,' Shubraatan said, 'our bai is lost in the world of her practice and recording, and in Ghulam Mohammad Shah Sahib's dramas. One day, that Punjabi smiled and winked at my Begum Sahiba, saying, "You should snag a role by getting close to this blind and rich miyan-ji! You aren't going to make a lot of money just by singing well. The other tawaifs are also acting along with singing, what's so special about you? If you say the word, I can arrange for you to get hooked up with that smart and handsome miyan."

'"Thanks, but no," our Begum Sahiba said, and got up. She was walking into the house when the drunk Jatinder Chaddha slapped her. Begum Sahiba said "Haaye Allah" and fell on the chair. But I got furious! I have also eaten the salt of Sherkothi. I came out of the kitchen roaring. I had been cooking and the hot ladle was still in my hand, so I hit that rascal so hard with it that he snapped out of his drunken stupor. He left the next morning, cursing.'

Ghulam Muhammad Sahib was of Kashmiri origin, but his ancestors had shifted base to Benares for the sake of trade. He had always been very colourful and used to visit kothas. He was greatly knowledgeable about music and had heard of Husna Bai and her daughter and my mother, Allarakkhi, who was making waves outside Benares. Since his wife died, he had been keeping himself busy writing and reading and in theatre. I did not have a problem with him. He was an educated and courteous man and was very loving towards Amma. We used to have very good discussions on the Benares-style music and cuisine at home. He wanted to stay away from the greed and decay that had entered the world of theatre with the advent of lowly prostitutes.

He had impeccable taste. Very fond of books like Amma. Soon, he started visiting us on the pretext of lending books. But he never looked in my direction. And if our eyes ever met, he was always sweet, kind and respectful. I'd be lying if I didn't mention that, with his arrival, the bitterness that Ghulam Haider Sahib's domestic disputes and the memories of Jatinder Chaddha's actions had created disappeared.

This was the first time since the death of her first and only love, Moti Pandit, that conversations with an educated and interesting artiste opened new doors between Amma and another man. Around this time, it so happened that Amma started getting these intense stomach aches. Doctors told her that she had kidney stones, and she should get operated soon. Amma went to meet Ghulam Mohammad Sahib before the operation, but he was not at home. She just left him two lines: 'I am going to battle death today. If I win, we'll meet again, otherwise, this is my last goodbye.'

The nurses were wheeling Amma in for the operation when Sahib also reached. In a very scared voice, he asked the nurses if they would allow him to take her to the operation theatre. All of them knew him and agreed. Before sending her in, Sahib held her hand and said, 'Allarakkhi Jaan, nothing will happen to you.' Then he recited a sher:

Sab kuch khuda se maang liya tujhko maangkar,
utthe nahi hain haath mere is dua ke baad.

By asking for you, I have asked God for everything,
my arms have risen for no other prayer after this.

By the time Amma returned home after recovering from the surgery, yet again Sahib's new play had turned out to be a hit. He put a diamond ring on Amma's finger and said it was to toast her health and his success. Then he recited the famous lines: 'All my life, I considered myself an incomplete couplet. But after meeting you, I feel whole.' But Amma was not to experience this happiness for long. Not even a week passed when we received terrible news. Ghulam Mohammad Shah Sahib had died of a heart attack in his sleep.

After that, my mother became disenchanted with Bombay.

'Let your education get over, then I'll put a stop to this profession of singing and dancing because of which any man can enter the house trying to hold my hand,' she said one day.

I don't know why, but all the anger simmering within me for all these years poured out.

'Why? Will I now have to keep roaming around all my life according to your desires? You can keep this love for begging in front of any man for money. Please excuse me. Enough is enough. The old nuns have agreed to give me an airy room in exchange for teaching the children dance and music in the mornings. Don't worry about me, I would have left tomorrow but I can leave now.'

When I later saw Shubraatan sobbing, I was ashamed of my outburst. I realized that it was because of Amma's talent and because she had left Sherkothi and moved here that I could receive this excellent education. I had inherited our family's legacy from her. But then a dark thought entered my mind: When did she consider me her own? If she stayed with me, we'd bicker all the time.

Amma started packing her things. I remained quiet. I did not apologize even when she was leaving. (Moti Pandit's stubbornness.) The only promise I made was that I wouldn't stop practising music and that I'd catch the evening local train to Bhindi Bazaar to my ustad's house.

Amma and Shubraatan were getting ready to leave, when suddenly a letter from Bundu Miyan's son, Wahid, arrived. He had been running a music and dance school in America. He wrote: '*Khala, the rajas and zamindars are no longer there. You should leave that world of cheats and pimps and come here with Haidari. The appreciation of real talent has started disappearing in India, but here, every Indian, Pakistani and Bangladeshi is ready to pay any amount of money to get their children trained in Hindustani classical dance and music. Your talent that has been cultivated over generations and Haidari's training in English will come to use. I have taken a big house here, and your arrival will light it up.*'

I thought this would be nice. We'd be able to leave this wild, decadent Bombay life behind and create a life anew. Who'd want to live in that accursed Sherkothi? But Amma did not agree. 'I am fine there,' is all she said.

It was decided that I'd accept the offer and leave the country and she'd return to Sherkothi with Shubraatan. A letter to Tapish Sahib was written. As soon as he received it, he came to take Amma away. After much thought, it was decided that Amma would settle everyone's accounts, get Shubraatan moved to the outhouse, and hand over Sherkothi to a big builder. After that, she'd take up a part of Tapish Sahib's house on rent. After some hesitation, Amma said, 'As Allah wills.'

My ticket to America was booked.

The first few days after reaching here were good, but then again, the same story. One fine day, Wahid Miyan said that he wanted to marry me. A qazi could come to the house to read out the vows. I was in a fix. If I refused, there would be strife at home, and if I agreed,

I would be going against my heart. Finally, I said tactfully that it was generous of him, but I was a tawaif. How could I become a householder? On top of that, he already had two wives, they would curse me. So I said my goodbyes to him and moved to New York. Two months later, Wahid Miyan died in a motor accident. He was a good man. May his soul rest in peace.

I will not say anything about Amaal's dead father. We were happy for a while and then grew apart. That was my destiny perhaps.

My daughter Amaal now runs The Oriental Dance and Music School here in America. Indians who have left the country send their children to us in fairly large numbers to learn traditional Indian music and dance. The truth is that only the soil on which we were born can hold our roots in place. Frankly, our music and dance do not interest most of these children born in America. The native flexibility of the body, after it has breathed foreign air and sunlight, has gotten lost somewhere; the language, too, has become different. Many vowel sounds have been lost and consonants changed. This language has neither nuktas nor subtle distinctions between various consonants. For instance, there is a difference in the way the 't' is pronounced in 'tabiyat' and the way it is pronounced in 'teka'. Even so, it is by God's grace that, despite raising the fee every four months, there is still a clamour for admission. Having left my own roots behind, I now want my children to become familiar with them. People here also know about Amma's songs from her playback days and fold hands in front of her picture.

Anyway! Looks like couples here are like us who have no assurance of a forever together. There are scores of houses with single men or women dealing with loneliness and sleeping only after taking pills.

Our films have caught the imagination of these newly rich people here in recent years. Last summer, the mother of one of my students took Amaal and me to an event with Bollywood stars. After a while, I came out. I have never been able to make sense of this kind of music and will never be able to. But that seems to be the only way now.

The songs sounded like crass Punjabi jokes, but they were described as compositions, and in the name of traditional Indian dancing, a group of emaciated boys and half-dressed girls shook their butts.

Both of us stayed awake all night next to each other. May God bless those darling girls whom we, mother and daughter, train every day. We, too, are searching for the same thing they are.

These are the only memories I have.

All the sadness and resentment that I could never express to Amma or Nani came out while writing this letter to you, and I feel lighter. Perhaps that's what Bi had wanted. If you don't like something I have written, please forgive Bi Allarakkhi's daughter.

Your sister,
Haidari

Kolkata

Dear Radha Dada, Sanjeev, Vidya,

I just returned from Sukumar Chacha's house, exhausted and uneasy. The brothers had arrived as soon as they received the news of their father's demise. Shantul's beloved and feisty Bagalamukhi Devi was in Paris for some seminar and could not come. Just as well. Not like she had kept Chacha in heavenly comfort while he was alive.

I was told over the phone that, after arriving in Kolkata, the brothers had left the airport for the mortuary with their pandit and from there they took the body to the crematorium without stopping at home for a last farewell. They just cremated him, and that, as they say, was that. Maybe Chacha himself would also have preferred being reduced to ashes and dust without any of the usual fanfare and family drama.

I could not resist visiting Chacha's house just one last time, though. The brothers were somewhat rattled to see me.

What about a memorial service or shraadh ceremonies, I asked, and was told that neither of them could stay for too long. And anyway, neither their dad nor either of them believed in those ancient and meaningless rituals. By way of informing Chacha's near and dear ones, they had already inserted two large-sized advertisements in the *Anandabazar Patrika* and *The Telegraph*, requesting everyone to pray for the soul of the departed one.

But I was still not satisfied. The two of them were sitting with a well-known builder, Surinder Khanna, and also Chacha's old solicitor and friend, Tola Sen. Maybe the brothers have already decided to do the necessary paperwork for selling off the house neither of them needs. My sudden arrival caused some consternation and disrupted their conversation. As a matter of fact, both seemed so tense that I could not even consider having tea. I cleared my throat and thanked them, uttered a few words of consolation, and left as quickly as I could.

Today, my driver has brought the news that Chacha's house has indeed been bought by Khanna the builder for many crores and the demolition will start within a week. Radha Dada, if you can rescue Chacha's music collection and related material, please do. As per his last wish, those documents must be sent to Vidya.

I am too upset to say more, so I'll end here.

Yours,
Putul

~

Kolkata

Dear Sanjeev, Vidya, Putul,

It is raining outside, and I am alone in my flat. On my lap is Sukumar Chacha's salvaged treasure, of which I could find only a part by the time I reached his place. I can't believe that a man like Chacha would leave so suddenly without saying a word.

When I arrived at Chacha's, some sort of supervisor in sunglasses was getting all the junk loaded on to a truck while

Chacha and Chachi's beloved home was slowly being prepared to get razed. A few trucks had already left, I was told. Before he left, Shantul Sahib had carefully selected what he considered worth salvaging. Then he ordered that a few select antiques be shipped to him in America. Bantul carried away the music system and record collection and told Khanna Sahib to sell the rest in Chor Bazaar and transfer the money to his bank account.

After many requests, I was given permission to search through a pile of papers fluttering in a corner outside. There were only two cardboard boxes left there, which I brought with me – just a few bits and pieces, that's all.

For me, the demolition of Chacha's house was like the destruction of a big, ancient laboratory. By the time I reached the place, an outsider like me could only find a few damp, tattered and dusty documents ready to fly in the wind. The formulae that could connect all the dots are lost forever, and the chemicals all gone, evaporated, or washed up in the rain.

I am sending whatever I found to Vidya. Maybe, if you dig deep enough, your trained eye might locate what Chacha had termed a lost pearl?

I wish I had known earlier that the sons were so keen on selling the house so swiftly. How can these people, who only value everything in terms of money, understand the immeasurable worth of these faded notes, photos, these yellowing tattered letters, that record a vast and tragic history? Bless the supervisor who looked puzzled but allowed me to take away a few things lying here and there! Now, only Vidya Rani can unlock the mysteries of this tangled skein. Even if she can connect some dots over time, some of the secrets of that period can be unlocked.

The writing can be postponed. But when a scholar like our Vidya has chosen to jump on to a tiny raft to navigate a vast sea with just one oar, the journey alone will be a unique experience, right?

So Vidya Rani, take the lord's name and go ahead. All I can do is bless you, saying what Kanva Rishi said to Shakuntala: '*Shubhastu te santu panthanah.*' May your path back be blessed.

Radha

~

Delhi

Radha Dada, Sanjeev, Putul Di,

I sit in my eternally disorganized room and stare at this dirt-encrusted and water-smeared treasure trove like a singer who has found a perfectly tuned tanpura and is taking a breather just enjoying its perfect sound. I consider this small and untidy room of an itinerant researcher the ideal place to negotiate the long journey through the time these documents record.

Being organized has never worked for me – neither in life nor in my writing. The perfection of outfits worn with great care and beautifully done-up faces or homes, hotel rooms or writing tables never appealed to me. I appreciate that the precious collection forwarded to me by Dada is disorganized and scattered.

Before his death, Chacha had talked to me at length. We also have the informative letters from Sherkothi and Ranikhet's learned triad. Now, as I take in the beauty and the mystery of this garden of surprises, I will continue sending you scans of these pages and photographs.

Writing and chronology come much later.

With love,
Vidya

Photo 1

Anjali Bai standing in a slight tribhanga mudra, with her hip jutting out and her hand cupping her chin. There is, behind her, another woman being presented a bunch of flowers by a turbaned man with sharp features. A few lines in Chacha's handwriting on the back of the photo tell us it was taken in 1911, at the site of the Great Delhi Durbar. The British regent had come to Delhi from England, and at this grand event organized in his honour, Anjali Bai had sung with Janki Bai in mixed ragas, 'Yeh jalsa tajposhi ka, mubarak ho, mubarak ho' *(Congratulations, and congratulations again on this occasion of coronation). Dressed for the occasion, Anjali Bai is wearing an expensive Calcutta Jamdani with a zari border.*

Photo 2

Anjali Bai sings with gusto, and like Parsi women, her pallu is stuck in place by a diamond brooch on her shoulder. Her face, an amused smile on it, is turned away a little from her fellow singer Janki Bai. Even years later, the proud upward tilt of her chin seems to say something in the photo.

Photo 3

Where was this taken? Standing politely next to a plump and regal Anjali Bai, Janki Bai looks like a bird, with her slight frame and slightly dark skin. But to mark the occasion, she is wearing a multi-strand gold necklace, a small nose-ring, and a thick maang-patti that straddles her curly hair shining with oil and combed very decorously under her anchal. A scared look is stamped on her face. It's understandable. For an amateur singer, singing and dancing next to a doyenne among singers like Anjali Bai, who could sing in twenty-two languages including English, must have been an overwhelming experience. That is perhaps why she looks so timid, maybe wondering if she should stay put or just run away.

The next fragment is a letter dating back to 1910. Probably part of a longish exchange between two old friends.

The name of a legal firm on top of the paper is somewhat faded but can be read through a magnifying glass. One Madhavkant Chatterjee, a solicitor from the legal firm of Messrs Chatterjee and Sons, writes in English to his friend, Kali Babu:

Dear Kali,

Considering your interest in music and singers, here's a very amusing case for your ears only. Last month, in the district court, the famous tawaif Hira Bai – who, as you know, has moved to Calcutta from Benares – accused, on behalf of her minor daughter, Anjali Bai, the latter's supposed husband Tajuddin Khan, son of Manawar Khan, that because of his depraved ways, she wants to divorce Tajuddin. Tajuddin's lawyer says that, according to the terms of their marriage contract, all of Anjali Bai's property belongs to her husband.

In the meantime, Tajuddin Miyan's party has floated a number of rumours, one of which is that Anjali Bai and he had a child from the marriage, whom Hira Bai quickly sent far away, somewhere in the hills, to be brought up by her relatives. Hira Bai has, as you know, watched over Anjali like a hawk. She had frowned on her marriage with Tajuddin, which she kept under wraps, waiting to get her daughter divorced and have her pick up the profession seriously. On behalf of Hira Bai, our firm has now filed a defamation case against the newspaper for printing Tajuddin's version of the story without any evidence, and also another one against Tajuddin for leaking information on a sub-judice matter and disrespecting the court. All of Calcutta is abuzz with the scandal, and even English officers have taken notice. Now that the case has reached the high court, I have been engaged on Bai's behalf. After discussions, the fee has been decided at Rs 510 per appearance. You will call it robbery. But miyan, this is the same pompous Hira Bai who had told this area's governor in public that she earned in one mehfil what his entire month's salary was. Easy come, easy go!

(On the margins of the letter, Sukumar Chacha wrote a comment in pencil: 'This is not a new practice. Famous courtesans have always commanded a high fee. In the times of the Buddha, the ganika Janpadkalyani's fee was equal to half of the entire annual earnings of the state of Kashi, and for that she was also known as "Addhakashi", or half of Kashi.')

Anjali Bai's husband and the father of their alleged child, Tajuddin, is a fair, good-looking Pathan with wavy hair and a great reputation as a young rake among bazaar women.

With the help of Hira Bai, we have managed to produce two witnesses against him. Both are from her settlement area. One a cook, Sadarat Khan, who is also said to be his secret lover. Another is a guard, Wali Muhammad, who stammers and had to memorize his statement for the court like a parrot. The matter continued as did the rumours. We kept getting dates from the court. Finally, when the bills were becoming rather heavy, Hira Bai agreed to an out-of-court settlement, and we went with that. We agreed to give the thug one of her big three-storeyed houses and wrapped up the case. Despite being so rich, Hira Bai kept haggling at every turn – on the fee as well as on the settlement. She also kept saying she was not a common prostitute but a deredar tawaif, how could she just give away her hard-earned money to such useless characters? Finally, we had to firmly explain to her that if the case of a rich tawaif, who earns thousands of rupees every night and owns half a dozen buildings in the city, goes to the highest court, then neither the court nor the genteel folk of the city will show her any sympathy. Her daughter Anjali is the talk of the town for her beauty and singing prowess, but her emerging career will only get ruined if this mud-slinging continues.

I caught glimpses of her hunter father's complexion and nature in Angelina's narrow eyes with the thick unibrow. She is well-mannered but very self-centred and arrogant like the mother. She is fluent in both English and Hindustani. I have heard that she can sing in almost twenty languages. If she keeps getting her worldly-wise mother's training, she'll be a big-time earner for her mother and scale greater heights than Hira Bai.

After examining all the aspects, I advised Hira Bai to not lose any more time. The other party is very greedy and will keep dragging the case. We advised her that it would be best if she handed over her three-storeyed house on Chitpur Road, near the Nakhoda mosque, to her son-in-law and got rid of him forever. I saw to it that as soon as the house was transferred in his name, Tajuddin and his family were introduced to a big buyer. To clinch the deal, they were made to promise that, after collecting the money, they'd leave the city and would never return to it. My plan worked well. As soon as he heard of a good price, Tajuddin agreed to the terms. One of my zamindar clients was on the lookout for a house in the city to stay in, and I quickly arranged for a deal that satisfied both sides.

This is how Tajuddin and company were ejected from Hira Bai and Anjali's lives. Maybe we'll never know if that said child was actually born. My heart says that it must have been a son, which is why Hira Bai hid him. Had it been a girl, she would have kept her. But as my brother says in Sanskrit, nobody can know all the faces of a woman, nor a man's fate.

When are you visiting us next?

Yours,

Madhavkant

Here's another fragment in Kali Babu's handwriting:

Calcutta's Hira Bai sang a rare song yesterday at the mehfil in Chulbul's house. Her sidelocks have started greying and the old grief is now marking lines on her face. She sings seldom these days, and pushes for her Anjali more and more now, but the old wine is still so heady.

After the usual greetings, she lifted listeners' spirits with her pure Malkauns, '*Ae baraj rahi main toko...*' (Oh, I forbid you my love...) Her voice seared my very heart. Who was pleading with whom here? Was it a Radha asking Krishna? Or a mother beseeching her out-of-control daughter? I had heard she forced Anjali to divorce Tajuddin and threw him out of the city. Now I know the whole sordid story and why the daughter is so angry with her mother that she is not talking to her.

But what a Malkauns! May you live long, Hira Bai!

A letter from Shivcharan from Asansol:

Dear Sukumar Babu,

You had asked me to collect some information on Calcutta's Hira Bai and her daughter, Anjali Bai, which I present below.

At that time, there were three famous singers named Hira Bai: Mirzapur's Hira Bai, the flirtatious Hira Bai of Benares, and Calcutta's Hira Bai. The first two sang in the mehfils of rich men in Mirzapur and Benares. But after moving from Benares to Calcutta, the third – that is, Calcutta's Hira Bai – made a name for herself among the rich with her divine voice and graceful and clever ways. The Awadh durbar now ensconced in Matiya Burj was also kind to her.

Calcutta remained the capital of the country until 1911, and during those years, the splendour and prosperity of the city were unparalleled. There were four things in the city the people were proud of: paan, keeping a courtesan, fighting court cases and debt! These new sons of zamindars steeped themselves in debt to keep fighting court cases for generations. Thanks to their generosity, lawyers of Calcutta and Patna continued to thrive. You would know that the ancestors of your friend Madhavkant had created the money-minting law firm Chatterjee and Sons for their successors by squeezing out such stupid but proud, spendthrift clients.

But let me go back to Hira Bai. After spending a few days in a rented house, Bai bought the house of one Haji Sahib on Dharmatala Road for forty thousand. It seems that, after being thrown out of everywhere and moving places, Bai had grown a great hunger for owning real estate. When she felt a little settled in Calcutta, she started buying property, and in a few years, the total property owned by the mother-daughter duo became an object of envy among other singers and musicians.

Bai loved to display her money like her flashy patrons. It is said that she spent twelve hundred rupees in the wedding of one of her cats. She spent twenty thousand on the reception feast. In private dealings, however, she was a skinflint. She kept her staff of twenty or so on a tight leash on almost slave's wages.

When she moved to Calcutta, Anjali Bai must have been some fourteen years old or so. Tajuddin, who married Anjali Bai without her mother's knowledge before her nath-utarai, was perhaps the reason for the cancellation of her nath-utarai. Whether he arrived with them or not, I do not know, but I have heard that in the initial days, Feku, the spoilt son of Hira Bai's closest servant Rahimun, and Tajuddin troubled Hira Bai a lot. There was all of Bai's money and property, and to top it, a rumour that Taju had got Anjali pregnant. Whatever it may have been, there was constant bickering between the mother and daughter.

Finally, one day, Tajuddin was seen in the city, and it was discovered that he was moving the court, demanding that he be given a share in his wife's property. The case dragged on for a long time, dividing the city's tawaifs, reporters and lawyers into two camps. One with Hira Bai, the other with Tajuddin. But nobody talked about what the young Anjali Bai had to say. Finally, Bai gave her three-storeyed house near the Nakhoda mosque to Tajuddin, who immediately sold it to a zamindar for a lakh and left Calcutta after that.

Then came enemy number two, meaning Feku. Hira Bai had opened a china shop for him on Rahimun's pleadings, but the brat spent all the money from the shop on weed and hash within just a year. Just a few months after Rahimun's death, Feku suddenly disappeared, and a few days later, his rotting corpse was found near a dockyard. Whispers abounded in the city for days. Then, people forgot. But it is said that Hira Bai's health started failing after these two deaths, and by the end of the year, it was her daughter who started performing at mehfils under her guidance.

It is said that Anjali was an arrogant and cunning courtesan. She had become very careful with her money, having seen her mother being fooled so many times at such a young age. Her nath-utarai did not happen after coming to Calcutta, but it is said that she lived with a zamindar in Ghutiari Sharif for a few months and then spent a few months with Chaggan Sahu, the owner of a Banarasi sari shop in the city. But she did not get along with Sahu for too long, and the two had a falling out. Anjali had also started getting reports of her mother's increasing alcoholism and liver disease. Finally, she returned home to join the trade.

She must have been around nineteen, bursting with the juices of youth and her rare Eurasian good looks outshining other young performers. She had no lack of lovers or patrons. Money was showered on her. She had a lovely voice, and her flirtatious mannerisms were to die for. She had inherited a fair, rosy complexion and grey eyes from her father, and a sharp nose and tall, slender frame from her mother. But after Tajuddin's betrayal, Anjali Bai's heart had turned into ice. It is, however, said that she was in shock for many days after her mother's death, the woman she hated and loved the most, her sole anchor in life.

I personally don't keep well, so have moved to my younger son's house in Asansol. What's left in Calcutta now?

Everything from that time is now in ruins. As they say, there's nothing left in Vrindavan since Krishna left.

Chaggan Sahu's cousin, Shibban, who lives near the Nakhoda mosque, might be able to tell you some more about the mother and daughter.

Please convey my regards to Bhabhi.

Yours,
Shivcharan

Photos 4 & 5: Two old photos of Hira Bai in sepia tone.

In one, Hira Bai is dressed in a traditional Pahadi attire, with her scarf worn like a turban around her head. She stares straight into the camera. Her finery also includes an expensive necklace of gemstones around her neck and a gold bulaank nose-ring dangling between her nostrils. She wears bangles and an armlet on each arm, many rings on her fingers, and her posture is straight and regal. She has a determined chin, an aquiline nose, and large, haunting eyes.

The other picture was taken after Hira became Hira Bai. She is seated on a futon in the traditional attire of a prosperous Benares courtesan, with pearls around her neck and wrists. On either side are two of her trusted maids, Khairun and Nazmun. They are sitting on the ground, close to Hira Bai. Their heads are covered demurely in a somewhat crumpled but fine fabric.

A letter from Shibban Babu, Kolkata:

Bhai Sukumar Babu,

I am lucky that you have remembered me after so long, and I am very happy to have received a letter in your noble hand.

I don't have the kind of information Shivcharan has, but in our younger days, we were all moths to the flame that Anjali Bai was. I met her after 1911, by when the nation's capital had shifted from Calcutta to Delhi. And with the shift of the capital, it seemed as if the wealth of this grand city had also begun to shift westwards.

Anjali Bai was an experienced, worldly-wise, and shrewd woman. She had realized early that these old digs in the east would stop yielding oil. So she was ready to move out when the government did. She took away her money and trusted band of servants from Calcutta. The old bai could see that once the mehfils of the rich in Bengal and Bihar ended, English music and the sahibs' language would take over, and many old dialects that fed the pool of Indian classical music would run dry for lack of speakers and singers. Bai herself was proficient in English, and kept polishing it more and more with the help of her English tutor, who also taught her how to conduct herself in mixed company.

By now, times were changing, influenced as they were by memsahibs and a clergy deeply seeped in Victorian ethics. Soon, under their influence, the government began to consider all traditional native singers and dancers as cheap prostitutes, and bands of memsahibs roamed red areas with padris ordering the houses of ill-repute be shut down.

By now, either the older generation of zamindars were impoverished, or their offspring educated abroad or in Jesuit convents had started to keep a distance from native mehfils and tawaifs. At this point, Anjali Bai began a round of meetings with the owners of various German and British recording companies. They wished to enter the lucrative Indian market, but the bull-headed pandits, ustads and gurus of gharanas had rallied against recording their precious music for the gramophone. The situation was such that there was a big market for recorded Hindustani music. But the snooty Indian singers stayed away from the British recording companies. At this delicate juncture, when our Anjali Bai sent word that, for the right price, she was agreeable to record for the companies, they were delighted. For a few days, both parties haggled hard, and finally arrived at a recording fee of Rs 1,000 per recording for Anjali Bai.

Within a year, Anjali Bai's voice was playing in every household that could afford a gramophone. She sang songs from '*Mone mone moner maane*' (The meaning of the heart in my heart) in Bengali, and also 'God save the King' in English. Soon, she was also recording popular songs for Marathi musicals and melodious bhajans to please the older members of Hindu households: '*Radhe Krishna bol re mukh se, kya lagega mol manva, kya lagega mol*' (Chant the names of Radha-Krishna, it will cost you nothing). After winning over Calcutta, she had set her eyes on conquering the music market in Bombay. By this time, big-ticket international recording companies had started investing in the industry. English and Indian merchants were collaborating in many new areas, from shipping to textiles. Some sharp Indian sahibs were handpicked as high officials in these firms and started to earn fat salaries. Indian lawyers were also making a killing in the native courts, where the British laws had almost totally overtaken customary Indian laws.

All these newly rich men would now invite bais for all their celebrations – from weddings to mundans – as a marker of their having 'arrived'. Bais were booked with money sent to them in bags in advance. The lavish baithaks they organized attracted a lot of listeners. I first heard Hira Bai's daughter sing at one such gathering at the house of a rich Parsi seth, the owner of a big shipping company. I still remember Anjali's rendition of the rarely heard Raga Lakshmi Todi sung to Jhaptaal, '*Tum Hazrat Khwaja, sab rajan ke raja*' (O Hazrat Khwaja, you're the king of kings) and another of a combination of two morning ragas, Paraj and Kalingada, with which she ended her presentation in the early hours of the morning.

Those were the days.

Music was everywhere in the megacity, flowing from mehfils to film screens, the theatre, and even in the politically volatile meetings called by supporters of self-rule for India, the Swarajists.

But the new generation cares nothing for all our old love. Recently, my own grandson sent an email to his father saying that, in order to avoid his FB wall so full of crappy Hindustani music, he was closing his old home page.

So, dear Sukumar Babu, this old friend hands over that crumbling wall to you.

My regards to Bhabhi, and love to my naughty friends, Bantul and Shantul.

Your old friend,
Shibban

A letter from a Babu Jagatnarayan of Allahabad addressed to Chacha:

Dear Sukumar,

My music-loving engineer chacha was an employee at the Allahabad Radio Station during the era you mentioned. Allahabad is a strange city. English political expediency dictated that, instead of rebellious Lucknow, this peaceful, religious city in the east be made the capital of the United Provinces. So a high court, a university and many churches were created here almost overnight. The city that came up was strange. It was a hybrid born out of the Anglophilia of the rising middle classes and the original tunnel-visioned conservative Brahminical mindset. It was befitting that it stood at the sacred confluence of two holy rivers in the north, Ganga and Yamuna, next to Emperor Akbar's fort. Colonies sprang up with names like Mumford Ganj, Colonel Ganj, Dara Ganj, Civil Lines. They still contain within themselves the story of a city that oscillates between its Indian past and its British legacy. A city where people will still discriminate on the basis of race, caste or language, but at times, will turn into a stronghold of socialism revolting against the authoritarian ways of Delhi. Its famous garden is still called Company Bagh and it has a Victoria Memorial embedded in it, and also a bust of a young man named Chandra Shekhar Azad, twirling his moustache. Azad – it means 'free' – a rebel who shot and killed a British officer and was chased and shot dead by the British.

It was while sitting here that Chacha narrated countless stories of the memorable musical performances he had been witness to after 1910. There were some unforgettable anecdotes about Anjali Bai too. It is no secret from you that, like many other young music lovers of that generation, Chacha was obsessed with Anjali Bai who had recorded songs in more than twenty languages. She wasn't just beautiful but was also the most intelligent and well-informed, market-savvy member of her generation. Chacha tells me that in one of her radio interviews, she presented such a refined analysis of thumri singing that he was speechless with wonderment. According to her, thumri was not developed in Lucknow. It was a genre that came into the north from Gwalior. She had lived in Lucknow and Benares, but the refining of what must have been a string of popular folk songs could only have been done in Gwalior, the source of the purest compositions of traditional music. Then, by singing two or three thumris, she clarified her point further.

Anjali Bai was a very capable critic of poetry. She understood the heart of the qalaam that she sang. Without that, you can't move hearts the way she did. A witty conversationalist, she decided on the course of her singing not based on the current trends but by gauging the mood of her audience.

The last time he met Anjali Bai, Chacha found her looking forlorn and tired. He had heard that her income had been coming down but the number of hangers-on kept swelling. She had to sell two of her houses to settle loans because of the number of cases she was fighting in courts. I heard that the people of Pathuriaghata also helped in secret, but Anjali Bai was a self-respecting tawaif and she was tired of all her worldly troubles. She had read out this sher to Chacha at this meeting:

Hum toh mar kar bhi kitaabon mein rahenge zinda,
gham unhi ka hai jo mar jaayein toh guzar jaatein hain.

I will live on in books even after my death,
sigh for those who pass on and just fade away.

Near her end, with the help of a professional devadasi friend from South India, she joined as a court singer at one of the few remaining big princely states somewhere in the region. She died there.

On hearing of her death, my chacha killed himself in the room of a dharamshala in Shimla by sealing off all the doors and windows and lighting a charcoal burner in the room. But the family refused to believe he did it for her and insisted on calling it an accident. It is an inside story that, on a blue pad in the room, Chacha had written a few lines by Amir Khusro on the back of a photo of Anjali Bai's: '*Gori sovey sej par, mukh par daare kes, chal "Khusro" ghar aapne ren bhayi chahun ya des*' (The fair one lies in slumber on the bed, hair covering her face; it's time, Khusro, let's go home, this land is shrouded in darkness). To save the family's reputation, the police officer did not speak about this piece of evidence in public and wrapped up the case by calling it an accident.

That's all I remember now. I'll write to you if I gather any other information. Hope you have been well.

Yours,
Jagatnarayan

EPILOGUE

Dear Radha Dada, Sanjeev, Putul Di,

I was piecing together all the information when I got this email from Haidari's daughter, Amaal.

When the book gets written, this letter from Amaal can probably be its epilogue.

With love,
Vidya

Queens, New York State
Dear Vidya,

You had written that I should write to you my experiences, memories and dreams about my past and future. Thank you for your kindness.

I have always lived under the care of my mother in an alien country. I stopped asking her about my father after never getting a real answer. My story may probably appear somewhat strange to you compared to my grandmother's and my mother's. But please remember, it is all based on secondary information.

As soon as I was old enough, I realized that, living in the Indian and Pakistani ghetto filled with the white poor of Jackson Heights, we did not really have anyone to call our own. The only thing common among all of us Indian and Pakistani families was that we had all left the Indian subcontinent to settle here. That's all. In the initial years, my only acquaintance with the country was through books and stray exhibitions. The first exhibition that Amma took me to had a display of a French photographer's photos of Rajasthan. Every face, every haveli and every cactus seemed to have been clicked through an orange filter and was bathed in a strange tangerine-coloured light. In one photograph, a few brown people were staring at the camera with musical instruments in their hands. An old man whose eyes were closed had his hands raised, as though he were pulling something out of space. It was difficult to tell the real colour of the orange sky above.

On our way back, Amma told me that my grandmother, Allarakkhi Bi, and her mother, Husna Bai, had been famous singers and experts on traditional North Indian music in their heyday. Most of Amma's childhood was spent with the families of old servants, and later, her grandmother sent her to a boarding school in Bombay to get an English education that changed her life.

It was in school that Amma first learned from her German nuns not about love but about independence and about earning money. Amma was a smart kid, and it did not take her too long to move away from the Indian ways the nuns disapproved of. By the time school was over, Amma was more immersed in English literature and moved away from her old self. For her, the old life had probably ended at Sherkothi. Amma persuaded her mother, my nani, to move to Bombay from Sherkothi and look for work in films and theatre instead. After that, mother and daughter lived in Bombay for many years. But unfortunately, their relationship remained strained and rather incommunicative. The first reason for that was the unfamiliar atmosphere of the new city, and the second, the suppressed, unspoken anger both carried within their hearts.

They quarrelled frequently, and that affected Amma's training in gharana music. Amma had a good voice, and she was an intelligent woman, but the two of them could not move past their egos.

As for me, because of being twice removed from my great-grandmother, I could only receive a fraction of the training that my Amma had received. But the one thing that I inherited from the women in my family was a strong desire to survive, no matter the setbacks, and to adapt to the times like a true tawaif.

During my childhood, I always found Amma unwilling to talk about her other relatives. I realized the reason for it when I went home after Nani's death. All these people who had very lovingly invited Amma to America belonged to families of traditional singers who had to bear a lot of humiliation and work very hard to make a name for themselves in the courtly music tradition that was eroding in India. After numerous efforts, they did manage to reach America, but the insults and ugly experiences they had along the way made them all rather quarrelsome and selfish. When they came running to America, they had hoped to make big money, but upon their arrival, they found that it wasn't so easy for Indian artistes to establish themselves in this alien land, one with a different culture and with musical traditions of its own. They did not have the training or education to be able to change and could speak in English only haltingly. Only a few artistes survived here with their art. Many became shop assistants or worked in farms. Those who continued to survive as musicians had adopted stratagems of all kinds to attract white sponsors. It brought them customers, but ultimately ruined their talents and their health. Amma was more keen to use her English than her music. My educated, cultured and sensitive Amma could never be comfortable around these uncouth and loud men who were hypocrites, expecting women to earn for them but to be their slaves inside the house.

Initially, these people entered our home whenever they liked. But no sooner had an acquaintance been established than they would start misbehaving. For them, all traditional singers remained sources of carnal pleasure, not intelligent colleagues whom they could respect or with whom they could share professional information.

The way most of them looked at Amma, and later, me, there was honestly no familiarity there, just pure lasciviousness. When Amma reprimanded a few, they would respond with, 'Bi, you are behaving like a respected householder after arriving in America, but we know of your origins.'

When it all became too much, Amma got out and we came here. She has always been hardworking. She started her own Hindustani music school, went door to door to collect students, got me admitted to the county school and continued my training in Hindustani music in addition to Western music at home despite my protests.

I had not liked her disapproval and suspicion of all men; her strict disciplinarian attitude irritated me. But in retrospect, I realize that, like Nani, she was a far-sighted woman out to secure her child's future.

Today, music, other than my fatherless daughter, Koel, is everything to me.

A little about my daughter's father. I had started getting close to an American boy here while in school. David was also the son of a divorced mother. Katherine had managed to run away from David's abusive father one day with her infant son. Here, she became a good friend and a close confidante of Amma's. Amma saw that the once-smart Katherine had taken to heavy drinking to deal with the abuse and now wanted to recover for her son's sake. Amma took her to a de-addiction centre. Finally, Katherine bravely managed to beat the addiction, but by then, alcohol had ruined her health. With great difficulty, she was somehow managing to make ends meet and raise her son in our poor colony. But by the time her son turned seventeen, she met someone and moved out of the colony.

David did not get along with his new father, so he spent most of his time with us. When Katherine was staring at the abyss, his friendship with Amma had deepened, and Amma was very fond of him. He would often say that Amma was the glue in his relationship with his mother. He had probably never experienced such warmth and love even in his own house. By then, Amma's school had also taken off, and my ambitious mother wanted me to join college. But I was adamant that I wanted to be a homemaker.

David and I got married as soon as we graduated from school, and I became pregnant. College was no go now. Meanwhile, David decided to join the army and died in a war in Iraq.

Today, it is only our daughter, Koel Katherine, within the confines of whose being rest every one of those memories. She is my life, its purpose too. In our embattled lives lived upon alien shores, where do we have the time to dream of anything bigger? To dream, one needs to have a footing too, so that in the earthen pot of desires, we can keep safe that which we wish to preserve – be it music or language.

When I listen to Amma's sweet Hindustani while she explains the compositions, I often wish that the language had also reached me. But every time I tried, the words would slip away like house lizards, leaving their tails behind in my hands. Losing your language after coming to a foreign land is like looking into a dried-up riverbed hoping there may be a little moisture trapped somewhere under its stones.

As the music unfolds in my ears, the dusky girl of Sherkothi who used to run behind the train carrying me to Mumbai still runs inside me all night. But I realize the gaps in my language, and whatever I have managed to retrieve by now may never be able to capture the elusive notes that play within me constantly.

This is also a kind of emptiness that we are all trying to fill up in our own ways. Last year, one Akash Agarwal in Brooklyn informed me on social media through his website that he had joined hands with many other music lovers to form a group called 'The Indi-Raga Massive' and they performed at the best local pubs. Would I like to join them?

I said, why not?

Agarwal Sahib is a very successful businessman and runs a hedge fund. He plays the drums and the tabla in his free time, and does not forget to make some money on the side from it with the help of social media. But he is honest and distributes the earnings equally. So, many musicians and music lovers, be it from among the gharana musicians or those who follow Western music genres such as Indo-chic, grunge and jazz have joined him. Like him, some are software engineers, some bankers or doctors. There are a few old people, too, who chased money in their youth to this land and are now turning to their roots in their time of leisure. They don't mind earning some money on the side.

So now, after discussing among ourselves, we decide on a time and meet at a pub in New Jersey or New York on a weekend, and sing and play and have jam sessions. After a session, if we like a new musician's level, we exchange cards and induct them officially into the Indi-Raga Massive.

Agarwal Sahib is a very intelligent businessman. He has inherited moneymaking in his DNA. We try to match step for step with this changing and mixed society and create fusion music. And we are making good money from this talent and also get to travel for fun.

These days, Agarwal Sahib is looking for ways to compete with matrimonial sites and doesn't hesitate to tell the youngsters on his fairly popular website that they can come for our jam sessions, and that if they hit it off with a good singer, shehnai- or tabla-player they can make them their life partners too.

To increase the number of hits, we have dispensed with many of the binding rules of Hindustani and Carnatic music. When the time here is twelve hours behind and the weather is different, then why shouldn't we adapt the raga-based music created on Indian soil to this place and play it at every hour, in every weather, in temples and school premises and open spaces of all kinds, and make it more approachable?

Truth be told, Amma is a little hesitant about all this talk of liberalizing the borders of our traditional ragas, but after attending many of our sessions, Amma sensed that only after matching new techniques with new sounds and beats can new listeners be found for salvaging what remains of the old music that's fast eroding.

Now, I spend a few winters with the band in Delhi, and Goa too, where they have bought traditional houses in the villages. The deals were made piecemeal for crores. And now we are turning them into four- or five-star hotels with the help of international designers. Agarwal Sahib says that villagers left farming a long time ago. Why would they mind selling whatever land they are left with and the ancestral properties that are turning into ruins for lack of money? Name your price, they simply say, and most times, we are pleasantly surprised at the low prices they quote.

Such heritage hotels that sprung out of villages and traditional Goan homes are like exotic gardens of orchids for our Indian and international audiences. Today, in the villages, every other shop is either a pub or a restaurant. Here, in this strange new bubble we have created with our music, evenings are not evenings and nights aren't entirely nights, and the Indi-Raga Massive music can fly in every week for two days from New Jersey or Oregon for music-loving customers. Who knows what tones and microtones are being used in the classical or semi-classical compositions in Hindustani, English, Moroccan and god knows how many more languages that are coming together and melding in this ocean of YouTube.

And why shouldn't they be?

Now, even in America, which is thousands of miles, seven seas and fourteen rivers away, insomniacs like me can listen to anything on the internet with just the click of a button. An Indian rapper from Punjabi Bagh or Matunga dressed in a colourful Jodhpur turban with a 'Save the Tiger' T-shirt, singing with his eyes closed, a flat-chested European girl swaying by his side, while a tabla plays somewhere in the background, link us suddenly to aggressive fighters trying to sing of love and freedom in a mixed language.

Ji bharke rounga ik din, khushi ke aansoo rounga ik din,
Gurgaon ki kisi building mein…

I'll cry my heart out one day, I'll cry tears of joy one day,
from a building in Gurgaon…

A slightly dubious tune in Raga Mishra Khamaj. The song is guaranteed to go viral.

The links get posted all night long.

In a world where the share market never sleeps, how can there be a lack of listeners? A market full of insomniac traders and a world of late-night cinema shows – that's what Agarwal Sahib looks for and finds everywhere.

Perhaps the offspring of the midnight's children like me were destined to be insomniacs, no matter where they live in the world. The grammar of the music we are creating today is born out of the old lanes and bylanes of India's sleepy small towns, redolent with their own nightmares, mud, piss, sweat, jasmine gajras, perfumes and attar. The music of our mothers and grandmothers still speaks to this new global virtual world. Here is where refugees from the biggest ruined cities of the world, from Iraq to Korea, Afghanistan to Sri Lanka, will manage to find a place for the music that speaks to their worn-out souls in between dim sums and chicken tikka masala, pancakes and ratatouille.

All inhibited and forbidden notes can roam like Naga sadhus at a Kumbh mela, uninhibited and free, here, in this digital world, when the old quiet of the night is speared by the sounds of a city that never sleeps.

These new ragas are a creation that come riding the broadband. They don't lovingly tap on your ears like an old friend knocking on the door of another. They bang on them. A spaced-out drummer's beat, *dhadak-dhadak*, takes you along a road made of steel girders on which a mad music charges fiercely ahead like a train gone rogue.

Yes, sometimes passing you by is another train, in which the sad ragas crouch, all bundled up, inside compositions that get unmasked in the yellow light for a split second before disappearing.

And sometimes you see beats and tunes lying inert upon the path of your train – all flattened out like a coin placed on a railway line by some child.

Vidya-ji, our sleep-deprived generation, which has seen homes, families and even countries melting away in a span of months, is like a homeless cat stuck on a tin roof. Sometimes it stares at the moon shining overhead and howls at its fate, but then sometimes, it just arches its back and pirouettes like a graceful dancer giving her last performance.

A strange celebration this. I can't understand the words, nor the rhythm of the beats, and it isn't like the listeners are totally unconscious. Even in this maddening cacophony of sounds, one stray sound may suddenly light up your insides and that's all…

'Where are you?' – this question was sung in Arabic by Umm Kulthum for the beloved she hadn't seen, in English by Mariah Carey and the blind Surdas-like American singer Stevie Wonder. All of them keep repeating: Where are you? My world is empty without you.

Truth is, all of us singers and musicians are standing on some faraway platform in an unknown land. The last train has left, and there's no knowing when the next one will arrive.

But we wait in this arrhythmic, atonal time, holding on to our hearts and the blood they send coursing down our veins regularly, and call out to some unseen companion:

'*Sahela re, aa mili gaayein…*' – that is perhaps all the bonding that's needed for this one birth.

Yours truly,
Amaal

TRANSLATOR'S NOTE

After having translated Shivani's *Bhairavi*, it almost seemed like a logical progression to translate her daughter Mrinal Pande's work, but it wasn't all that straightforward. In the year following my submission of the final manuscript of *Bhairavi*, I jumped from book to book, recommendation to recommendation, trying to find that one book that would make me its own. After kissing a few frogs, my darling friend, the publisher–poet Dibyajyoti Sarma gifted me a copy of Mrinal Pande's magical *Sahela Re*, a slice of nostalgia told through letters, and I knew I had found the one.

I grew up around music, much like many Bengalis do, but having grown up in small-town Udaipur, it was a second-hand experience. Dida, my maternal grandmother, started her day playing Shyama sangeet on the tape recorder, followed by Rabindra sangeet, by which time I would be wide awake. I had heard from Dida and from others in the family that Ma had learnt the sitar from the Dagar brothers when they were in Udaipur, but her broken sitar never made it out of the loft and I never heard her play it, probably in protest against the injustices of life. She has never cared to give her reasons and I haven't pressed either. She had learnt Bharatnatyam too, and I saw her dance on more than one occasion. She had insisted that I learn a dance form and I got enrolled for Kathak, but I quit after a few months because my self-respect could not take the caning that the process, or so

Ma had tried to explain to me gently, necessarily entailed. Dida had wished that I learn singing, but Ma and I shot the proposal down because my singing can be very effective in chasing people out, though I do wish I could sing. I don't know why nobody ever thought of training me for an instrument, not that I myself was terribly inclined to learn one either.

My childhood was also filled with stories of Dida's maiden home in Birbhum. She always insisted that she came from a proper zamindar family while my grandfather (Dadu), her husband, was from a chasha family, a petty peasant's. The truth, however, was that hers was an impoverished though educated family while Dadu's were landowners, just that they were also involved in farming and were not as educated or 'cultured'. My grandmother resented the situation anyway. I'd like to believe that Dadu was just amused by her anger, that it was their love language.

It was probably all these stories and memories from my own childhood that brought *Sahela Re* so alive for me. The bitterness and resentment within families, the differences, the layered and complicated mother-daughter equations – all spoke to me. And then, at the heart of the story are the twin enigmas, Hira Bai and her daughter Anjali Bai. Peeling their story away layer by layer, meeting Eddie Sahib, and learning about the mehfils of yore added to the joy of solving the puzzle. At times, the narrative reminded me of Dida's stories – never chronological, often contradictory, sometimes tragic, but always interesting.

With the mystery surrounding the bais at its core, the book also comments brilliantly on language, writing and translation. And since Mrinal Pande is a renowned translator herself, her insights are always incisive.

In the translation, I have attempted to retain as much of the nuances of language that she has mentioned in the book, sometimes talking about the inadequacy of translation. Thus, we have cracks made at the expense of Sukumar Chacha's assistant's limited understanding of Hindustani and terrible translations. My favourite bit though is when she talks about how the beauty of the lines "'*Aaye haaye! Yeh toh Huddu Khan Sahib ki gamaktaan hai!*"; "*Arre vaari jaaun, is adayegi mein toh ayn-mayn Patiale ke Faiz Mohammad ki chhab hai*"; "*Wah! Kya rangeeli firat hai, jiyo raajjja!?*"' is untranslatable, for it *is* truly untranslatable. You also have the gem in Haidari's last letter where she comments about how the native language the children from India and Pakistan speak on foreign shores has undergone a change; how it has neither nuktas nor subtle distinctions between various consonants, such as between the pronunciation of the 't' in the words 'tabiyat' and 'teka'. Many vowel sounds have been lost too.

The author also talks about the tussle between the old order and the new, and she's not always disparaging of the new world. While in parts of the book she captures a certain dismissiveness about the modern world and its relationship with music, be it through Tapish Sahib's assistant's using earphones or in the digs at the easy accessibility of classical music through YouTube, it is in Amaal's letter that one finds how a collective in America is trying to keep classical music alive. This is the letter with which the book ends, and I found it to be one of the most sensitive and balanced pieces of writing there can be.

Hira's story is set in the pre-Independence era, while the actual reporting and solving of the mystery of her origins happens in more recent times by our protagonist sleuth, Vidya. As she travels from Delhi to Rampur to Kumaon to Kolkata, she takes us along on the journey and gives us a peek into the lives of ustads, deredar tawaifs, music companies, Baadi singers and women from genteel households.

I am grateful to Maaz Bin Bilal for sharing with me and letting me use his translation of the couplet: '*Taaillah Benares chashm-e-baddoor, bahisht-e-khurram-o-firdaus-e-mamoor*.' To modern technology, read Twitter, or rather the author Mrinal Pande's Twitter page, for the translation of the colourful '*Paani pul kul poochna nahi sayano kaam*' as 'It is unwise to ask about the server's lineage after having drunk the water'. To Saif Mahmood for explaining the nuances of Urdu words. Saumya Agarwal and Shabari Choudhary for reading a very early draft of the translation. Anish Chandy, Amruta Byatnal, Teesta Guha Sarkar and other friends in publishing for their friendship and for keeping me gainfully employed as I worked on this translation. Arpita Kuila for her warmth and encouraging words. Rahul Soni for being an amazing publisher, and Rinita Banerjee for her close editing and handholding through the entire process. Thanks to everyone at HarperCollins.

When I sent Mrinal Pande the first draft of my translation, she sent it back within a week with her comments and corrections, especially about music, which I much appreciate. That added to the translation a rich cadence, a musicality. Last but not the least, I thank her for writing this book and transporting me to a different world.

AUTHOR'S ACKNOWLEDGEMENTS

I did not think *Sahela Re* could be translated into English. When Priyanka Sarkar offered to do it, I was a little hesitant, but she was persuasive. She created a draft on which our editor, Rinita Banerjee, and I worked some more. In the process, these two young women taught me a lot about translating fiction. I am equally indebted to both.

MRINAL PANDE is a veteran journalist, television personality and author. She was the first woman in India to be the chief editor of a Hindi daily, *Hindustan*; the first woman chairperson of Prasar Bharati (2010 to 2014), the apex body of the official Indian Broadcast Media; and the founder-president of the Indian Women's Press Corps, a national body of India's women journalists. Pande has authored several books in Hindi and English, including *The Journey of Hindi Language Journalism in India: From Raj to Swaraj and Beyond, The Other Country: Dispatches from the Mofussil, My Own Witness: A Novel, Devi: Tales of the Goddess in Our Time, Daughter's Daughter, That Which Ram Hath Ordained or the Tale of Manna Seth* and *The Subject Is Woman*. She has also translated into English *Gathering the Ashes*, written originally in Hindi by Amritlal Nagar, and *1857: The Real Story of the Great Uprising*, written originally in Marathi by Vishnu Bhatt Godshe Versaikar. Pande has studied Hindustani (vocal) music from the Gandharva School, and drawing, design and the history of art and architecture at the Corcoran School of Art, Washington, DC. In 2006, she was awarded the Padma Shri for her services in the field of journalism.

PRIYANKA SARKAR is an editor, translator and writer. She has translated Shivani's *Bhairavi* (2020) and Chitra Mudgal's *Giligadu* (2019) into English. Her translations of short stories from Hindi to English have appeared in anthologies published by Yoda Press, Oxford University Press India, Women Unlimited, *South Asian Review* and Macmillan. Her translations have also featured on Scroll.in and Audible. As an editor, she has worked with Oxford University Press and Random House India, and was also the head of editorial at Konark Publishers. She is currently associated with the Rama Mehta Writing Grant, which aims to encourage creativity in English, Hindi, Urdu and Rajasthani among unpublished Rajasthani women writers.

30 Years *of*

HarperCollins *Publishers* India

At HarperCollins, we believe in telling the best stories and finding the widest possible readership for our books in every format possible. We started publishing 30 years ago; a great deal has changed since then, but what has remained constant is the passion with which our authors write their books, the love with which readers receive them, and the sheer joy and excitement that we as publishers feel in being a part of the publishing process.

Over the years, we've had the pleasure of publishing some of the finest writing from the subcontinent and around the world, and some of the biggest bestsellers in India's publishing history. Our books and authors have won a phenomenal range of awards, and we ourselves have been named Publisher of the Year the greatest number of times. But nothing has meant more to us than the fact that millions of people have read the books we published, and somewhere, a book of ours might have made a difference.

As we step into our fourth decade, we go back to that one word – a word which has been a driving force for us all these years.

Read.

Harper Collins · 4th · HARPER PERENNIAL · HARPER BUSINESS · HARPER BLACK · हार्पर हिन्दी

HarperCollins *Children's Books* · HARPER DESIGN · HARPER VANTAGE · Harper Sport

